A Closer Look

For Pat,
with all my love
∞

A Closer Look

Karen DelleCava

WestSide Books®
Lodi, New Jersey

Published by WestSide Books
60 Industrial Road
Lodi, NJ 07644
USA

This is a work of fiction. All characters, places, and events
described are imaginary. Any resemblance to real people,
places, and events is entirely coincidental.

Library of Congress Cataloging-in-Publication Data

DelleCava, Karen.
 A Closer Look / by Karen Dellecava. -- 1st ed.
   p. cm.
 Summary: Fourteen-year-old Cass, a high school freshman and track star, struggles to
cope with the news that she has alopecia, and may go completely bald.
 ISBN 978-1-934813-49-2
 [1. Alopecia areata--Fiction. 2. Self-esteem--Fiction. 3. High schools--Fiction. 4.
Schools--Fiction. 5. Family life--Fiction. 6. Track and field--Fiction.] I. Title.
 PZ7.D3849Clo 2011
 [Fic]--dc22

                                                                    2010053727

International Standard Book Number: 978-1-934813-49-2
School ISBN: 978-1-934813-50-8
Cover design by Amy Kolenut
Interior design by Chinedum Chukwu

Printed in the USA
10 9 8 7 6 5 4 3 2 1

First Edition

A Closer Look

One

It was New Year's Eve, but I didn't care how I looked—jeans and a sweatshirt, hair in a ponytail—done deal. Babysitting for a two-year-old could be messy so that outfit was a safe bet.

Too early to leave, I wandered into my younger brother Kyle's room. He was packing video games for a sleepover at his friend Rob's house.

"Got big plans for the night?" Kyle asked.

"While you're frying your brain playing those stupid things, I'll be making a cool ten bucks an hour."

"For babysitting a kid that's asleep?"

"It *is* New Year's Eve. I could've gone to a party or done something else instead."

"Yeah, right—as if anybody asked you."

Jerk. I hadn't expected any party invites, and besides, I'd accepted this job over a month ago, so I was already booked even if something else had come along.

"Bite me," I told him. "Next time you're hard up for cash, don't come to me looking for a loan."

"Aw, you know I didn't mean it," he said. Then he

Kyle-smiled me. That always worked on Mom, not on me. But I never could stay mad at the brat for long.

"Tara sitting, too?" he asked.

Tara Speziale and I had always been friends, but since we both ran freshman track this fall and had some classes together, she's become my *best* friend.

"Yup, and then she's coming back and sleeping over."

A car horn blasted from the driveway and Kyle went to the window.

"That's me—I'm outta here," he said. Then, with one arm in his ski jacket and the rest of the coat dangling, he zipped his backpack and flung it over his shoulder. He flew down the hall, his backpack bumping into every picture along the wall.

"Have fun at Rob's," Mom called to Kyle.

"I'll pick you up tomorrow around noon," Dad said.

Kyle bounced down the stairs, shouted *"Hap-py New Year!"* and slammed the front door.

On my way down the hall, I stopped in front of the crooked frames and straightened the first one: our family portrait. It showed four perfect people, frozen, held hostage there forever under that pane of glass. We may have looked great, but it was *so* not the real us.

I straightened the next picture—Kyle in his communion suit, his hands in the prayer position and a halo practically glowing around his head. That one always cracked me up. Talk about false advertising.

The next was one of Mom as a teenager; she'd modeled in a bunch of magazines when she was my age, and even did a European TV commercial for Pepsi. I had no idea how she could stand all that fussing with make-up and hair, and all that posing. No way could I ever sit still long enough—not that anyone would ever ask me.

Dad told me I looked a lot like Mom at that age. She looked pretty in that picture, but I didn't think I looked like anyone other than me, not special like my mom. But my hair was longer—it reached the middle of my back—and I also had Mom's full lips, as she called them. *Whatever.*

I poked my head into my parents' room on my way out.

"What do you think?" Mom asked when she noticed me watching from the doorway.

She lived for nights like this and showed off her cocktail dress as she glided across the room.

"Real attention getter, no?" she said, obviously pleased with her reflection in the mirror.

"Wow," I said. Compliments were like crack to my mother, and I wanted to feed her addiction and keep her happy.

"Thanks, honey," Mom said dreamily, until she looked at me. "Oh, Cass—you're not going out like *that* are you? There's a stain on your shirt." She pointed to the bottom edge of my sweatshirt; an ordinary person would need an electron microscope to see the tiny speck, but not my mother.

I scratched at it, trying to scrape it away. What did it matter, anyway? I wasn't going out in public—just babysitting.

Dad was absolutely no help; he just gave me that look, the one that said he'd learned to choose his fights—and this wasn't one of them. He took the path of least resistance when it came to Mom's pickiness, and even though I should've been immune to it by now, I wasn't.

My father stood in front of the mirror, fiddling with his bow tie.

"There," he said. "Got it—after only seventeen tries. My New Year's resolution should be to learn how to tie one of these things right the first time. How 'bout you, Cassie? Any important resolutions?"

"Only to sweep the one-, two-, and four-hundred-meter races this spring."

"Whoa—that's a tall order. Bet you can do it, too."

Dad was the one who got me into track in the first place. His company sponsored a 10K race every year and I ran in the last two. The first time I crossed the finish line with energy to spare, I knew I wanted to run track in high school.

"Track again?" Mom tsked. "Cassie, what about cheer-leading, tennis, or the drama club?" Her voice always perked up when she talked about those things *she* did in high school. "Dawn's a cheerleader, and I'm sure she'd be happy to give you some pointers for the next tryouts."

"But I'm good at *running*, Mom," I mumbled, still trying to scratch away the tiny yellow stain on my sweatshirt. "Maybe this spring, you'll make it to one of my meets."

"All I ask is that you keep an open mind about other activities," she said.

I crossed my arms. "I guess" was all I could manage. No point starting a fight now. The Dawn she mentioned was not only a cheerleader; she'd been my best friend in elementary school. Her mother and my mom had remained friends ever since; in fact, her parents were celebrating New Year's Eve with mine. And Mom was always trying to ram me down Dawn's throat, only to have my former friend gag politely and spit me out.

It was nearly eight when the doorbell rang.

"That'll be limo with the Coopers," Mom said. "Tell the driver we'll be right down."

"Okay, but first I have to change my top."

"Good girl," Mom chirped.

I gave Dad a peck on the cheek, then leaned over to kiss Mom, who was still primping.

"Oh, honey, my make-up!" she said. That meant I should kiss her *near* her cheek, not *on* it. Mom's brand of affection was mostly hands-off, doled out in the form of compliments. I had no clue how Dad ever got close enough to actually *make* Kyle and me, not that I wanted that picture in my head. Eww!

After we wished each other a Happy New Year, I changed and bolted downstairs, put on my coat, went out and talked to the driver, and then hustled down the street to my babysitting job at the Vetrones'. As I rang the doorbell, Mrs. Spez, as I called Tara's mom, pulled up with Tara.

Mrs. Vetrone opened the front door and greeted us, then we followed her into the kitchen. She pointed out the list of phone numbers she'd left on the table, which in- cluded everyone from Nick's grandparents to the National

Guard; I had no doubt we'd be able to track her down in case of an emergency. Then the Vetrones told us they'd be back soon after midnight, showered Nick with hugs, kisses, and choruses of "Be a good boy," and left.

I scooped Nick into my arms and took him to the door to wave bye-bye; then, before he could think about crying, I started a round of "Where's Nicky?" in front of the foyer mirror. It worked every time.

Tara plopped on the couch and started channel surfing. She just came along to keep me company once Nicky conked out. Since there was no way she'd ever change a diaper, I didn't have to split my pay with her.

But right now my job was to play with Nicky, so I crawled around on the floor, saying, "I'm gonna get you." Nick screamed and laughed every time I popped out from somewhere. And after a few rounds, my ponytail holder slipped out and I became the hairy monster from Dogwood Drive. I stalked him to his room and back, and his diaper crackled under his penguin pajamas as he padded away at top speed.

"Don't get him all wound up," Tara said. "He'll never go to sleep."

"He will if I wear him out." I grabbed the remote, popped in a sing-along video, and Nick settled down in front of the TV.

"How about some milk, Nicky?" I asked as I headed to the kitchen.

Suddenly Tara gasped, then called out, "Cassie, come here and take a look at Nicky's hands."

I turned around to see his fingers laced with loose

strands of my hair. It was a lot—way more than when I comb it out after washing it.

"Gross," I said, as I untangled the hair from his fingers.

"He pulled all that out?" Tara asked.

"I guess, but I didn't even feel it."

When Nick finished his milk, I changed his diaper and carried him to the living room to say goodnight to Tara. He waved, then I brought him back to his room and tucked him in with his favorite blanket and bunny. I turned off the light, whispered, "Goodnight," and slipped out. I listened from the hall for a few seconds; he whimpered a few times, found a comfortable position, and that was it.

"Finally," I said after heading back to Tara. I opened a bottle of iced tea, nuked a bag of popcorn, and asked, "What's on TV?"

"Video countdowns to the New Year," Tara said, flipping through the channels. "Take your pick."

"It's Shantique!" I said—my favorite singer. Tara had just given me her latest CD for Christmas.

We sank into the couch, psyched to watch the countdown and bopping our heads as we sang along to the next few videos. Tara's feet, clad in bright holiday socks, tapped the coffee table. She had the most extensive sock wardrobe of anyone in the known universe.

"Shantique's so hot," I said, looking down at my lanky limbs and barely visible boobs.

"That's her job," Tara said, munching. "Plus, she's got a team of experts who get paid to make her to look like that. Hose her down and she's probably just like the rest of us."

We both perked up when Side Step's video came on. The lead singer almost never wore a shirt.

"Ooh, baby," I said.

"Niiice," Tara said.

We watched TV, trying to guess which of the videos would make the top three. Every so often I got up and listened at Nicky's door, just to be sure he was still sleeping.

The Vetrones got back close to twelve-thirty.

"How'd it go?" Mrs. Vetrone asked as Mr. Vetrone peeked in on Nick.

"No problems," I said, pulling on my jacket.

"I'm glad," Mrs. Vetrone said as she dug through her wallet and handed me two twenties and a ten. "Thank you very much."

Yes! She always rounded up.

Mrs. Vetrone dropped us off in my driveway and we thanked her for the ride.

"Do you want to hang out at my house tomorrow?" Tara asked as we went inside. "I mean today?"

"Sure. Your house is okay with me," I said as I shut the door. Stray pieces of tinsel blew across the floor and when I picked them up, the image of Nick's fingers tangled with my hair popped into my head.

I'm sure I would've felt it if he'd pulled it out. I shrugged. *Weird.*

Two

New Year's morning, I rolled out of bed and remem-bered my resolution—all three races. I wondered if a fresh-man had ever pulled that one off. And the start of a new year made it feel like anything was possible. I slipped on Darlington High sweats and went to Kyle's room, where Tara was sleeping.

"Come on, get up," I said, nudging her shoulder.

"Five more minutes," she mumbled.

"Okay, five more minutes," I told her and left.

Downstairs, the branches on the Christmas tree drooped under the weight of its ornaments. Later, Kyle and I'd take them off and pack them away while Mom and Dad de-Christmas the rest of the house.

In the kitchen, the scent of cologne and cigarette smoke greeted me as I passed Dad's coat slung over a chair. I poured two glasses of OJ and decided to let Tara sleep while I checked my e-mail. Consolidate my debt. DELETE. Lose forty pounds. DELETE. Enlarge my penis. Eeew. DELETE, DELETE, DELETE. I did find one non-spam message, from Tara, sent yesterday afternoon. I clicked on the link to find a dancing blue hedgehog tossing confetti and wishing me a Happy New Year.

Tara walked in, yawning and rubbing her nose. "Okay, I'm up, Miss Early Bird."

She may have been half-asleep, but her bouncy, telephone-cord curls that fell over her shoulders always looked wide-awake.

"This for me?" she asked, then sipped her juice. "Ya know, I never noticed before, but you look just like your mother in that picture upstairs."

"You think so?" I was skeptical.

"Sure—don't you?"

I shrugged and shook my head. "No, not at all." Despite what Mom hoped, there still was only one glamour girl in this house—and it wasn't me.

"Want to listen to the Shantique CD?"

"It's upstairs," I told her. "I'll get it."

Tara took my seat at the computer and I went back to my room, where the sun, slicing through the blinds, fell in a strange swirly pattern on my pillow. I walked over to check it out.

Holy shit! That weird pattern wasn't from the sun.

I ran halfway downstairs, leaned over the railing, and shouted, "T, get up here—quick!"

"Can't find the CD?" she asked.

"Never mind that—just hurry!" I shrieked.

Tara came upstairs, but not fast enough; I nearly yanked her arm out of the socket dragging her into my room. We stood at the foot of my bed and I pointed.

A lace doily of hair covered my pillow.

16

"Geez," Tara said.

"Tell me about it."

I grabbed a comb off my dresser and thrust it into Tara's hand, then plopped down in the chair in front of her. "Check and see what's going on up there, okay?" I begged.

She combed and parted my hair in a few different places, then said, "I feel like a chimpanzee looking for bugs."

"Well?"

"Just some lice," she joked.

"Cut it out, T. Seriously—what the hell is going on?"

"I don't know, Cass—I don't see anything."

But there was an awful lot of hair on that pillow.

A moment later, Mom was standing in the doorway, her fingers pressed against her forehead, her eyes two slits.

"G'morning, girls. Do me a favor and keep it down, okay? We need a little more sleep after our late night." Then she turned to walk away.

"Mom, wait."

She turned back and leaned against the doorjamb.

"My hair is—I don't know, something's wrong with it. Last night and this morning, too. I mean, *look at that*," I squeaked, pointing to my bed.

She inched toward my pillow, eyes wide, put her hand to her chest and ran out of my room. I followed her to her bedroom.

"Chet!" Mom said as she shook Dad awake. "Cassie's hair—it's starting again."

Again? What did that mean? "Did you say *again*? What's happening to me?"

Now Dad was up. "Everybody just calm down," he said, twisting his robe belt into a loose knot. "Let's go downstairs and talk about this."

We filed into the kitchen, then Mom dropped into a chair and buried her face in her hands. Tara sat in the far corner of the family room and picked up one of Mom's decorating magazines, trying not to intrude. Dad got the coffee started, then turned to me.

"Honey, when you were three—" he said, digging his hands into his pockets, trying to gather his words. He glanced over at Tara, not wanting her to hear what he was about to say.

But I didn't care. "Just tell me!" I hissed. "She's going to find out anyway. Now what's going on?"

"When you were in preschool, your hair started falling out in clumps."

What? "Are you trying to say I'm sick? Like cancer-sick?!"

"No, no, slow down," he said. "It's nothing like that."

I tried to swallow against the knot growing in my throat.

"You have a *condition*. It's called alopecia areata," Dad said. "There's something in your body that rejects your hair. It's sort of like having an allergy."

"There was nothing we could do," Mom said with a tremble in her voice.

No way. It didn't make sense.

"Maybe I accidentally pulled it out in my sleep."

Dad grimaced and rubbed the back of his neck as coffee filled the pot. "They told us it could start again at any time."

Mom shook her head and rambled. "You looked like you were in a fight and had your hair torn out. You were so little, and you wouldn't wear a hat."

"A hat?" My eyes shot open wider. "I needed a hat?"

Dad put his hand on Mom's shoulder. "Victoria, you're scaring her."

Mom blinked. "Oh—sorry. I was just caught off guard with this happening again, after all this time. The doctor told us then that it could grow back," she said, calming herself. "And it did, thank God—right in time for you to start kindergarten. Just like that." She snapped her fingers.

Arms crossed, I squeezed fistfuls of my sweatshirt and held on tight to keep my heart from pounding out of my chest.

"I don't remember any of this, but you're telling me I *was bald*. Is that it? And that's what's happening to me *now*?" I was shaking. "Why didn't you ever tell me about this?"

I felt like we were talking about someone else.

"Oh, honey. We didn't want you to worry," Dad said. "There was never a right time to bring it up as you got older. And up until now, we thought it wasn't going to happen again."

I couldn't believe they'd been keeping this secret from me for eleven years. I'd never heard of this condition, and my brain scrambled for another explanation—*any* other.

Maybe my hair was too dry from blow-drying or flat

ironing, and that had made it break off. Maybe a new sham-
poo or conditioner had caused it; Mom was always buying
me all-natural, top-of-the-line shampoos—her way of try-
ing to groom me into a show pony. I paused for a millisec-
ond. *Could that be it? Or a reaction to something I ate?*
Or maybe a vitamin deficiency? Anything was possible,
wasn't it?

I wanted there to be a different reason for this. "You're
wrong!" I snapped. "You *have* to be wrong!"

But nobody said anything.

"No," I insisted and started to cry. "This is a mistake.
I don't feel sick. I'm fine."

My parents still said nothing and Mom rubbed the side
of her face.

Tara's eyes were riveted on us and she looked horrified by what she was hearing. As the coffeemaker sputtered
the last few drops into the pot, she made a quick exit and
headed upstairs.

"But I feel fine," I told my parents. My words came
out like a plea.

Maybe I'd misunderstood. Maybe they'd say some-
thing to clear things up.

Still, they said nothing.

Losing my hair? It couldn't be. Heat washed over me
at the thought.

But Mom's and Dad's faces confirmed it. The faint
taste of orange juice in my mouth soured and all I could
think was, *No. I'm fourteen years old. I can't be losing my*
hair!

"Does Kyle know?" I asked.

"He wouldn't remember. He was just a baby."

"Does he have it, too?"

Mom shook her head. "I don't think so. He's never shown any signs."

"Great—just me." I sniffled and wiped my nose.

"Did it ever *all* fall out?" I choked on the words, afraid of the answer. But I needed to know.

"No," Mom said, looking at the ceiling. "I don't think I could've handled it. The other mothers at your school would look at you, then they'd turn their pathetic smiles on me, as if to say, 'Poor thing.' I could tell how relieved they were that it wasn't happening to their kids. I couldn't sign you out of that school fast enough—I had to get you out of there."

"Were they mean . . . the other kids?" I asked.

"You never said they were," she told me.

"Whatever this *peesha* condition is, it'll stop again. There's a cure, a special medicine or shampoo, right?"

Neither of them answered me.

"Right?" I demanded.

"Cass, take it easy," Dad said. "We'll make an appointment with Dr. Barnett. She's the dermatologist we went to when you were little. Everything'll be fine."

"That's easy for *you* to say! You didn't wake up with loose hair all over your pillow! This is such bullshit!"

My eyes blurred with tears as I ran out of the kitchen, up the stairs and to my room. I slammed the door, startling Tara as she stuffed her pajamas into her backpack.

"Can you freaking believe this?" I asked her.

21

"Cass, I don't know what to say. I'm so sorry."

I raked the hair off my pillow and squeezed the soft, spongy handful. My hand disappeared under the pile of hair.

"There *must* be a cure by now," she said. "A new medicine."

But I just stood there and cried.

"This is sick," I said, wiping my cheek. "What if it won't stop?"

There was a knock on the door—it was Dad.

"Tara?" he said, "Why don't you get your things together and I'll take you home."

"Sure, Mr. D."

Tara said, "I'm sorry, Cass—I gotta go." She grabbed the shoulder strap on her backpack and headed toward the door.

"What?" I said, not having been able to focus on her words.

"I'll call you later," she said.

"Huh? Okay. See ya later."

After Tara left, I dropped the clump of hair in the bathroom wastebasket and washed my face. I kept running my hand down the length of my hair, as if that'd help me figure out what was going on. Then Mom came in and stopped me, pressing her hand over mine on the vanity.

As we stood in front of the mirror together, I had a déjà vu that we'd done this before, but then it was gone.

Mom spoke to our reflection. "It'll be okay, honey. It didn't last that long the first time." She closed her eyes for a moment and shook her head ever so slightly. "I'm sorry, Cass, but I have to lie down. Please try not to worry."

Try not to worry? As if.

When I went back downstairs, I felt disconnected from my body, like I was guiding yet following myself through the quiet house. I wasn't sure where I should go or what I should do, so I curled up on the couch, turned on the TV, and watched the infuriatingly cheerful Rose Parade, coming to me live from beautiful, sunny, Pasadena, California. It didn't take long before I couldn't stand even the thought of roses.

That afternoon, Kyle and I stripped the Christmas tree. But the whole time, the word *alopecia* gnawed at the edge of my brain. I was so distracted that I dropped two crystal ornaments, shooting glass shards in every direction. It was just how *I* felt—shattered.

And I could only imagine what Tara was thinking, after that earful she left with this morning.

I finally got so desperate for a diversion, I played video games with Kyle. His eyes were glued to the screen as his thumbs whizzed over the game controls when he said, "Pretty scary, about—you know—your hair."

Dad must've given him the scoop earlier because the kid was letting me win.

"I know," I said.

"You okay?" he asked.

"I don't know. I guess."

I realized I needed to do some serious Googling about this condition I supposedly had. But every time I went to use the computer, Dad was banging away on it, catching up on work after taking time off between Christmas and New Year's.

When I'd had enough of the video games, I stopped by the kitchen to see what was for dinner. I leaned against the counter as Mom wrestled with steaming sheets of lasagna noodles.

"Want me to make a salad?" I asked.

"I'll take care of it," she said.

I opened the cabinet and pulled out the dinner dishes.

"I *said*, 'I'll take care of it.'" She sounded ticked off now, like I'd done something wrong. So I just left the stack on the table and sat down again with Kyle.

"Did you hear that?" I asked him. "I was only trying to help."

"Dad said she's taking your hair thing pretty hard, and that it's tough for a parent to watch their kid get hurt."

"I guess. But you weren't here this morning when they were telling me the wonderful news. Mom was definitely upset, but…more like for herself, if that makes any sense."

"Well, you know how she is," he said.

He was right. Everything had to be so perfect all the time. Sometimes that made it hard to breathe, because who could be perfect—like her—all the time?

"This'll get her all OCD for a while," Kyle joked, like he was reading my mind. "But she'll chill out eventually," he added.

I wasn't so hopeful.

❧

When we sat down to dinner, a thick, let's-all-pretend-nothing's-wrong silence hung between polite requests to pass the grated cheese. Kyle's dragging his fork through his teeth seemed amplified by a thousand percent and it made me cringe.

Mom, one elbow on the table, took one deep drink of red wine, then another as Dad twisted an impossibly stretchy piece of mozzarella around his fork. They both seemed lost in thought.

"It's your turn to clean up tonight," I told my brother.

Kyle groaned at the pile of pots in the sink.

"I'll clean up," Mom said, stacking her barely picked-at plate on top of Kyle's empty one. She couldn't have eaten more than two bites of her dinner.

"Thanks, Mom." Kyle wiped his mouth on his shoulder and took off before she had a chance to change her mind.

I didn't bother to offer to help before I got up and left the table. In my room, I stood in front of the mirror and slid my fingers through my hair. It felt the same. With a hand mirror I examined my head from every angle. It didn't look any different.

This can't really be happening. Can it?

Then my phone rang—Tara.

"Hey, girlie. You okay?" she asked.

"I've had way less suckful days, thank you very much," I said and dropped onto my bed, still checking out my reflection in the mirror. "Um, listen, T," I said, "please don't tell anyone about this, okay?"

"No way—I won't say anything," she vowed. "You know, I was thinking—there must be a cure for your aloe-um-hair problem. The news is always talking about genetic engineering, cloning, reattaching limbs. They've had a long time to come up with a breakthrough since you were a baby."

"But wouldn't my parents know about it?" I asked. "They haven't said a word. Still, there must be *something* they can give me for this, right?"

"Maybe herbal medicines? Holistic healing—" Tara suggested.

"But what if this really *does* happen? What'll I do? I mean, how do you cover missing patches of hair?" My heart hammered as I spewed out the possibilities. "Barrettes, scrunchies, headbands? Hats? A scarf? And walk around looking like a fortuneteller? I can't do that!" I started to cry again.

"Did you hear my mother? It was so bad last time, she had to take me out of school." I choked on the sobs and wiped my nose. "So really, what am I looking at here? A wig? Football helmet? Brown paper bag?" I whimpered into the phone.

"Oh, Cass. Don't cry. Maybe—"

"T—" I choked. "—I gotta go."

Three

The next morning I woke up long before the alarm went off, my heart pounding wildly in the stillness of my dark room. *Calm down. Deep breath*, I told myself. That helped before a race, but not in the middle of an all-out sprint, which was what my heart was doing. *If it happens again—if it all falls out—what will I do?* I couldn't move.

Morning seeped in around the edges of the window shade as the alarm buzzed. I bolted upright and hit the snooze bar, then reached back and ran my hand over the pillow—nothing! I didn't realize I was holding my breath until the lack of oxygen forced me to breathe. But thank God there was nothing on that pillow.

I rushed down to the kitchen to give Mom and Dad the scoop.

"Morning," I said, smiling.

Mom's expression relaxed when she saw me.

"Good morning to you," Dad said. "Is everything okay?"

"Nothing fell out last night."

"That's great, Cassie," Mom said with an uneasy smile as she clutched the collar of her robe.

Dad put his arm around my shoulder and squeezed, then said, "I still want to get you in to see Dr. Barnett."

"Couldn't we wait? Maybe it's over. Why jinx it?" How I wished it was over, or better yet, that it had never gotten started.

"Let's see what she says," he reasoned.

"I'll call this morning," Mom said.

After breakfast, I passed Kyle on my way back upstairs to get dressed for school. He had a severe case of bed head; flat on both sides, with the rest straight up like a shark fin. I was just glad mine was still attached.

Later, when the bus dropped me off behind the school, Tara and I met in the corner of the cafeteria that faced the parking lot. We crossed the length of the cafeteria on our way to Tara's locker, where the smell of floor cleaner mingled with a hint of Falcon burgers and chicken noodle soup.

"I didn't mean to freak out on you last night," I said.

"Hey, no biggie. I'd be seriously stressing, too," she said. "Feeling any better today?"

"Nothing happened this morning, if that's what you mean. But my father still wants me to see a dermatologist. Can we change the subject?"

"No problem. Shall we discuss global warming, foreign affairs, Adam Faber's sweet ass?" Tara had been totally into him since fall track.

"Get this," I said. "On the ride in, I heard Scott and Suzanne talking about this great New Year's Eve party. It sounded like the entire track team was there. So much for us lowly freshmen."

"You mean Robin's party?" Tara asked as she spun the combination on her locker. Robin Lakewood was a junior and co-captain of varsity track; she always acted like she was way too cool for me.

"Were you invited?" I asked her.

Tara tucked her chin inside her turtleneck as she jiggled the locker handle without answering me.

"So, was I the only one *not* invited? How nice."

"The invitation probably got lost in the mail. Once my mother got a birthday card that was postmarked the year before. Talk about snail mail."

"Like I'm gonna believe that."

The last warning bell rang before homeroom. I said goodbye to Tara, then squished my jacket into my locker and pulled out my books for my first three classes: Biology, Algebra II, and French. Then I jogged down the hall and slipped into homeroom just as Mr. Marsh was about to close the door. No one was allowed in after the bell without a late pass, something I learned on the second day of school when I got lost.

As everyone stood for the Pledge of Allegiance and the national anthem, I gazed out the window at a small, scraggly courtyard, where papers, candy wrappers, and a filthy gym sock decorated the bare branches. *Tara had turned down Robin's party to babysit with me.* Big deal if *I* wasn't invited, but Tara missed out on a party with the team and the chance to hang with junior and senior guys, especially

Adam. Then there was the whole hair thing; I bet now she wishes she'd gone.

It was totally off the wall. My hair couldn't be falling out like they were saying. It just didn't seem possible. But all I could do was wait. And I'd hit the computer lab in the library right after I ate lunch to see what I could find out on the Internet.

The morning announcements were brief; next month, track practice would begin, and soon after, the first meets. Some high schools were all about football or basketball, but here at Darlington High, it was all about track and field.

I cruised through Biology and Algebra II, and usually, I looked forward to French class. It was fun, kind of like going to preschool. We learned our colors, days of the week, and how to count to twenty—it was an easy A. But I was in no rush to get there, and for a good reason.

That's because my conversation partner was none other than one Robin Lakewood. Some conversationalist she was. Usually, the most I got out of her was *Je ne sais pas*—"I don't know" in French; otherwise, it was *J'ai oubliez*, meaning I forgot. It was the class favorite, and it always got a laugh when Monsieur Haus asked someone about their homework.

"Bonjour," Robin said as I sat down.

"Bonjour, comment ca va?" I responded politely.

Yes, I was sure my lost invitation would be arriving any day. But I refused to let on that I knew anything about her party as she studied my face, no doubt hoping for a re-action. And she may as well have waited for France to in-vade Australia, because she was getting nothing from me. Finally, she turned and faced forward. Like I needed any crap from her. *What did she have against me anyway?*

Monsieur Haus wrote a ton of verbs on the board that needed to be conjugated. As I worked, I stopped to think up alternate spellings for aloe-peesha. Luckily, by the time the teacher got through the verb families, there was no time left for conversation. *Merci, Monsieur Haus.*

At last I got to the library and went online. *Alopecia Areata* wasn't the spelling I'd come up with, but two clicks later, I was there. The first website I found showed a group of people with bald heads—all smiling.

What the hell could they possibly have to be happy about?

This couldn't happen to me.

As I read through the FAQs, I kept thinking, *not me.*

"Alopecia is an autoimmune disease," it said. Disease. Dad had called it a *condition.*

This was really freaking bad; I got more upset as I scrolled down, my hand shaking and tears threatening.

"Hair follicles are mistakenly attacked by a person's own immune system. Four and a half million people in the country have it. At present, there is no cure." I read it and sucked in my breath.

My God, no cure. Tara was so wrong.

I pressed my fist against my mouth to muffle the sobs rising in my throat, but it was useless. I was losing it right there in the school library.

"Treatment depends on a person's age and extent of hair loss. Treatments are most effective in milder cases, but none are universally effective." As I read this, the blood rushed in my ears; I was on overload from re-reading those terrible words.

What did it mean? Okay, so there was no one treatment that worked for everyone, but something must've worked for me because I had hair now.

"Hair can grow back even after extensive hair loss. And it could fall out again." It sounded like a giant merry-go-round of losing and growing hair. No matter where I clicked, I found the same bad news.

I'd been through this once already, not that I even re-membered it; but the thought of becoming a member of this hideous club of happy, bald aliens made me feel sick. And the more I read, the more I wondered: *Why hasn't anyone found a cure?*

Furious about everything I'd read, I yanked the mouse out of the computer tower and slammed it repeatedly on the keyboard. The screen flickered and went black.

Suddenly, an ancient teacher hobbled toward me, wag-ging his finger. "What are you doing? Stop that, young lady!" he said. "You're destroying school property."

I got up and bolted from the library without looking back.

This couldn't happen to me—I wouldn't let it.

I was distracted all day, and my teachers had to reel me in from outer space and back to their subjects. In Eng-lish, Miss Troy dredged up yet another bleak Sylvia Plath poem, and while she was totally getting off on the poet's misery, I was trying to shake Internet aliens out of my head. It wouldn't take much more to send me to the nearest bridge, where I'd end up just like Sylvia.

Finally, the bell rang and Tara and I headed to art class.

"Hey, girlie," she said. "You seemed kinda out of it in English."

"Sylvia Plath isn't the most uplifting poet, is she?" I think Tara knew it wasn't the poetry that had gotten to me, but I didn't want to tell her about the website pictures I'd seen. I shuddered and just said, "It's been a long first day back."

"Well," she said, "Mr. K's class is what you need."

Tara was right. I needed something—anything else to keep my brain occupied. Even though I wasn't very good, art was mostly a lot of fun. I sifted through the pile of pencil drawings we'd started before Christmas break, trying to find mine. The assignment was to draw our own hand. Some of the more creative people posed their hands doing something, like holding a can or giving a thumb's up sign; Alex's was flipping the bird. I kept looking and found Tara's drawing first. When I got to my own, I cringed.

"At least yours looks like a hand," I said, handing over her paper. "Mine looks like a branch with fingernails."

"It's not *that* bad," Tara said. "Try adding a ring."

I practiced on tracing paper.

"Hey, thanks for babysitting with me," I said. "Robin's party must've been awesome. I feel bad you had to miss it."

"New Year's was fun. I mean—"

"Anyway, thanks." I said and sketched a ring onto my

33

drawing. "Ugh—forget it. Now it looks like someone's building a tree house between the branches."

Tara giggled. "How 'bout adding a mitten?"

I rolled my eyes. "Thanks a lot."

⌒

Mom wasn't home when I got back from school, but she'd marked the calendar with my doctor's appointment for Friday. And I was surprised to see she'd made a facial appointment for herself at the end of the month at her favorite spa. While I couldn't focus on anything but losing my hair, Mom had still managed to think about booking a facial. Why was she so determined to be perfect all the time, no matter what else was going on? I just shook my head and left the room.

All week I tried to push alopecia deep down and out of my thoughts, but it was like trying to hold a beach ball underwater. Every morning I woke up panicked, wondering if there would be more hair on my pillow. But so far, there was nothing.

On Friday morning, the day of my doctor's appointment, I showered at the usual time, dried off, pulled on a robe, and twisted my wet hair into a towel. The plan was to go to my first two classes, then Mom would pick me up and take me to the doctor. I tossed my clothes on the bed and went back to the bathroom to plug in the blow dryer, then untwisted the towel.

And there it was, more horrifying than blood—a massive amount of lost hair.

My legs collapsed and I bashed my shoulder on the

towel rack as I tried to catch myself. Then I straightened up and angled a mirror over my head, frantically searching until I found a bald spot on top of my head. It was toward the back, and about the size of my fingertip.

I screamed and then Mom burst into the bathroom.

"Look!" I pointed to the towel full of hair that lay on the floor.

"All right," she said. "Let's not panic." She took me by the arm and positioned me in the doorway, then said, "First, let's get rid of this," and raked the hair off the towel with two fingers. She was all business, like she'd just killed a giant spider. She dumped the hair into the garbage and tossed the towel in the hamper, and you'd never know anything had gone wrong. Satisfied with her cleanup, Mom walked me back to my room.

I sat on my bed, touching the naked spot on my scalp, my fingers drawn to it like a magnet. It was creepy, touching skin where there should have been hair.

"What am I going to do, Mom?"

"Just cover it up," she told me as she dashed out of my room. She was back a minute later with mousse, a comb and a handful of clips, barrettes, and ponytail holders. "Here," she said, dropping them on the bed next to me and patting my shoulder. "No one has to know, honey. It'll be okay."

I picked up the comb and suddenly the idea of getting ready to leave the house terrified me. "But what if more comes out?" I asked her, feeling so confused.

"Listen, Cass, if you don't mousse your hair soon, it'll dry into a knotty nightmare. You have your appointment later this morning, so let's get through that, okay?" She gave me a stiff smile and repeated her question. "Okay?"

I nodded and thought she'd help me, but she didn't wait around.

I sprayed a blob of mousse into my hand—double the usual amount to avoid having to drag a comb through any knots. Working a small section at a time, I started from the ends and combed up to the roots, my hands trembling. I worked carefully, slowly, and got through it, then finished by smoothing my hair back and clipping it into a loose ponytail.

I stepped into my jeans, threw on a shirt, and stood staring at my reflection. Then I used the hand mirror again to examine the back of my head, praying that this shedding had been a fluke and wouldn't get any worse.

At school, all through Algebra, the minute hand on the clock seemed like it would never move, and then it'd jump six minutes. Between jumps, I scribbled equations in my notebook in a kind of delayed reaction just before Mrs. Furmanchek erased them and moved on. Restless, I pulled out Mom's note excusing me from school and read it over. Ten o'clock—it wouldn't be long now. And then I'd find out what the dermatologist had to say about my problem.

When the bell rang, I had just enough time to go to my locker, then head straight to the office with my note. I handed it to the secretary, whose desk hosted a Beanie Baby convention. She read the note, put it aside, and spun around in her chair, leaving me standing there. I felt out of place and didn't know what I should do next; I'd never left school early before, other than for an away track meet.

"Should I wait here?" I asked.

She turned back around. "Either that, or you can wait by the front door. Is that where you're getting picked up?"

I wasn't sure. After practice, Mom always came to the back of the school, but that's where the track was so it made sense. I thought about it, then said, "I'll wait in the front. Thanks."

I left the building and stood on the front steps, next to one of the cement falcons that roosted proudly at Darlington's main entrance. I'd see Mom's car and head her off before she drove around back. I picked at the threads inside my coat pocket.

Okay, let's think positive. The doctor will give me some medicine and everything'll be fine. It has to be, I thought. *This morning was a fluke. Everything'll be fine.*

In no time, I'd picked open the seam and could shove two fingers through right through the pocket to the lining of the coat, my fingers as relentless as my thoughts.

Then Dad's car pulled up.

"Where's Mom?" I said, as I opened the door and slid in.

Four

"Mom called me at work," Dad said.

I clicked on my seat belt. "She all right?"

He pulled away from the school and told me, "She isn't good with this sort of thing."

What sort of thing? Mom was the one who always took Kyle and me for our checkups, and went with me to mother-daughter night in fifth grade for "the period talk." But when I really thought about it, Dad was right. When Kyle got stung by a bee and his finger blew up like a hot dog, *Dad* was the one who raced him to the ER, not Mom. And that summer after first grade, at the town pool, when I climbed out over the side, slipped, and sliced open my chin, Mom had stayed with Kyle and *Dad* rushed me to the doctor. He was the one who held my hand while the doctor sewed me up. That night, when Mom tucked me in, she spun soft circles on my forehead and cooed, "My poor girl. Let's be thankful that you didn't need stitches on your face." For her, it was all about appearance.

"So Mom didn't take me to the dermatologist when I was little?"

"I guess it was just easier for her to stay home with your brother."

Hearing that, I got that same weird feeling as when they first told me about my losing my hair the first time. Then, before I could stop myself, I blurted, "More came out this morning."

"Oh, babe, I'm so sorry." He glanced in the rearview mirror and switched lanes.

"Do you think it'll stop? There must be something they can do by now."

"You'll be fine," he said, in his typical glass-is-half-full way. "I know it."

Okay. Maybe this morning was a one-shot deal and I'd worked myself up over nothing. But I'd read all that information on the website. It said there was no cure, and now I didn't know what to think. I just prayed this doctor would know something the Internet didn't.

Dad exited the highway in a dizzying loop and soon we pulled up to an elegant brick building. It could've been a fancy restaurant, with its large arched windows and potted topiary trees lining the front steps.

At the entrance, I scanned the directory. My doctor was first on the list, DR. LESLIE BARNETT, DERMATOLOGIST. She was on the second floor, suite three. I took a deep breath to steady myself. This was it.

When we got to the office, I took a seat in the waiting area and Dad went to the receptionist's window and gave her my name. Nothing was familiar, but I was only three the last time I was here.

The receptionist handed Dad a clipboard and forms to

fill out. Dad pulled a few cards out of his wallet and started filling out the forms. Meanwhile, I noticed a rack of pamphlets on the wall: Acne, Chemical peels, Ringworm, Melanoma, Warts, Basal Cell Carcinoma, Eczema, Psoriasis—some pretty disgusting stuff. The rest may as well have been written in Greek; that's how little the names meant to me. And as far as I could see, none of them were about alopecia. Dad handed the clipboard back to the receptionist, who told him the doctor would be right with us.

Two *People* magazines later, a door opened and an old man stepped out, followed by a nurse.

"Cassandra Donovan," the assistant said. "Please come right this way."

We followed her trail of fabric softener fragrance to an examining room, where she opened a folder that held the papers Dad had just filled out.

"How are you today?" she asked me.

"Fine, thanks." *Not. That's why I'm here.*

"Any allergies?"

I shook my head and she made a note.

"And the first sign of hair loss was about a week ago?"

"Yes," I told her. "Then it stopped." I lifted my hand to the back of my head and jerked it away like I might get burned if I touched that naked spot. I swallowed hard and went on, "It started up again today."

"Okay, hon. The doctor will be right in," she said as she left.

When the door opened again, a short, pudgy woman stepped in. She held out her hand, saying, "Hi, Cassandra, I'm Dr. Barnett."

She had clear skin—that was a good sign. Otherwise, it'd be like trusting a dentist with bad teeth—it'd make no sense. She was also wearing a thumb ring, which was cool.

We shook hands. "Cassie," she said. "I'm sure you don't remember me."

"Sorry, no—I don't," I told her.

"I wouldn't have recognized you either," she said, smiling. "It's been a very long time." She shook hands with Dad, too. "What are you now, a sophomore?"

"Freshman."

"That's great—time flies by quickly enough, and before you know it you'll be off to college." She rolled a stool out from under the counter and the vinyl squeaked as she sat and shifted to find a comfortable position. She clasped her hands in her lap, then said, "So, Cassie, your history suggests that alopecia areata runs in your family."

"It does?" I turned to Dad and he nodded.

Dr. Barnett lifted a page inside the file. "Let's see. Yes, your maternal grandfather had it, too."

I questioned Dad, "So Mom has this? It happened to her, too?"

"Not that I know of," he said. "Let's let the doctor go on."

Why didn't they tell me about Grandpa? I remembered that he was balding, with a fringe of hair around his head. But a lot of old men get that way.

"Do you understand what alopecia is?" Dr. Barnett asked.

"I looked it up on the Internet."

"That's good. Basically, what happens is that the white

blood cells in your body that are normally responsible for fighting off infection somehow get the wrong signal and attack your hair follicles. When this occurs, the hair can't enter its growth stage and you're seeing the results. This condition may also affect facial hair."

Why is she telling me this? I wondered. I wasn't planning on growing a beard.

"That means eyebrows and eyelashes can also fall out," she explained.

Oh, shit. This just keeps getting worse.

I tried so hard to understand, but now the words seemed to be coming at me like Jell-O thrown against a brick wall. She went on about *alopecia totalis* and *alopecia universalis*, and I felt as lost as when my Algebra teacher tried to explain some weird new way to solve for *x*.

Dr. Barnett continued reading the page in my folder. "I see that this time, you've had two incidents of hair loss, and they weren't concentrated in any one area on your scalp."

"There were three incidents," I said. "And the third time—today—left a bald spot."

"May I see?"

She stood up as I searched with my fingertip for the spot under the stiff, dry mousse. Then I tipped my head forward so she could see where I pointed. "Here."

Dr. Barnett tugged the hair in the surrounding area; I totally didn't expect that and started wondering about my doctor's sanity. Weren't we trying to *save* my hair?

Her lips puckered a bit as she examined my eyebrows and eyelashes.

"Mm-hmm. I can't be certain what's triggering it now. We still don't know very much about this condition, except that it's very unpredictable. The fact that your hair grew back the first time is a big plus."

Not what I wanted to hear. Was she saying I should *expect* my hair to fall out, then wait around for it to grow back? My foot jiggled as I waited for her to get to the part of this appointment where she actually came up with a way to save my hair, or at least gave me something to fix the problem.

The doctor tipped her head to the side and said, "Sometimes it helps to know you're not alone. Something like two million young people live with some degree of hair loss."

I flipped out. "Is that supposed to make me *feel* better? Besides, if there are two million of them, where the hell are they? *I've* never met one. You don't even have a stupid brochure about it outside!"

"Cass!" Dad's tone was sharp.

"It's okay," Dr. Barnett said to Dad. "I understand. It's a lot to digest. Listen, Cassandra, one of my patients runs an alopecia support group. I'm sure he can put you in touch with a teen group if you're interested."

I crossed my arms. "I am *not* some kind of whack job, and there's no way I'm going to join some group of bald people, my age or not!" Then I started bawling again.

"Maybe I'm getting ahead of myself," she said, patting my leg.

Dad plucked a tissue from a box on the counter and

handed it to me, then put his arm around me as I let out an-other round of sobs.

I wished she'd have said it was something else. Not this. Not alopecia.

After a while, I managed to calm down and wiped my face.

Dad asked, "You okay, babe?"

Far from it. But I nodded anyway.

"All right, then. Let's talk about treatments," the doc-tor said. "There are a few things we can try."

That's better. Now hold it together and listen.

"It's best to start with the least aggressive treatment, so we'll start with a topical lotion."

I sniffed and rubbed my nose. "Can't we just start with the one that works?"

Dad gave Dr. Barnett a look like, *she's got a point there.*

"Some people *do* respond well to the topical," she said. "So let's give it a try for a few weeks, okay? You'll use a drop or two on the bare spot twice a day. The skin should be clean and dry before applying the drops. We'll try to stimulate the hair to grow in again." She scribbled out a pre-scription in hieroglyphics and handed it to Dad.

"Minoxidil?" he asked.

She nodded. "If the minoxidil does its job, new hairs should appear as a soft, downy growth, like baby hair. Oh, and don't hesitate to call me if anything changes, okay, Cassie?"

When she spoke, Dr. Barnett chose every word care-fully. She didn't answer yes or no. She didn't give the impression that this was a hopeless situation, but she didn't come off as, 'Hey, it's no problem. This happens all the time.' And after a few weeks, *maybe* I'd end up with some baby hair? *Damn. That wasn't much at all.*

"Thanks, Doctor," Dad said.

Dr. Barnett closed the folder and extended her hand to Dad, then to me.

"Hang in there, okay?" she said.

On our way out, I peeked into Dr. Barnett's office from the hall. Diplomas, plaques, and important looking certificates cluttered a whole wall. But I couldn't help feeling let down. All that education, all that knowledge, and all I got was, 'We'll see what happens'? Seemed like a total rip-off to me.

Dad and I rode home, and we were on Meadowbrook Road when he turned into the Willow Square strip mall, then parked in front of the pharmacy. I wished he'd dropped me off first.

"Can I wait in the car?" I asked.

"Sure. I'll be right back."

I slumped down in the seat and propped one foot on the dashboard. Eventually Dad came back with a small white bag and put it between us on the front seat. "Swisher's Pharmacy," the bag read, "Caring for our community for the last forty eight years."

My head felt dull and fuzzy, like I hadn't slept in forty-eight hours. "Do I have to go back to school?" I asked.

"It's still early enough," Dad said, then turned to me. "But I think it'll be okay to hang out at home for the rest of the day." He shifted into reverse and winked. "Maybe I'll play hooky, too."

Mom met us at the front door with a nervous smile.

"So what did the doctor say?" she asked.

"I have medicine," I said, wanting to be optimistic. I held up the pharmacy bag to show her. As long as I could remember, Mom's mantra was always 'How you look when you leave this house is a direct reflection on me.' I got a strong sense that she didn't want a daughter who looked like one of those Internet space aliens. And I didn't want to become one. All I wanted was for everything to go back the way it was.

I said, "She said my hair will grow back in a few weeks."

"That's…good news, then…," Mom said, almost like she suspected I was lying, but was willing to go along with it. She nudged the crooked doormat with her toe until it was realigned with the front door.

"Cass?" Dad said. "I think what the doctor meant was—"

"Yes," I said to Dad through gritted teeth. I planted a fake smile and nodded, saying, "Good news."

"Babe, I know it's important to stay positive," Dad said. "But—"

I turned and dashed up to my room, suddenly pissed off that I was clutching that white bag, pissed that I could lose more hair—that I'd have to 'wait and see.' But what really killed me was that Mom made me feel like I had to lie about it. It wasn't like I'd ever purposely called nega-tive attention to myself, like hitting the streets in a metallic space suit, rubber wading boots, and a Statue of Liberty crown or anything. This was beyond my control!

I ripped open the bag, and under the box of medicine I found a pack of ponytail holders and butterfly barrettes. The ponytail holders were made of soft, squishy chenille. Dad probably thought they'd be gentle on my hair. The barrettes might look cute if I was still in second grade and I tucked them into my jewelry box. But it was nice of him to try.

I examined the box that held the medication, turning it over in my hand. The label said, "To stimulate new hair growth and prevent further hair loss." I opened it and pulled out a bottle, a dropper, and the directions. I unscrewed the cap and took a whiff: nothing. I strained to understand all of the fine print: "Temporary hair thinning may occur to prepare for new growth. Noticeable results should take about four months but could take up to eight months. Discontinue use if any irritation occurs."

Four to eight months? That was a helluva stretch from a few weeks! Waiting another hour to try it wouldn't make a difference, so I changed into my running clothes, fished through the downstairs closet for my sneakers, double-knotted them, and bolted out of the house.

The cold air tightened the muscles in my neck and back, and the slick, cool spandex hugged my legs. I rolled my head and scrunched my hands inside my sleeves. I should've stretched first, but my legs were already carrying me away.

I found a comfortable rhythm as my arms pumped to the soft thump of my sneakers on the pavement. Icy January air filled my lungs, and puffs of warm air pushed out, moistening my lips.

My feet knew the route: to the edge of the neighborhood, toward the winding path in the woods. With my body on automatic pilot, I could drift outside of myself and think about anything or nothing. Over the metal footbridge, along the stream, up another path to the next neighborhood, I needed nothingness. The steady thumping, breathing, and thumping released me and I finally found some peace.

Before long, I'd run the full circle and was headed back up Dogwood Drive. I slowed to a shuffle, then to a walk and up the steps to the front door. My ears were pounding—my own fault for leaving them uncovered in subfreezing weather.

I went to the kitchen, peeled off my sweatshirt, and poured a glass of water.

"I made you some lunch," Mom said.

"I'm not hungry."

"I'll leave it here. Maybe after—"

"Whatever," I snapped. Then I felt bad. She was trying to be nice. "Thanks, I'll have it later." I started up the stairs and my insides twisted and tightened. It wasn't an empty stomach that was bothering me—far from it.

I stepped into a steamy shower, where the hot water stung my cold hands and face as I smoothed shampoo into my hair. Afraid to scrub, I let the shower rinse away the thick coating of shampoo. Foamy lather slid over my shoulders and rushed down my back. I added conditioner, then washed my face. Water pooled around my feet and I cleared away soap bubbles with my toes. That's when I saw it.

A wad of hair was covering the drain.

Noooo! The tile walls closed in on me as I slid down and melted into a ball in the corner of the shower, crying. Mournful, guttural sounds rose up, twisting with the steam over my head. I covered my ears against the horrible echoes. I huddled there so long, the hot water eventually got cold, making me shiver. By now, my chest and shoulders ached from the heaving sobs.

"Cassie!" Dad knocked at the door. "You okay in there?"

I wobbled to my feet and turned off the water.

"Cassie!" He knocked again, harder.

I quickly dried off, threw on my robe, and opened the door. "Please make it stop. Please, Daddy, please make it stop," I said, pointing toward the shower drain.

Dad's arms surrounded me and squeezed me tight, his chest pounding against my cheek. When I was little, whenever he'd held me when I was upset, everything would be fine by the time he let go and the problem would disappear like magic. I wished I could go back to that time. I wanted to stay right there, where I was safe.

Five

By the time Dad finally let go of me, I was exhausted from all the crying.

"God, this sucks," I said.

"Want me to send Mom up to help you?"

I pulled my robe tight in front of me. "No. I'm okay."

Back in my room, I just sat on my bed for the longest time, flicking my thumb over the teeth of the comb. I knew I had to hide this. Tara would never breathe a word, but how long could I keep something like this a secret? People were eventually going to notice, and then what'd happen? I could understand how they'd get all grossed out, and I still couldn't shake those bald Internet pictures from my brain.

I hurled the comb across the room.

This isn't fair! I'm not a freak!

No. Get a grip. Pick up the comb and get started.

It took forever to comb out my hair because I had to be extra careful. Halfway through, my arms felt so heavy; it was like I was holding fifty-pound weights over my head. The whole time, I kept praying, *No more. Please don't let anymore hair fall out.* I caught a knot and tugged at it instinctively and then my heart dipped. But there was nothing in the comb this time. I let out a deep sigh of relief.

As I let my hair air dry, I felt a draft on the back of my head, up near the top. I angled the mirror to find a shiny new circle of bare scalp, smack in the center of my head. It was about the size of a quarter and I traced it with my finger.

So smooth. So creepy.

Anyone who was a few inches taller than me couldn't miss it if they were behind me. I shifted some hair to cover the new bare spot, but it wouldn't stay put; changing my part wouldn't camouflage it either. I figured out that I'd have to pull at least the top part of my hair into a ponytail to hide the bald spot, letting the rest hang straight down.

When my hair was completely dry, I went to the bathroom to apply the first dose of medicine. On the first try, I spazzed out and dripped it onto the floor, but then I managed to make contact with that first bare patch of scalp. I applied two drops with the tip of the applicator and it evaporated with an icy zing.

That's it, I thought. *Get in there. Start growing some hair.*

But this morning's patch was harder to get to, and as I tried to hold the surrounding hair out of the way with the hand mirror, I zapped my finger with the liquid instead of my head.

Great, now I'll have hair growing on my finger. How strong is this stuff? I wondered as I fought back more tears.

Finally, I got coordinated and used bobby pins to hold the hair back, then finished the job.

Downstairs, Kyle was home from school, digging around in the kitchen for a snack. My turkey sandwich was still sitting on the counter as he sat down with half a sleeve of chocolate chip cookies and a glass of milk. As he shoved a cookie into his mouth, it sounded like he'd asked, "So how'd it go at the doc's today?"

I snagged a cookie from his package and dipped it into his milk.

"Get your own," he said, and formed a wall around his stash with his hands.

"Wanna see?" I said, and tipped my head to give him a look.

"Holy shit!" he said, then cringed as we waited to see if Mom was in earshot. Lucky for him, she wasn't.

"Tell me about it," I said. "One minute everything's fine. The next minute, I'm staring at a wad of hair and I'm a basket case. I feel like I'm totally losing it."

"Man, that sucks."

"Royally." I stole another cookie.

Kyle dipped his next one too long and it sank to the bottom of his glass.

"Hey, guess what we did in Social Studies?" he said. "We had a sub today." He started cracking up. "And me and Rob passed a note around to the whole class. It said, 'Fall off your chair at two o'clock.'"

"And you and Rob were the only ones who did."

"No, it was awesome. They all did it! Even the girls! Oh, man. That sub went wild. She didn't know what to do with the whole class rolling around on the floor laughing."

"Excellent."

"When we got back in our seats, we couldn't stop cracking up so she couldn't teach. She was fuming. I mean, steam was coming out of her ears."

We were both laughing now.

"And guess what! Then she walked out and never came back!" Kyle laughed harder. "I don't think she'll ever come back to our school, no matter what." He banged his hand on the table.

Mom walked into the kitchen. "What's so funny?"

Kyle shook his head.

"Nothing," I laughed.

Mom came around the table behind us and dropped the dishcloth in front of Kyle. She slid my lunch in front of me and I felt her hovering for an extra half a second. We'd quieted down just enough to hear Mom gasp.

My hand sprang up to cover the patches as I whipped around to face her. "It's not that bad, is it?" I asked.

"Uh—um, no," she said, turning away and tugging at her earring.

"You won't be able to see it when my hair's tied back," I told her.

Kyle stood up and looked again. "Maybe you can draw a smiley face in there. Or, you know what would be so cool? Make it look like two eyeballs, so people'll think you have eyes in the back of your head."

I gave him the death stare. *That was not even remotely entertaining.* Then I pushed my dish away.

I promised myself I'd wait at least two weeks before checking for new hair. That lasted about two days. Before applying each dose of medicine, I prayed: *Maybe today*. It was hard to get close enough to the mirror to see if I was making even the tiniest bit of progress. But if I was going to be able to find any soft new hairs, I'd need a microscope. The skin always looked so shiny; it was never fuzzy, and it still felt smooth.

A week later, on Friday night, I found Mom in the kitchen getting dinner ready and humming to herself. The mouth-watering fragrance of rosemary chicken filled the room.

I scraped a chair away from the table and sat down and said, "Mom, what other things did you try when I was little to get my hair to grow back?" Then I leaned forward on my elbows and waited.

She opened the oven door and added salt to the tiny gourmet potatoes surrounding the chicken. "There weren't a lot of options, really. Just remember to keep up with your medicine. Do you need a refill? Because your hair looks fine," she said.

"No. I'm good."

Next, she started hacking at a head of broccoli, the blade moving at sharp angles as she deposited the chunks in a colander. She patted the pile after it grew to reach the top of the colander.

"Um, Grandpa had this, right? Did it ever happen to you?"

The next thing I knew the colander hit the floor and

broccoli flew all over the place. *Whoa. That was quite a reaction!*

I swooped in and started collecting the big pieces.

"What a mess," Mom said. She picked up the last piece and threw it into the sink. Then she took out the dustpan and went to work on the bits of broccoli confetti dotting the tile floor. She put on a fake grin after she swept up the last green speck.

"Well, did it?" I asked again. My voice sounded tiny and far away.

Mom ran hot water over the colander and wisps of steam rose from the sink. *Damn, you could brew a cup of tea with that water.* Bare handed and unfazed by the heat, Mom scrubbed each piece of broccoli feverishly, shaking her head.

"I think Gramma would've had cardiac arrest if that'd happened, especially when she was dragging me in and out of the city five nights a week, hitting every modeling agency under the sun. Even the sleaziest agents were turning me down, but she was determined and we never missed a cattle call. How many times I paraded in and out for a go-see, without so much as a call back. Thank God for that one commercial. For Gramma, it was like she'd hit the lottery."

With the broccoli sufficiently washed to within an inch of its life, Mom wiped her sunburn-red hands on the dish towel. I never knew about all the rejections it took before she got that commercial made. I mean, she always seemed so *into* it. Mom usually managed to work her modeling into conversations even with complete strangers.

"Oh, I almost forgot," Mom chirped, switching gears. "Mrs. Vetrone called earlier. It's a little last minute, but she asked if you could babysit Nick tomorrow night."

"Tomorrow's cool. As long as she wasn't calling for tonight."

"That's right. Mrs. Cooper mentioned that Dawn's going to Battle of the Bands, too. So you'll get to see her there."

"I'm going with Tara, Monique, and Amy, and some girls from track."

Simply put, we used to be a group of four: Monique and Amy, who are still best friends and practically conjoined twins, and Dawn and me. But somehow in eighth grade, Dawn passed through a secret portal into the mystic realm of popularity, and the rest of us were *not* invited along.

"I thought it'd be nice for you two to spend some time together again," she said, ignoring the fact that I had real friends who actually called and *liked* hanging out with me.

"I already have plans."

"Either way, just make sure you give Mrs. Vetrone a call before you leave."

I left a voice mail for the Vetrones and got ready. I'd recently cracked open the cosmetic gift pack Mom bought me two years ago, and put on a touch of mascara, blush, and lipstick. Then I tried to think of a different way to wear my hair. But I settled on my new standard, with the top part of my hair pulled into a ponytail. For a little pizzazz, I worked with the crimping iron down the length. My ride was already waiting outside when I triple checked my head.

Mom called up to my room. I paused again—just one last look.

I heard the driver honking impatiently and thought, *Keep your panties on. I'm coming.* Then I rushed outside.

℮

The Battle of the Bands raged on in the Driscoll gym, all original music, ranging from teeth-rattling heavy metal, which I strategically saved for bathroom breaks, to rock, to a jazz band with a girl drummer. Each band had its own small following, with girls who danced in front and swayed and sang along.

After a jackhammer and machine-gun love song from Tears of Frustration, the jazz band Silk City took the stage. They had a polished, sophisticated look, and a sound to match. A mellow instrumental washed over the room and I was surprised by my own reaction. The full, rich tones of the horns seeped inside me and simmered in a way that made me feel warm all over.

"Omigod," I said to Tara. "Check out the sax player. It's Tommy Sweeny. I haven't seen him since eighth-grade graduation. I thought he ended up going to County Vo-Tech instead of here."

"First-kiss Tommy," Tara said, nudging me with her elbow.

Yes. My first and so far *only* make-out kiss was with Tommy. And Tara was the only person on earth who knew that, when Tommy and I were making out, I let him feel me up—over the shirt, just a little, before I got scared and pushed his hand away. *I mean, who lets a guy do that the first time you kiss? Probably everyone—that's why I'll end up dying a virgin.* I could see the scarlet letter emblazoned on my tombstone, P for prude. *Damn.* And feeling up aside, I really liked him.

My eyes were glued to the stage. Tommy's fingers fluttered over the shiny throat of the saxophone, and his shoulders tensed and released as he hit the soulful notes. He wore a Frank Sinatra-type hat, brim folded up in the back. Yes, the boy had style.

"The song's over. You should go talk to him," Tara said.

The band set their instruments aside and left the stage.

"I can't do that," I told her.

"He's leaving the gym," she said. "Hurry up. Go say hello."

"No, but maybe we should take a walk."

"Like go undercover and follow him?" Tara asked.

"Zack-ly."

We made like Sherlock Holmes and followed the crowd out of the packed gym in time to keep tabs on Tommy. We kept a safe distance back as he walked the length of the annex, a dining area reserved for juniors and seniors, and finally into the main cafeteria. And was that boy turning heads! I always thought he was cute, but there was definitely something about musicians. Girls flocked around them like seagulls around a French fry.

We reached the mobbed cafeteria and I imagined Tommy being devoured by the ever-popular Dawn and her new BFF Kelly, or even worse—by some hot junior or senior girl. *I mean, really. Can't they leave the younger ones for us freshmen?*

"Crap," I said. "Where'd he go?"

"Let's get a drink and sit down," Tara said. "He'll turn up."

We got iced tea and sat opposite each other at the table, then waited. I was about to call it quits after what seemed like forever, when Tara glanced over my shoulder and jerked back in her seat. She started bouncing her leg so hard, the table probably registered at least a seven on the Richter Scale.

"Don't turn around." Her eyes flashed wider. "I think he's coming over here."

Omigod! This was good. But then I thought about the back of my head and how he was approaching from behind. I'd checked my head before I left the house and was sure I was safe—at least that was what I hoped.

"Just act normal," Tara whispered.

"Cassie?"

I turned around and did my best to seem surprised when I said, "Oh—hi, Tommy."

"I thought that was you," he said, and hooked his thumb on his belt loop. "Hey, Tara," he added.

Boy, he's still cute. Maybe even cuter than last year.

"Your band sounded great," I told him.

"Thanks, but it's my brother's band. Eric's the one who plays keyboard."

"You know what?" Tara said. "I have to go. Amy's waiting for her drink." She grabbed *my* cup.

What's the big idea? I wondered. *I'm going to need that!* Already, my mouth felt like it was lined with a towel.

"I'll meet you upstairs," she said and disappeared.

This was a classic example of 'be careful what you wish for.' Somehow, my previous knowledge of the English language had somehow been sucked out of my brain and I felt hot, sweaty, and practically mute. I sat there with my thousand-watt smile, but if I didn't say something soon, he'd think I was too stupid to waste any more time on and find someone who could actually make conversation.

A sophomore girl breezed by and flashed a seriously flirty expression at him. *Take a hike, girlie.*

"You know, I forgot you played an instrument," I said. "You were really good."

Tommy slipped into Tara's empty seat and I snuck a better look at him. He had the kind of long lashes that most girls would kill for, and with that mop of wavy black hair, he was totally hot. I watched his bangs dance on his forehead every time he blinked.

"Wasn't too long ago, my sax was on the way to eBay."

"What do you mean?"

"Me and Eric were always tight, ya know? Then he started Silk City and working part time at the dry cleaners…and now there's Eric's girlfriend, Dina, too. Who's totally cool." Tommy ran his finger along a deep scratch in the ugly Formica tabletop. "Anyway, last year, once he had the band going, I dug out my sax and started practicing again. I mean, it's not like I don't have plenty of friends and all, don't get me wrong but—"

"You missed him," I said.

He nodded his head and gave a shy shrug, having offered me this bit of inside information about himself. *Amazing.* I'd have guessed most musicians are in it for the music first, followed closely by the screaming female groupies. But for Tommy, it was mostly about staying tight with his big brother.

He adjusted his hat and went on. "So I've been rehearsing with Silk City for about six months. Eric's hoping that if we kill tonight, we might be able to land a paying gig somewhere—a backyard party, a coffeehouse, or crafts fair, something like that." He unscrewed the cap on his water bottle and asked, "Want a sip?"

"No, thanks. I'm fine." *That is, if you consider heart palpitations, cotton mouth, and sweaty palms to be fine.* How cruel the human body is to siphon the moisture out of the one place you need it and put it where you totally don't want it. I wiped my moist hands on my lap.

The conversation flowed as we began comparing schedules. Our classes were mostly on the opposite sides of the school. Darlington is a regional high school, and with all the new faces from two other towns, it was possible to never run into some of them at all. The time passed quickly, but then Tommy glanced at his watch.

"I have to get back upstairs. The judges'll announce the results soon—I don't want to miss it if we won."

"Yeah. Me, too. I need to find Tara and the others."

We started walking and I noticed he was a lot taller now than when I knew him. *Yes, the testosterone gods have smiled upon him.* His shirt was unbuttoned enough to tease me with the chiseled outline of his pecs. I liked having to tip my chin up to make eye contact.

"So, where did you find a girl drummer?" *Please don't say she's your girlfriend.*

"You'd be surprised. There are a lot of them out there. Elaine goes out with one of my brother's friends."

Good, good. Stay calm.

We walked to the lobby where the four sets of double doors outside the gym barely contained the noise blasting from inside. Someone was making an announcement over the microphone, and Tommy slipped his hands into his pockets, then leaned against the wall. I got out of the swirl of traffic and moved closer to him.

We heard another announcement being made, and Tommy said, "I really have to get going. Maybe I'll see you around again, sometime." He said this, but he didn't actually move.

"I hope so," I told him, wondering if I sounded lame.

He smiled at me, then said, "I'll give you a call then, okay?"

I nodded. Then, before he took off inside the gym doors, I touched his arm and said, "Good luck."

Seconds later, Tara rushed toward me shouting, "I caught that!"

"Spying on me?"

"Nope, just happened to be in the right place at the right time," she said.

"That makes two of us."

Six

Saturday morning, I was up early and tried to stay occupied while I waited to see what would happen next. I didn't want to miss Tommy's call, but there was only so much tidying up of my room I could stand. I dusted the shelves, straightened out the clothes in my closet, and put away my laundry. Vacuuming was out of the question—too noisy. I might not hear the phone! Any time my phone rang, I let it go on for a bit before my calm, cool, and collected attitude flew out the window and I pounced.

But it kept turning into the same conversation, over and over.

"Did he call yet?"

"No, T."

"Call me as soon as you hear from him."

I didn't know who was getting more frustrated, Tara or me.

I waited until late in the day to go for my run, finally convinced that I wouldn't be hearing from Tommy any time soon. Even Tara gave up.

As I ran my usual three-mile route, I wondered if he'd changed his mind. Maybe he'd met someone else right after we parted. After all, the place was swarming with girls.

I showered before dinner and was thankful there was no hair fallout to speak of. I was carefully combing my hair when Kyle banged on the bathroom door.

"Phone for you."

"Who is it?"

"I don't know him. Some guy named Tommy."

My insides melted and I was elated. He *called*!

I picked up the cordless in Mom and Dad's room and waited with my finger on the mute button until Kyle hung up, my heart fluttering and my hands trembling the entire time.

After I heard the click, I ducked into my room and said hello.

"Hey, Cassie. What's up?" he said.

"Nothing much." *Besides the pounding of my heart, that is.* "I just got back from a run."

There was a click on the phone—Kyle! "Kyle, hang up," I said.

I heard giggling.

"Kyle! Get off the—"

Then came the click.

"Little brothers can be such a pain," I said.

"Oh, real-ly?" Tommy said in mock astonishment. "Did you forget I have two older brothers?"

"Sorry 'bout that."

"For what? Dissing little brothers?"

"No, that you're probably a pain."

The way Tommy laughed at this made me wish I could think of something else clever to say, just to hear it again, but my joke well had run dry.

"Jason told me you're on the track team," he said.

Wow. He did his homework.

"Yeah, we had a great season, too," I said. "We took second place, all county. So, how did your band do last night? We had to leave before they announced the winners."

"Tears of Frustration won."

"That heavy metal band? They were terrible. But not so frustrated anymore, huh?"

"My brother says these battle gigs are mostly for the head bangers anyway. He warned us not to get our hopes up too high. But the night wasn't a total loss."

Whoa. Did I catch that right? Did he mean hanging with me? Dizzy with the idea that he might actually be interested, I forced myself not to let out a whoop. Instead, I squeezed the phone and my huge grin started to make my cheeks ache. But I played it cool.

"You'll get 'em next time—really. You're awesome."

Omigod, I was totally flirting in code!

"Well, uh, I just wanted to call and say hello."

We hung up and I let out a high-pitched squeal. This was *so* big! I couldn't punch in Tara's number fast enough.

After I'd given her the rundown and we analyzed that conversation from every possible angle, she said, "So, is he going to call you again?"

"I guess. I don't know, really."

"Well, what did he say?"

"I told you."

"Why else would he say that the night wasn't a total loss?"

We were cracking up when I caught a glimpse of my medicine on the dresser, an instant buzz kill. I tried to pretend that this wasn't the worst possible time to start something up with a guy, then I thought about Tommy's eyelashes, how sweet he was last night when we talked, and how he leaned against the wall, saying he had to go, but still didn't budge, and his great laugh a few minutes ago.

Everything pointed to *go for it*. But adding a boyfriend to my life right now didn't seem like the smartest move either. *Argh*. For now it was out of my control. For all I knew, maybe he'd never call again and I wouldn't have to worry about him finding out about my hair. For the next few days, I tried but couldn't ignore the truth: I *totally* wanted him to call.

On Wednesday, I was sitting in the cafeteria with my Falcon burger, going over notes for my World Cultures test, when Tommy appeared across the lunch table with a grin, then said, "Hi, can I join you?"

I nodded and could feel the heat of a major case of nervous red blotches creeping up my neck. It always happened, no matter if I was nervous and happy or having an anxiety attack; at least this time I was mega psyched.

"What are you doing here?" I asked him. "You cutting class?"

"Me? Never." He unbuttoned the side pocket on his cargo pants to give me a peek at a full pad of hall passes. "A gift from my brother, Richie," he explained. "He *found* a

whole stack of these in a supply closet right before he graduated."

*How great was that? He could come and go as he
pleased, as long as he was able to forge some teacher's signature.*

He buttoned the pocket, and with his hand over his
heart, he told me solemnly, "A Sweeny never cuts."

"Yup. I hear those Sweeny boys are real model citi-
zens. Theft and forgery. You'll be playing sax for your in-
mate friends some day at this rate. You know, 'Jailhouse
Rock'?"

Oh, man, what a killer smile.

"Anyway," Tommy said, "Mr. Frost is cool if you're a
few minutes late for band." He adjusted his hat and shook
his head at his unintentional pun.

He cleared his throat. "So, um, I wanted to ask you
something."

I offered him a French fry. He declined and doodled a
tornado squiggle on his paper book cover.

Then he said, "You want to go to the movies tonight?
I'm going with Jason and Glen, and I thought if you invited
some of your friends, we could hit the mall for a while
first."

A date! My Falcon burger turned a happy little cart-
wheel in my stomach.

Then common sense kicked in. *What about, you
know? Are you ready for this?* But it was just one date. I
didn't see how that could hurt. Looking at that hot guy sitting there in front of me, there was no way I could ever turn
him down.

"You're not going to see *Grave Lies* are you? I'm not into scary-bloody-gory-slasher movies," I told him. And yet, how sweet would it be to have to hide my eyes on Tommy's shoulder the entire time?

"No, the action flick. The one with Brad Carter."

"Okay, that'll work. I can get a couple people together."

I knew I could count on T. And Monique and Amy were a no-brainer—Brad Carter was their top pick to-lose-their-virginity-to, as if they'd have a chance to even get near a Hollywood type.

"You better get going," I told him. "You don't want Mr. Frost to have a *meltdown* if you're missing for too long."

"Ha, ha," he said, gathering up his books. "See you at Center Court at seven?"

I managed to keep my hysteria caged in long enough to say, "Cool." But inside, I was shrieking and dancing around.

❧

When I got home, Mom and Dad agreed that it was okay to meet the guys at the mall, since Mom had worked on a PTA fundraiser with Tommy's and Glen's mothers and felt comfortable about it.

"It's fine, as long as you stay in a group," Dad said at least ten times.

Mom popped into my room as I was getting ready. She sat on my bed and gave me the once over, and during my pirouette, I knew she was checking out the back of my head big time, but I had it covered. All was quiet on that front, so we didn't talk about it much lately. I'd read on the website that some people only ever have one or two bald patches, and no news was definitely good news.

"It's great that you're getting out with some *new friends*," she said, meaning guys.

I had a feeling Mom has been looking forward to becoming my dating coach and tonight was my first lesson. Her feeling was that you must sacrifice all comfort to avoid the embarrassing pitfalls of fashion *don'ts*. And this was no exception.

"How about wearing your new boots?" Mom suggested.

"These are more comfortable," I told her, indicating my Sketchers. "We're going to be walking around in the mall and I don't think my feet would last in the boots."

"I've hardly seen you wear them."

Not wearing them was a blatant insult to her sense of high fashion, since she picked them out for me.

"But, Mom, they're kind of dressy, don't you think?"

"It's a shame." She crossed her legs and laced her hands over her knee. "The salesman said they were the hot item this season. And they featured them with jeans or skirts in all the magazines. Come on, Cass, why don't you just try them on and see how they look?"

I was getting picked up in a few minutes and it wasn't worth it to leave wearing sneakers and have Mom looking disappointed over it. I knew it wouldn't kill me to wear the boots. They were really very nice and I think pretty expensive. So I nodded. Mom jumped up, took them out of my closet and presented them to me like they were the ruby red slippers from the Wizard of Oz.

"See?" she said, beaming. "Much better."

Monique's mom dropped us off at the mall and we met up with the guys, who were sitting on the edge of the fountain, waiting. We wandered around for a while and one of the boots was rubbing against the back of my heel. So much for fashion statements.

After a while, Jason, Glen, Monique, and Amy led the way toward Macy's. Tara, Tommy, and I, blister-in-progress, trailed a few steps behind. As we walked, the conversation turned to track.

"We're lucky," Tara said. "Last fall Coach let us try all the events to see where we'd fit in this spring."

"Tara's an awesome hurdler," I said.

"Do you do hurdles, too?" Tommy asked, shifting his attention back to me.

Tara stifled a snort. "Puh-lease!"

"Put it this way," I said. "If they gave you points for knocking them all down like they do at a carnival game, I'd win hurdles every time plus choice of the stand."

We walked around, Tommy and I brushing arms along the way, as the rest of the crew peeled off to go into stores. Jason zeroed in on Spencer's Gifts, a cool store with black lights, neon posters, and a wide variety of naked gag gifts and cards. Tara and I have browsed in there plenty of times but it's too embarrassing when you're with guys, so I pulled Tommy back by the hand. Then he squeezed my hand to make sure I wouldn't let go. As if! The other girls wouldn't go in with them either, opting for the nearby pet store instead.

Suddenly, Tommy and I were alone. From the doorway, we could hear Jason and Glen already cracking up and shoving each other.

"Those guys are going to be in there a while," Tommy said. "Let's wait over here."

We found a bench surrounded by hulking palm leaves as a cozy hideaway. Tommy rested his arm on the back of the bench and gazed at me intensely. We weren't touching, but I wanted us to be. Then he slid closer.

"You're so pretty," he whispered.

Wow! "Really?"

Dreamy-eyed, he leaned in a little and swept a strand of hair from my face.

Panic! I couldn't move, not toward him or away from him. He touched my hair and I resisted the urge to pull back and explain the whole thing. Be honest right up front.

He thinks I'm pretty. Shit. Why did he have to touch my hair?

His lips, barely parted, came closer still. He closed his eyes. But that was as far as it got.

"Tommy! Cassie!" Jason shouted. "We're movin' on. Let's go!"

Tommy's eyes popped open. We'd been only a centimeter away...but the moment had passed and I couldn't decide if I should thank Jason for interrupting or pop him one for ruining our kiss.

Tommy slid back on the bench, grinned, and half

shrugged. "Timing is everything," he said. He sounded disappointed.

I sat back and said, "In the Olympics, the difference between gold and silver can come down to one one-hundredth of second."

He raised an eyebrow and skimmed his finger along my cheek, his eyes on my mouth. Then he said, "Next time I'm going for the gold."

This made me feel warm and shimmery inside. And I decided, yeah, I was *so* going to pop that Jason.

Tommy stood up and held out his hand. "Guess we should go."

At the theater, Tara, Monique, and Amy each paid for their tickets. Then Tommy slipped in before I could open my purse and bought two tickets.

Tara, her eyes wide, mouthed, *Omigod. He paid for your ticket!*

I gave Tommy a shy smile when he handed me a ticket.

We went inside, where Jason and Glen sat a few rows behind Tommy and me. They seemed to feel the need to pelt us with an occasional piece of popcorn. The girls, sitting off to the side, behaved much better.

Halfway through the movie, Tommy shifted in his seat and put his arm around me. I curled my legs to the side to get closer to him, and the ache from having the armrest jammed into my ribs for the rest of the movie was pretty much canceled out by the rise and fall of his chest and his scent mixed with popcorn.

When the credits started rolling, we scooped up our

things and headed for the lobby. As soon as my eyes adjusted to the lights, I found strands of fallen hair cradled in the hood of my jacket. My heart leapt to my throat when I realized Tommy had noticed it, too.

This can't be happening. Please, not in front of him. Shit. Shit.

I wondered where it came from. Was there now a visible hole in my hair somewhere in back? Or is it on top, where he can see? I stepped back. Since he didn't look shocked or horrified, I assumed there was no major change in my appearance that Tommy could see. I only hoped that this was only a minor shedding episode and not the beginning of something worse.

"Look at that," I said, trying to sound ultra casual. "My mother says that sometimes I shed like a dog." I folded the jacket over my arm, hiding the hood full of hair against my body. Tommy took it as a joke and didn't make more of it. But what a disaster! I totally wanted to dissolve on the spot. I was so flustered, I didn't even take his hand on the way out of the theater.

Back out in the mall, Monique and Amy were fanning themselves after drooling over their on-screen fantasy boy, Brad Carter, for the entire movie. Glen, wrist to forehead, made girlie fainting sounds and fell into Jason's arms. They were all having a good time except me, well, I was having a great time until I saw the hair, and I needed this night to be over—now.

That's when Jason's cell phone rang. "Dudes, come on," he said. "My father's here."

Tommy brushed his bangs back and sunk his hands into his pockets. I tried to smile as I clutched the jacket tighter in front of me. I just wanted to go home.

"So I'll see you tomorrow?" he said.

I nodded and Tommy ran to catch up with his friends. With the guys gone, the girls swarmed me as we headed toward the parking lot, anxious for juicy details of my time with Tommy.

"So what happened?" Monique asked. "Did you get a kiss?"

"Not quite," I said. As we walked, I discreetly raked the hair from my hood before I put my jacket back on. There wasn't a trash can in sight so I hid the hair in my pocket.

"Damn. Tommy is seriously hot. If you don't snag him fast, I will," Amy said, teasing. "And what's Jason's story? Maybe you can have Tommy put in a good word for me?"

We pushed through the outside doors just as Amy's father pulled up to the curb. I dropped the strands of hair on the ground before I climbed into the car. On the way home, I gazed out into the ink black sky. *This is never going to work.*

At home, I yanked off the pain-inducing boots in the front hallway and tossed them into the closet, not intending to ever put them on again. Then I slipped into my room to evaluate this latest hair episode in my mirror. Shedding, that's all it was. I wanted to be thankful that it wasn't another patch, but I hated the whole situation and scowled at my reflection. *It was so unfair! What did I ever do to deserve this?*

74

I didn't see how I could be with Tommy if he didn't know what was going on—but I couldn't tell him either. I mean, we barely knew each other. I flopped on my bed and hugged my pillow.

Since I couldn't control or trust what was happening on my stupid head…maybe I'd be better off if I just ended it now.

Seven

The next morning at breakfast, Mom took out cereal and a bowl, and set a place at the table for me, then sat across from me and tried to sound matter-of-fact.

"So how'd it go last night?"

I was starting to see that Mom was just as bad as Tara when it came to wanting details.

"The movie was good," I said as I poured milk into my bowl and dug in.

"So, this Tommy is a nice guy?"

I nodded, crunching away on my Apple Cinnamon Cheerios.

"So, um, will you be seeing him again?"

It was weird. She almost sounded like she was hoping I'd say no. What was up with that? She'd seemed so psyched about my date last night.

I wiped a dribble of milk off my chin and shrugged. I finished eating and stacked the bowl and spoon in the dishwasher and told her, "I have to get dressed."

I wasn't sure when I'd see Tommy next, but in my head, I didn't think I could handle it after what happened last night. And maybe that's what Mom had been hinting at. If I ended it now, neither of us would have anything extra to worry about.

But after lunch, I found a note and a hall pass shoved in the top of my locker. It said, "Roses are red. Violets are blue. Meet me at guidance at 2:02." The pass was signed—okay—forged by Mr. Reinhardt, my guidance counselor. Excitement flashed through me, but I forced myself to snuff it out. That was it! I'd tell him it was over this afternoon.

At the beginning of sixth period, I told Miss DeFeo I had a guidance appointment. I was sweating. What if she asked for the pass? What if Reinhardt wasn't even in or left early? Did Tommy know what he was doing with the pass forgeries? I could feel my red blotches starting up and de-cided I should try wearing turtlenecks.

Miss DeFeo tilted her head thoughtfully at my request, saying, "That's the middle of his lunch period," she said.

I took the pass out of my folder so she could see it was a pass, but without letting her read what was written on it, or who'd signed it. I tried to project positive thoughts such as, *I'm one of the good kids, Miss DeFeo. This isn't a fake hall pass. Really, I swear.*

I managed to choke out, "It says two o'clock."

"Okay, go, but make sure you get tonight's assignment from someone," she told me.

With that out of the way, I went back to my seat and waited for two o'clock.

After leaving class, I found Tommy leaning against the wall outside of the guidance department, plugged into his iPod and looking like he owned the place. Miss Lerner, the school's only hot young secretary, came out of the office and Tommy flashed his killer smile—the ultimate hall pass—and she smiled back, then continued on her way, her high heels clicking on the tile floor. One look at him sent what I wanted to say straight into the shredder, and my heart skipped a beat as I got closer.

"You're totally crazy," I told him.

He took the earbuds out and said, "Wasn't sure if you were going to make it."

He motioned to follow him and we ducked into a stairwell. You almost couldn't see the dust bunnies and crud in the corner, but my heart was so revved up, I couldn't imagine wanting to be anywhere else.

"I *had* to see you again. Hope that's okay." He handed me one of the earbuds to his iPod and said, "Check this out." He put the other one in his ear and turned it on. With our faces close together, we listened. I didn't recognize the song at first. It was a jazz instrumental and the piano was 'singing' the lyrics: *A silent, broken dream remains. Love held hostage by these chains...*

"It's Shantique," I said. "How did you know?"

"We Sweenys have our ways. Cool, huh?" Tommy bit his bottom lip and shot me that gorgeous smile. All I could think of was having those lips on mine.

We were totally getting into the music when he put his arms around me and we swayed to the music, cheek to cheek. Tommy exhaled and his lips got closer to mine. And finally, contact!

Damn, this boy can kiss. And better than I remembered. I put my arms around his neck and kissed him back, just the way I'd been practicing—slow and neat, and definitely not slurpy.

Get back to class, an annoying voice inside my head urged. *You were supposed to break up with him, not kiss him—and certainly* not *fall for him.* And oh, was I ever falling for this guy!

Suddenly, footsteps echoed from the top of the stairs and a man cleared his throat. And that was the end of our kiss. It was over way too soon.

"Hate to kiss and run but…" Tommy tipped his hat and started *up* the stairs.

"You really *are* crazy," I whispered after him.

Then I heard Tommy say, "Good afternoon, Mr. Reinhardt. How's the guidance biz these days?" I cupped my hand over my mouth and listened, still tingling from that amazing kiss.

"Where are you supposed to be, Mr. Sweeny?" the counselor said.

"I thought guidance people were more concerned with their students' future, not so much the here and now," Tommy said.

"I can arrange a detention for your future, Mr. Sweeny," he told Tommy.

"That won't be necessary, Mr. Reinhardt. I have to get to class."

"Good choice, Mr. Sweeny."

A shriek of laughter escaped me as I rushed down the hall, barely making it to English on time. Miss Troy had a picture prompt posted on the board for free writing. It showed a guy in a grocery store, coconut under his arm, talking on his cell, and browsing the greeting card aisle. The words *dialogue* and *go* were written beside it.

I unfolded the pass and Tommy's note. It was so romantic that he found a Shantique song between last night and this morning. It was a perfect blend of the kinds of music we each love. Elbows on my desk, I hugged my shoulders, pretending to brainstorm some fabulous dialogue to go with the picture on the board, but in reality I was still under the stairs with Tommy.

Tara flung a pencil across the room to get my attention. Her expression said, *What's with you?*

I mouthed back, "Tommy."

Tara nodded her approval, then started jotting words in her notebook. The rest of the class was improving dialogue aloud and laughing. Coconuts and their hairy exterior, as it turned out, are extremely funny to guys. I wrote *nada*, except for Tommy's and my initials in a heart with lacy edging, then I added some musical notes.

At the end of the period, people tore out their notebook pages to hand in. I claimed writer's block, which, when used sparingly, was okay with Miss Troy. She always told us that creativity cannot and should not be forced. And who was I to try?

After class, Tara and I shuffled through the crowded halls to art. Walking shoulder to shoulder, I kept my voice down.

"I think I'm seeing Tommy now. I was with him a few minutes ago, and was going to end it, but...."

"Wait a second." Tara grabbed my elbow, clearly confused. "So which is it?"

"Given my *situation*, I didn't think I could handle being with a guy right now. But when we kissed, everything else sort of disappeared, you know?"

"You *kissed*?" Her voice rose ten octaves.

"Shhh! I mean, shouldn't I be allowed to have a boyfriend? I can make it work as long as my hair cooperates. Agh! God, I hate this!" I started picking up speed, weaving in and out of the slowpokes, accidentally clipping one kid in the back of the arm.

"What was I thinking, T? I never should've kissed him. I'm being totally irrational. Now it's going to be that much harder when I have to tell him it's over. And what excuse will I use? It's obvious that I like him, because whether he knows it or not, I don't go around making out with random guys under the stairs at school."

Tara was trying to keep up—with her feet and her brain.

"Cass." Tara stopped me before I zipped passed the door to art class. "Why don't you just explain to him what's going on with you? Seriously, if he's the right kinda guy, it shouldn't matter so much."

I felt tears welling up in my eyes. "He had no right to make me like him."

"Just tell him," Tara urged.

I leaned against a locker, my chin quivering. "I don't think I can."

Eight

After school I needed to think.

And I needed to run.

I changed as soon as I got home and hit the pavement. As I ran, I tried to imagine how Tommy would react about my hair.

There were two ways he could find out: Tara's way, by sitting him down and explaining the whole mess, or else by him being there and seeing it when it happens again. Geez. I'd barely dodged that bullet at the movies—I may not be so lucky next time.

I could explain to Tommy about how unpredictable alopecia is—God, how I hated that word! And I could tell him that for the rest of my life, I might have to live with random bald spots. I could even say something like, 'I bet you didn't know that I have two right now that you can't even see. It's just something I'm dealing with and I hope you can, too.'

Maybe he'd be okay with that. I'd hope so, anyway. And then I'd tell him the rest—that there was chance I'd end up without any hair at all.

By this point in my musings, I'd run the length of Meadowbrook Drive, so I veered toward my old elementary school. I ran a few more blocks before I was able to see the school sign ahead.

A girlfriend without hair. Tommy would be sweet about it, but he'd also be thinking that *Geez, is this what I signed up for? Why didn't I pick a girl with something simple, like acne?* And that'd be fair, because it'd be a butt-load of information to process about a girl he barely knew. But if he backed out now, he'd look like a total insensitive creep. I hadn't realized how tough it might be for him, if he knew everything up front.

I ran up the circular driveway of Washington Park Elementary School and picked up the path that led to the playground equipment in the back. I sat on a low-to-the-ground swing and my knees practically hit my chin. Two little kids were passing a football on the dry, chewed-up field. I pushed against the ground and swung a little.

So I guess I don't tell him—yet.

And then, if we're together when I lose a massive wad of hair, he could (A) Freak out and break up with me; or (B) Get mad at me for not telling him sooner—and use that as an excuse to dump me because he really *was* freaked out; or (C) Hug me and tell me it's okay because he's into me— not just my hair, and I'd act surprised, and then he'd get all mad because I assumed he couldn't handle it, and *then* he'd break up with me because he really *was* freaked out. Or maybe it'd be (D) He'd be perfectly cool with it and we'd go on like before, as if I'd never said anything.

I dragged my foot on the ground to stop the swing, then got up and ran back toward my neighborhood. Once I was back at the house, I sealed myself in my room and applied the medicine to the bare spots. *Losing all my hair wasn't definite,* I thought as I spread the drops around. *Only a possibility.* I wanted to believe so badly that it wouldn't all end up gone that I ached. Some days felt harder than others and I wished I could install a pop-up blocker in my head for those awful images of bald people from the website that plagued me so often. I was glad I never could quite conjure a clear picture of myself bald. That image was always distant and fuzzy, and that was exactly where I wanted it to stay—as only a far-off possibility.

My phone startled me.

"This is crazy," Tommy said. "I can't stop thinking about you."

"Me, too," I said, but it came out with zero enthusiasm. Shoot. I shouldn't have admitted that out loud. I still had no idea what to do about him. About us.

"You okay?" he asked.

"Totally. Hey, that was a great song you found," I said. "I think it was the song that put Shantique on the map." Nice recovery, but why was I making this harder for myself?

"Precisely," he said. "It was her first gold single that turned double platinum. I told you last night that the next time I had the opportunity, I was going for the gold. So you liked it?"

I detected the flirtiness in his voice and was responding like a moth against a lighted window. I wanted in.

"Oh, the song?" I asked, my voice lilting. "Yup, one of my favorites."

"Anything else you'd like to add?"

"Hmm, nothing comes to mind."

"Yeah, me either," he jabbed right back. "Just another boring, uneventful, lackluster day at Darlington."

"Hey!" I laughed. "Take it easy already!"

"You started it."

Kidding around with him was as easy as hanging with Tara, but with the added bonus of kissing. But I had to sort things out about how to handle this situation with him and my hair. Tommy and I obviously liked each other, but I just couldn't tell him about me. Not yet, anyway.

I decided to take a chance with him and see what happened.

As we talked, I fluffed my hair over the bare spots. But it just fell away, leaving the two spots exposed. I knew it wasn't going to be easy, but I had to try and disguise the problem until I was ready to tell Tommy what was happening.

I redirected the conversation away from our teasing, then asked, "Do you ever write any of your own songs?"

"Attempt to? Yes, but unfortunately, they're responsible for killing three of our fish."

I pictured Tommy serenading goldfish with their faces pressed against the glass bowl and forming interested o's with their mouths. *Talk about a captive audience.*

"I doubt that," I said. "You have to let me hear them."

"Okay, maybe I'm exaggerating. Yeah, I've written a few things, but it's weird. I guess I'm not ready to put myself out there yet. It's so personal, ya know? Like, what if my songs are terrible?"

"But," I countered, "what if you're depriving the world of your musical genius?"

"I assure you, the world is doing fine without me and my songs."

"Well, if you ever think you want to play for a human instead of a fish—I mean, I don't know a lot about jazz but…when you're ready…no pressure of course…I'd love to hear them."

"That's really cool," he said. "Thanks for the offer."

"Anyway," I said. "I bet the fish died of natural causes."

"That's what we said at the funeral before we flushed them. Hey, listen, if you want to hear the band play again, you can sit in on our rehearsal tomorrow after school."

Okay, no more debating. "Count me in," I said.

That night after dinner, as Kyle was drying the last of the pots I'd washed, Mom and Dad were already settled in the family room. Dad was skimming high school sports stats in the local paper and Mom was watching the Home and Garden Network while leafing through a decorating magazine. I waited for a commercial to get their attention.

"Tomorrow afternoon, I'm sitting in on a band rehearsal."

"Something going on at school?" Dad asked.

"No. It's Tommy's band," I said. "They're rehearsing at his house."

Mom closed the magazine in her lap and motioned to

Dad to lower the volume on the TV. "So you *are* seeing him again," she said, as if accusing me of some illegal underground activity.

"I didn't think it'd be a problem," I said.

"Tara going?" Dad asked.

"I don't need a babysitter, Dad. I'm almost fifteen." I put my fist on my hip, but Dad's expression told me to try and appeal to him another way. "Tara wasn't invited, but other people are going to be there listening, not just me." I remembered about the drummer and said, "There's one girl, Elaine, who *always* goes." Okay, so I stretched that one a bit. "And Tommy's brother's girlfriend, Dina, will be there."

Dad sat forward in his chair and seemed willing to consider a scenario that included someone else's teenage daughters. But for Dad, it was all about being in a group.

But Mom was shaking her head. "Before you go running off to his house," Mom said, "I think your father and I should meet him first."

Whoa. *Running off?* My dating coach had pulled a complete one-eighty on me. "We all went to the mall, remember? What should I do? Have his mother drive him over here right now to meet you so I can have permission to sit in his garage tomorrow?"

"How about this?" Dad said, leaning his elbows on his knees, his fingertips forming a tent. "You go to the rehearsal, and when your mother comes to pick you up, then she can meet Tommy."

That worked for me, and Mom agreed. *Way to go Dad!*

Pots clanged in the kitchen as Kyle put them away.

Then he popped into the family room and started in on me in sing-song voice. "Cassie has a boyfriend. Cassie has a boyfriend."

"Dad," I said, hoping he'd make Kyle zip it.

Then Kyle turned around and hugged himself, sliding his hands up and down his sides to make it look like he was kissing someone while he made kissing sounds.

"Daaad!"

"Kyle," Dad warned half-heartedly. But he'd already refereed once tonight and probably wasn't in the mood for another.

Kyle wouldn't stop so I took matters into my own hands and chased him halfway up the stairs. "You are so *obnoxious*!" I growled.

"You are so in looove."

I lunged for his ankle, but the little weasel seemed to sprout wings and he disappeared up the stairs. "Next time, you're dead," I huffed and doubled back downstairs. Before I turned the corner to the kitchen, I heard Mom say to Dad, "I think this is a mistake. We shouldn't let her go." I flattened myself against the wall and listened from the hallway.

"Hon, I thought it was decided." Dad sounded tired.

"Just think about it for a minute. It's hard enough being a teenager," Mom said. "Wearing the right clothes, getting in with the right group of kids. You know I always try to steer her in the right direction. And now she's starting to date. Do you know how complicated this could get with alopecia?"

"The fact is, she has to live outside these four walls.

88

And while she's out there, at least to some degree, we have to let her make her own decisions. Because if you put all kinds of restrictions on her....Look, it's just a band rehearsal. We trust her, right?"

"You're missing the point," Mom said. "Boys can be so immature at this age. I think we should step in now, so she doesn't get hurt later."

Dad waited, then said, "I think you're overreacting here, hon. She's not in preschool any more, and we can't choose her friends. It doesn't seem like a bad idea for her to develop new interests and find new friends."

"I don't like it. It's not as if she's looking for piano lessons or something."

"I thought she said he plays the sax," Dad said.

"Piano, sax, bagpipes, whatever," Mom said.

"Listen, spring track will be starting up soon. And right now she's got a little time between seasons, so why not let her keep busy until then? The way I see it, Cassie's handling her condition pretty well, and we should take our cues from her."

Pretty well—as long as no more falls out.

Mom didn't answer right away. She must've been giving it some thought.

"All right," she finally said, but in a way that meant she just was letting Dad have his way this time.

I drew back from the hallway, shaking my head, and headed for my room.

Mom was right. *What if I am building myself up for a huge letdown? But I couldn't know for sure unless I took that chance.* I sat down at my desk and rested my chin on my hand. *It wasn't too late to back out.* I sighed. The only thing I could do was hope that Tommy would understand if he eventually had to find out. And if he doesn't understand…well, I couldn't bear to think about that.

Nine

The next morning when I rolled out of bed, the only thing on my pillowcase was the printed floral pattern. *Thank God!* With Tommy's rehearsal later that day, I prayed my hair would stay put.

I made my bed and arranged the kajillion coordinating throw pillows on top. *I swear they reproduce at night when I'm asleep.* Then I tried on three pairs of jeans and almost every top in my closet before I came up with an outfit worthy of the day's main event. The jeans hugged my hips and butt, accenting the curves I'd recently developed, and I hoped that the chunky V-neck sweater I'd picked made my boobs look bigger. I tugged at the neck and looked down, but I could see those curves were still under construction.

Then it was time to tackle the hair.

I hated that I couldn't just wear it down anymore, so to hide the bald spots, I carefully combed everything back into a full ponytail and wrapped that with a scrunchie. Hiding those bare spots made me feel guilty that I wasn't being straight with Tommy. As I ran my hand down the length of my ponytail, I knew that was the way it had to be.

I couldn't wait to get to school and talk to Tara, since I'd been a mess when it came to the subject of Tommy. We met in the cafeteria and sat at a table.

"We had to draw and label a plant *and* an animal cell? Oh, crap," she said as she hunched over and started scribbling in her notebook.

"Tsk, tsk, tsk. That is not your best work," I told her.

"Oh, shut up." She turned the page. "Define all these terms, too? Crap cubed."

"Chill there, girlie." I whipped out a typed set of vocabulary words for her.

She squealed and squeezed my arm. "Thanks, Cass. You're the best!"

"Hey listen," I said. "I know I've been obsessing over what to do about Tommy, and you're probably sick of me bouncing back and forth on it, but I've decided to go for it."

Tara's head popped up. "So you told him about your hair?"

"I'm going to his house after school. His band is rehearsing. "

"So you're *going* to tell him then?"

"You mislabeled that one," I said, pointing to her drawing. She swatted my hand away and waited for my answer.

"I'm keeping him on a 'need to know' basis. And as far as I'm concerned, *no one* needs to know anything right now. Don't get me wrong—it's cool that *you* know. It's actually been a relief that I can talk to you about it." I sighed.

Tara looked as if she was trying to understand, so I said, "Can't I just be a normal person going to listen to a garage band?"

"Normal?" Tara asked, teasing. "Don't you think that's stretching it? How many outfits did you try on today?"

"Um, all of them."

"Okay, maybe there's hope for you yet," she said and finished her homework.

The simple act of opening my locker during the day made me breathless, wondering if I'd find another note from Tommy. But there weren't any—I checked and double-checked to be sure. Then I remembered that Tara used my locker once a day, too, and it was strange to think of her reading a note that was intended for me. *Nah, she wouldn't.* But in art class, I asked her not to, just in case she ever found one waiting.

After eighth period, Tara wished me luck and I ducked into the nearest bathroom to examine my hair for the twentieth time, applied a sheer layer of lip gloss, and puckered up to the mirror. Then it was go time.

Tommy met me at my locker and we walked outside, through the parking lot, to his brother's car. Eric's scrubby silver Camaro, duct-taped taillight and all, was much cooler than taking the bus. Eric, a taller version of Tommy in tight jeans, leaned against the car door, playing keyboard on the sideview mirror and humming to himself.

"Dude," Eric said to Tommy as we approached. "So this is the girlfriend."

Girlfriend! Sweet.

Tommy glanced at me to check my reaction, as if he wanted to know if I agreed with his brother's assumption. I smiled at them, as if to say, "No argument here."

Tommy placed his hand on my lower back and said, "Yeah, this is Cassie."

"Well done, little bro."

Not too embarrassing.

Then another girl approached. I recognized her from school and the Battle of the Bands. Eric introduced his girlfriend, Dina, and she gave Tommy a knowing grin. I could tell I'd been the topic of conversation, which was kind of flattering.

"You're the runner, right?" Dina asked as Eric slung his arm around her shoulder. "You must know Robin Lakewood. She's in my homeroom."

"Yeah, and she's in my French class, too," I said, wondering if they were friends.

"She's supposed to be the one to watch," Dina said.

"Says who?" Eric asked.

"Says Robin," Dina said, and laughed. "That girl honestly believes the sun rises and sets for her, and that it's our privilege to occupy space in the same solar system. But someday, when she hits the real world, she'll be in therapy before you can name the planets." Dina leaned her head on Eric's shoulder and gave him a quick peck. She was clearly not a fan of Miss Lakewood either, and I had a feeling we'd get along just fine.

Tommy and I climbed into the back seat of the car with tunes cranked and we were off. Tommy had said at Battle of the Bands how he thought Dina was cool. It felt like the welcome mat had been laid out for me. Dina fluttered her long nails to the music and turned around once to smile at us. It was a short ride to their house. When Eric dropped us off in front, he told us, "Mom needs a few things from A&P" and gassed the engine, wrist slung over the steering wheel. "Guys'll be here in few. Be right back."

We went inside the detached garage, which served as Silk City's rehearsal studio. Tommy flipped on the light and fired up a space heater. "So this is it," he told me.

Mounted on the right side of the garage was a peg-board studded with hand tools and, below that, a grass-encrusted lawn mower hibernating until spring. Against the opposite wall was a hideous, plaid 'Salvation Army special' sofa. I shuddered. Mom's decorating shows must've infil-trated my subconscious. There were two metal folding chairs, a dartboard and some posters of babes in bikinis. In a corner and angled for optimum babe viewing was a slant board and rack of free weights. The place smelled of gaso-line, fertilizer, and potato chips, and here I was, a guest in Tommy's special world.

I walked to the back of the garage, where drums, Eric's keyboard, an amp for the guitar, sheet music stands, Tommy's saxophone case, and a couple of empty beer cans sat on a milk crate. I tapped the cymbal. "How about your brother Richie?" I asked. "Not musically inclined?"

Tommy plucked the darts out of the board and lined up behind a piece of duct tape on the floor. He tossed one. "Richie used to be the drummer, but playing for Silk City doesn't exactly pay the bills." Another toss—near bull's-eye. "Richie started working full-time after graduation to help my mother out, and our computer geek-a-tron is doing all right out there in the real world."

"That gets me," I said. "'The real world.' How many

times have you heard your teachers say that? Even Dina said it before. So what is *this*?" I waved a drumstick around in the air. "La-la land?"

"Tell me about it," Tommy said, holding out the darts. I joined him at the duct tape and my first throw was very respectable. "Before graduation, my father taught Richie how to take care of things around here. Ya know, fix a dishwasher hose, wire an outlet, spackle and paint if your brother punches a hole in the wall." He flexed his hand open and closed, then blasted a bull's-eye. "Richie said I was lucky I didn't hit a stud. I could've shattered every bone in my hand. That was two years ago, when my father left. How's that for living in la-la land?"

"I remember when your hand was all wrapped up," I whispered. "I'm sorry. I didn't know."

"Hey, it's all good, though." He cranked up a smile and shrugged it off as he collected the darts. "Who needs him, anyway?"

"Do you ever see him?"

Tommy shook his head.

I couldn't tell whose choice it was and was afraid to ask. "That's gotta be rough." I touched his arm. "I can't imagine what it would be like without my dad around. But you all seem pretty tight with music and your brothers pitching in around here."

"Like I said, it's all good." He put the darts down, hooked his finger in my belt loop, and pulled me closer. "Let's talk about something else," he said, and gave me a sly grin. Then there was no more talking between us.

He kissed me more intensely and his hands began to travel under my shirt.

"Mmm, no," I said, sucking in a breath, but still kissing him back.

His hand kept going.

I pulled away. "Really—No."

"Okay, okay." He held up his hands in surrender. "Damn. Can't blame a guy for trying. Look at you."

I smiled, relieved that he stopped, and hooked my finger in his belt loop.

He said, "I can't guarantee I won't try again…"

I loved that flirty tone, and his eyelashes caught a wisp of his bangs.

"If you do," I told him, "you might be at risk of shattering every bone in your hand *again*—this time, courtesy of *moi*."

"You're pretty tough, aren't you," Tommy said.

He kissed me and it sent tiny electric pulses all the way down to my socks. I was *so* not tough.

"We wouldn't want your sax career to end before it begins," I said.

"Actually, I've been thinking of taking up the triangle instead."

I rolled my eyes. "Great."

Then the side door flew open. "What's goin' on in here?" Eric said as he paraded in with an A&P bag. Dina was right behind him, carrying a Celestial Mocha-Chino-Grande. The rest of the band followed and whirlwind introductions started. There was Elaine, the drummer, Deek on guitar and his girlfriend, Amanda, who had a pinched face and green-tinted round glasses perched on the end of her nose. She reminded me of an angry bookworm.

Eric threw his arm around the last guy, and said, "This is Smoke, our musical genius. Plays trumpet, clarinet, and flute."

I'd seen him around school, too, but never this close up. I was guessing he was a senior whose nickname probably came from his incredible gray eyes. But when I inhaled, I thought again—he totally smelled like pot.

"This guy can make an empty toilet paper roll sing," Eric boasted.

And he probably just got done using one as a bong.

The thing that struck me was that nobody's last names were mentioned; only their instruments. That was who you were and how you were identified.

Dina elbowed Smoke out of the way, wrapped herself around Eric, and planted one on him. Amanda, obviously anxious to get into the music, gestured at the plaid couch, indicating I should go sit down. She'd obviously make an awesome stage mother some day.

The guys tuned up and heckled each other on noticeably sour notes. Tommy, goofing around, warmed up with that old song "Tequila." But when they got serious and really jamming, they had a great energy together that came through in their music. I wanted to capture every note pouring from Tommy's sax; they were like tiny bits of him and I wanted to take them home with me. That two-hour rehearsal flew by and I would've been happy to hang there and listen for another two, no problem.

The band was packing up when I called Mom for a ride home, and then Dina came up to Tommy and me.

"Cassie, we're all going to Montclair University for a concert and we have an extra ticket to DuValle in two weeks. Wanna come?"

"Who bagged out on the show?" Tommy asked.

"Smoke's girlfriend. She's pissed at him again."

Geez, I can't wait to meet her.

"If you haven't heard DuValle, you can borrow my CD," Tommy said. "It's in Eric's car. They're progressive jazz. Different from our stuff."

"Yeah—better if you come prepared," Dina said. She went to Eric and told him, "Cassie's coming with us. Who knows how long before Smoke can sweet-talk Natalya into coming around again. I swear, those two are like electricity and water."

"Guess I'm going to a jazz concert," I said.

"Guess so," Tommy said. He walked me out and got the CD from the car just as Mom pulled up and rolled down the passenger window.

Time to meet the parent. I introduced them and they exchanged hellos, then Tommy held the door for me as I got into the car. *Score!* He hunched toward the open window and I turned the CD over in my hands. I liked having something of his to take home.

"The band is awesome, Mom," I said. "Someday they're going to make it big."

"High praise," Mom said. "Sounds like you already have a publicist."

"That's a long way off," Tommy said with a shy grin.

For a goof, I crossed my eyes at him, but he managed to keep a straight face.

"Well, stay with it. You never know," Mom said as she shifted the car into drive. "Tommy, tell your mother I said hello."

That wasn't exactly the Spanish Inquisition, but it was over with. We pulled away and I tuned the radio to 101.9 FM, Smooth Jazz.

Mom took a breath, then said, "You know, you should not lock yourself into one relationship at your age. There are plenty of boys out there to date."

I knew what she was doing, preparing me in case Tommy bails when he finds out my secret. But I had a good feeling about him. I couldn't explain it, but it was there. But rather than get into that, I decided to mess with Mom's head a little.

"So I should be going out with a lot of guys at the same time? You mean like be a slut?"

She nearly choked. But then Mom regrouped. "No," she said. "I mean that you should keep your options open."

"So be available to date, but don't actually go on any dates."

Mom sighed and massaged the back of her neck. Then she glanced at me and asked, "So you like this guy?"

"Yeah, I guess I do."

That's when it hit me how much I meant it.

Ten

Three weeks had flown by since Tommy and I had become an official couple and I was enjoying the attention. He'd surprise me and walk me to class. He called at night after rehearsal and we'd talk for hours. And there were these moments—when we laughed on the phone or met for a kiss-and-run—when I noticed the sweet way he looked at me. Well, I felt so good with him that I could *almost* forget about my secret. But in the back of my mind, it was like an invisible fist was lurking, one that followed me around, just waiting for the chance to rip out more hair. And that could screw things up between Tommy and me.

Although my hair wasn't breaking any records for growing back no matter how hard I searched, the good news was that I had no new bald patches. My immune system was behaving for now, and my secret was safe.

On the night of the concert, Eric pulled into the driveway. I peeked out the upstairs window to see Dina in the front seat, and Tommy climbed out of the car wearing black jeans and a funky-patterned button-down shirt that hung out from his black leather jacket. He took off his signature hat before he rang the doorbell—the perfect gentleman.

I heard Mom and Tommy exchange hellos, then Mom came up to my room, where she'd instructed me to wait. "You don't want to appear too anxious," she'd said. My coach was back on the job.

One last check in the mirror showed I had nothing stuck in my teeth, and I was satisfied with my outfit that included one of the shirts Mom gave me for Christmas. I'd put the top of my hair up in a ponytail with the rest down and thought for sure Mom would commend my choice of her gift top, but no. Instead, she stood behind me and fluffed my hair over my shoulders.

"You did a good job," she said.

Loosely translated, she meant, 'The ugly patches are well hidden. Mission accomplished.' I didn't reply.

Mom handed me my purse and said, "Since when are you into jazz?"

Wasn't the gorgeous sax player I was going out with enough of a clue? But I had a snarky answer for her.

"Sometimes you have to expand your horizons," I told her. "I didn't want to lock myself into one type of music at my age."

Mom grimaced. Parents hate it when you spin their words around on them.

"Shall we go downstairs, then?" Mom said, giving up.

When Tommy saw me as I came down the stairs, he crushed his hat between his hands. That smile of his made me feel like gravity was optional, and as I reached the bottom step, he snapped his hat to restore it's shape. Then we started toward the door with Mom following.

"Where's everyone else?" she asked.

"We're meeting them there," I said.

"Be home by eleven o'clock, Cassie," Mom said, from the doorway.

I nodded and we climbed into the back seat. Dina waved hello, then proceeded to drum against her window in time to the DuValle song Eric had on. Tommy waited until we were out of my neighborhood before he leaned over to kiss me.

"So, have you been loving the DuValle CD?" Dina asked over the music.

"Most of it, yeah. Sometimes I didn't know where one song ended and the next one started, and I kept waiting for a singer."

"DuValle is hardcore," Eric said. "An acquired taste."

"You're going to love hearing them live," Tommy said.

We held hands, his thumb stroking back and forth over mine. I loved the way my hand fit in his and how our fingers entwined.

Eric pulled into one of Montclair University's parking lots and we hiked across the campus. Lamp posts lit the long sidewalks between buildings and people were moving in all directions, some carrying books. There were so many buildings all around us; I'd thought our high school was intimidating at the beginning of freshman year, but this place was like a small city.

Dina pointed to our destination, which was just ahead, and then we all went inside.

"Let's hit the ladies' room first," she said to me.

It was the perfect chance to get to a mirror and make sure all was well in the hair department, and we handed our jackets to the guys first.

"Why do girls go to the bathroom in groups?" Tommy asked.

Eric laughed. "In case one needs a spotter."

"No, that's not why," Dina said. "It's so we can talk about *you*." And she poked her talon into Tommy's chest, which wiped the goofy smile off his face. It was funny watching those two busting chops. Then I tossed my head back in mock superiority and followed Dina through the crowd.

"I actually may need a spotter after the mocha grande I just had," Dina said. "Oh, man. How long is this line?" She did the 'I-really-have-to-pee' bounce, then said, "There's never a line for the men's room."

She'd better not get any ideas about dragging me into the men's room, because that was *never* going to happen. "Try not to think about it," I said. Then four more girls got in line behind us, and for some reason, that always made me feel better—no longer being last.

"So you and Tommy, eh?" she said. "That boy has it bad for you."

I smiled. *Yessss!*

"You know, he took it the hardest when their father left." Dina craned her neck to see how far we still had to go. "You know about that, right?"

I nodded. "He told me he punched his fist through a wall when it happened."

"Hey, I never met the guy, but it doesn't take a brain surgeon to figure out he was a total dick after he moved out. Like he'd promise to take Tommy somewhere, then blow him off at the last minute. And *then* he started pulling no-shows altogether. Shit. It's one thing when the parents have issues, but do you have to mess with a kid's head like that?"

A stall opened up and Dina darted in, then let out a moan of relief.

I pulled out a mirror and checked my camouflage job—so far, it was all good.

Dina, lighter by one mocha grande, washed her hands and said, "All I'm saying is, it's great to see Tommy happy."

That clinched it. We were *both* happy, and I wasn't going to take a chance on ruining it by telling him about my hair. We finished up and headed back to our respective Sweeny brothers.

"So what'd you two talk about?" Tommy asked, one eyebrow raised. "Me?"

"Geez. What an ego!" I said.

Dina gave me a knowing wink and we got in line to enter the auditorium.

As we stood waiting, Tommy slipped his arm under my hair and around my shoulder, and I moved inside his jacket to be close to him. I was hoping his cologne would rub off onto my top so I could take whiffs of his cologne afterward.

When he shifted his arm, some of my hair was caught and the weight was pulling on it. I tried to wriggle away, but we were crammed together too tightly. As we crept toward the entrance, his arm was still there, and it was still pulling.

"Have your tickets ready," the usher said.

Pleeease, get off my hair was all I could think about.

"Do you have the tickets?" I asked.

"Uh-huh. In my wallet."

We took a few more steps forward, and I couldn't stand it. I needed him to get off me.

"You'd better get the tickets out. We're almost there." I said, then I plucked his hand off my shoulder, accidentally flinging it into the person behind him.

"Take it easy. I have them right here." He opened his wallet and handed me a ticket, adding, "Is something wrong?"

I just smiled and shrugged, then, as sweetly as you please, I said, "No, of course not. Nothing at all."

But my mind was racing. I'd felt the pull, which meant the hair was still attached to my scalp, but I wasn't sure if any fell out. I ran my hand over the back of my head, ready to gather any loose strands, but we were packed together so tightly. How would I drop the loose hair down to the floor without anyone noticing? And we were too close to the front of the line to make another excuse and dash to the bathroom. I tried to force myself to relax. I couldn't feel any difference and had no evidence of any 'fallout.' So I hoped and prayed everything was okay.

At last we got to our seats, where we met up with the two other couples from Eric's band. Elaine had brought all her DuValle CDs and a drumstick she'd bought on eBay in the hopes of getting them autographed after the show.

We sat down and, like a ninja, I blocked every potential arm-around-the-shoulder move until Tommy finally took the hint and backed off. Only when the house lights dimmed did I manage to calm down. I let out a breath and reached for Tommy's hand.

I recognized the opening number, but so did the entire auditorium and the crowd roared with excitement. A light show bounced in sync with the dramatic rush of pure sounds that wrapped around me and pulsed in my chest. Progressive jazz was like heavy metal's more sophisticated first cousin; not *my* fave, but it was great being there as the crowd was swept away.

Tommy was totally caught up in the night and the music, and half the fun was watching him and the guys in the band as they cheered and grooved. They were having a blast as spotlights chased each other across the sea of faces and more than once lit up Tommy's smile.

He didn't seem to notice or at least mind that I needed a little space. During intermission, I checked around me for loose hair and was relieved that all was clear. I didn't want to mess up tonight for Tommy by having a meltdown if I found half my hair on the floor.

After the show my ears were buzzing from the amplified music and I knew the clock was ticking. It was pushing eleven o'clock already, so Eric rushed us to my house so I'd make it on time. I didn't want to give Mom any reason to keep me from seeing Tommy.

We squeezed in a mini make-out session in the back seat on the way, and Eric smooched with Dina at red lights. When we got to my house, Tommy walked me to the door.

"How 'bout one more for the road?"

We kissed again, deeply. Then he pulled back and gazed at me.

If I were a cat, I'd have been purring.

"You better go in," he said.

And after *one more* kiss, I did.

Inside, I closed and locked the front door, then leaned against it. I could still smell him. I licked my lips to taste him—mmm. Being involved with Tommy had to be the right choice when I got to feel this way, like I was brimming with total happiness.

After checking that Eric's car had pulled away, I turned off the porch light and started upstairs to my room. Things had gotten a bit shaky for a while, but overall, I thought I'd handled myself pretty well.

This was what I'd promised myself—to take things one day a time.

Eleven

The next morning at school, Tara and I met in our corner of the cafeteria that faced the parking lot. I kept hoping to see Eric's car pull into its assigned space, along with Tommy.

I gave Tara the play-by-play of my date, editing out my panic attack and how I wouldn't let Tommy put his arm around me during the show. And I didn't tell her the part about his father and how hard it'd been for Tommy. It was so sad, I didn't think he'd want the whole world to know about it. We're all entitled to our secrets, after all.

"I can't believe Dina told you how much Tommy likes you," Tara said. "You're so lucky to get insider information like that."

"She's great. She acts like she's his big sister or something."

Then the first warning bell rang and I noticed Eric's space was still empty.

"C'mon," Tara said, coaxing me away from the window. "All guys have to do is roll out of bed and brush their teeth. No way is *your* boyfriend making *me* late for home-room."

I loved the sound of that. *My boyfriend.*

We started to our lockers, cutting through the cafeteria annex, where we found Adam Faber with his arm around Robin Lakewood.

"Shit," Tara said, under her breath. "When did *those two* hook up?"

I don't know why, but for some reason, Robin zeroed in on *me*. Her mouth curved into a cocky grin and she slipped her hand into Adam's back pocket, like a cat marking her territory.

I ignored her and looked toward the school spirit mural, grateful I was with Tara because she was going to be seriously bummed about Adam, who she'd been crushing on for months. As we left the annex, Tara peered back over her shoulder.

"What's so great about her, anyway?" she asked sourly.

Let's see. Pretty face, gorgeous smile, great body...I can't imagine. But that's not what I said to my hurting best friend.

"I'm sorry about them getting together, T," I said. "But you gotta remember, she's one of the fast ones—on *and* off the track. Or so I've heard."

That seemed to make her feel better.

"And what was with her giving *you* the stink eye?" she asked.

"Oh, you caught that, too?" I thought for a second. "I don't know. She started acting like a jerk to me after that practice last fall, when I raced her in the four hundred. I don't think Miss Lakewood likes taking a beating from a freshman, and I beat her good that day."

"Greedy witch," Tara said. "She gets the guy *and* wants the glory, too. Maybe I'll throw her a beating myself. And I don't mean on the track."

"I'm sure Adam would be really impressed."

"Fine," Tara huffed. "Then how about an Italian curse? I can ask my nana if she knows any. Something gross like turning her teeth black or making her gain fifty pounds—all in her ass."

Tara plotted the curse all the way to homeroom, and when I got to my seat, I shuffled through my homework as the announcements came over the loudspeaker. I only half listened until I heard "Track and field practice begins next week. Team members report to the gym on Thursday, February twenty-eighth, immediately after school."

Yesss! I was dying to get back on that track again and see what kind of a team we'd turn into this season. I couldn't wait to see what my times would be, especially with all the running I'd been doing the last few weeks. That ought to count for something.

My first two classes of the morning were yawners and mostly were in review mode. But in the hall, directly outside my French class, a big show was going on. It was none other than Robin, flaunting her new dating status in front of anyone who might be paying attention. It was impossible not to notice.

She was laughing too loud, tossing her long black mane over her shoulder, and playing with Adam's gold chain. She just couldn't decide if his cross should go over the shirt or under the shirt. Over? Under? Over? Under? Finally, she decided on over the shirt. Halleluiah!

I did my best to ignore them as they made out and quickly got into the room and over to my seat. From where he sat, Monsieur Haus glanced sideways out the door and cleaned his glasses. They were probably fogging up from watching Robin with Adam.

They were one of those perfect couples—the kind where all the girls wanted to be her and all the guys wanted to be him. And Robin knew it. But when Robin finally decided to grace us with her presence and join the rest of us in class, I caught Adam tucking the cross inside his shirt before he took off.

I barely stifled a laugh—I couldn't help it.

"Something funny?" Robin sniffed.

I shifted awkwardly in my seat and she went on.

"You won't be laughing much out there on the track next week."

"Who said anything about that?" I said.

"Spring training is brutal," she said, sweetly. "You have no i-dea."

"Bonjour, mes eleves," Monsieur Haus said and we opened our *livres de vocabulaire* to complete a written exercise.

I gave Robin a sideways look as she started matching words. Ha! She got the first one wrong. I wished I had the nerve to say, *Okay, Miss Lakewood. I'm on the lowly freshman team. You're on the high and mighty varsity. So what is your problem?* I wondered if I could hijack some eye of newt from Bio lab to help out with Tara's curse.

Near the end of class, I noticed Tommy waiting for me in the hall. He was leaning against the lockers, tapping his pen to the tune on his iPod. I got that fluttery feeling inside when our eyes met. *God, he's so cute in that hat.* And here was my chance to show Robin *I* had a boyfriend, too.

When the bell rang, I rushed out the door and pounced on my guy. I wanted to plant a kiss on Tommy that would knock his socks off, but instead I knocked his hat off and our front teeth collided. We both pulled back with our hands over our mouths. I ran my tongue over my teeth to check. *Damn, that hurt.*

Then Robin strolled out of class looking amused. I picked up Tommy's hat and dusted it off. *Yeah, that was really smooth, Cassie.*

After we recovered, Tommy and I held hands and started down the hall toward the auditorium. The cast list for *Godspell*, the senior play, was posted, along with a sign-up sheet for stage crew and orchestra. I scanned the list for Tommy's name, but he just kept walking.

"You and Eric going to sign up?" I asked.

"Mr. Frost has been trying to rope us into it for a while now, but it's too much rehearsal time when we're busy with Silk City," he said. "And playing for both would mean even less time to hang with you, now that track's starting." He gave me a half-smile.

"We'll still get to see each other," I said. "Sure, I mean, practice takes up a lot of time, but it's so worth it when I do well at the meets." He nodded, but he looked disappointed.

I totally didn't want him to think I was ditching him, especially after what he'd been through with his father. But he couldn't possibly think that, could he? He knew track was important to me, just like being in the band meant a lot to him.

"Not to worry," I said and tapped his hat down over his eyes.

He adjusted it back and said, "Right. Where there's a will, there's a way."

We'd reached my next class, so he gave me a quick, clash-less kiss, and then pushed through the stairwell doors and disappeared down the stairs.

During the day, I sneaked many spot checks of my hair. I mentally high-fived myself each time I didn't find a new naked spot, and I felt as if someone must have been smiling down on me.

When I got to my last class of the day, art class, Tara and I set our canvases near each other on our easels. The latest project was acrylic paintings, and I stood back to study my canvas as if I was considering buying it. *Not bad.* It looked like a tree. Cool, because this time it was *supposed* to be a tree.

As we painted, Tara invited me over after school. After class I called home and Mom gave me the green light and said I could stay for dinner if I was invited, which was good because Mrs. Spez usually asked me to join them.

We left the building and were almost to Tara's bus when she had to endure another Robin/Adam sighting. We climbed into the bus and Tara watched them through the window.

"So how goes it on that curse?" I asked.

"I'm workin' on it," she said. "Tomorrow I'm wearing skull and crossbones socks in protest of this relationship."

"That'll show 'em." I told her.

She gave me a weak smile.

I wanted to cheer her up, so I asked, "Psyched about practice?"

"Running laps and up and down the bleachers? Are you nuts?" Tara asked.

"Builds strength," I said, deepening my voice and flexing my biceps. "And stamina. Anyway, this is what we've been waiting for all winter! You're going to kill them on hurdles."

"Hey, I didn't mean to whine. Yeah, I'm actually kind of psyched for spring."

It was a short ride home to Tara's—the second stop in fact. She was lucky. My bus probably stopped at least a hundred times before it was my turn to get off. When we got to Tara's, we dumped our books on the kitchen table and I strolled into the living room while she rustled up a snack for us.

I liked looking at all the pictures of when Tara was little and I picked up a frame. "I love this one," I said. Tara must've been in first grade, and all you could see was a giant jack-o'-lantern smile, except jack-o'-lanterns usually have more teeth.

"I hate that picture," she said. "I look like the poster child for fluoride toothpaste. 'Brush your teeth or you'll end up like this.' I've asked my mother to put it away a million times. It took forever for my teeth to come in. Agh! It's so embarrassing. *Your* mother doesn't keep pictures like that around."

"No." I thought for a minute. "I guess not." Most of the pictures that were out were pretty nice—perfect, in fact. And Mom always took plenty of pictures. Vacations, school plays, birthday parties. And none of the goofy ones ever ended up framed.

What about when I lost my hair the first time? I knew those pictures had to be around somewhere. That is, if there were any. I decided to look around and see what I could find.

Twelve

Back home later that night, when Mom and Dad were in the family room watching TV, I snuck into their room. On the floor in Mom's closet I found all the photo boxes. Each box had a range of dates, and they were stacked in chronological order. I searched for the year I was age three and slid out that box. Going through some old pictures wasn't exactly a punishable offense…so why did my pulse quicken as I carried the box to my room?

I closed the door behind me for privacy and had barely lifted off the lid when there was a knock on my door. I jumped and tossed a T-shirt over the box.

"Can I borrow ten bucks?" Kyle asked through the door. "Whatcha doin' in there?"

I opened the door a crack and crossed my arms, leaning against it.

I narrowed my eyes. "You're already into me for eight bucks. When are you going to pay me back?"

"Please?" he said as he bounced on his toes.

"Don't you have something you can sell?"

He Kyle-smiled and shook his head no.

"Ask Dad," I told him.

But he wormed his way in and snuggled his cheek against me shoulder. "Pleeease?"

Ugh! "Fine," I said and gave him a look. He knew to evacuate the area immediately if he wanted the cash.

"Duh, I already know where you keep it," he said from the hall.

"Here." I shoved two fives at him and said, "Take a hike."

He grabbed the cash and disappeared.

I shut the door again and opened the photo box, my fingers walking over each envelope. They had notes on them like *Feb-Snow storm/Cassie & Kyle/sleigh riding*. I kept going until I came to *Sept-Cassie 1st day Pre-K*. I flipped through the stack. Pictures of Dad and me. Mom and me. Kyle and me. Me and a backpack twice as big as I was. My hair looked fine in all of them.

There was still nothing unusual, until I got to the stack marked *Dec-Xmas card photo shoot*. There were Kyle and me, in matching outfits and Santa hats. Kyle pulling his hat off. Kyle pulling my hat off.

And there it was—the start of it, right in the front of my head: a bald spot.

My hands started to shake. Did I really want to see myself without hair, even as a little kid? But I kept going. The next five or six envelopes were all of Kyle and nothing of me. It was like watching a horror flick, knowing the goriest part was coming, something that'd give me bad dreams about for months, but I still couldn't look away.

Wait a minute. There was a gap in the picture sequence.

I rifled through what was left in the box and I wasn't in *any* of the photos. They couldn't have been misfiled—Mom was way too anal for that. June, my birthday, should've been next, but a batch of envelopes was missing.

I snuck back into my parents' room and started poking around in Mom's closet, checking over my shoulder to be sure I didn't get caught. My cheeks burned anyway, knowing how pissed she'd be if she caught me going through her things. But I had to find those pictures!

I opened shoeboxes, bags, and an old sewing basket—nothing. *Maybe she trashed them years ago.* But I wasn't ready to give up. I kept searching, all the while listening for someone coming up the stairs. And then I noticed a gift bag on the top shelf in the corner. I hooked the bag's handle with a hanger and lowered it down.

Bingo. *June-Cassie's 4th Bday.* I opened the envelope and in the first picture, I'm smiling behind a 4-shaped candle, wearing a hat—and not a pointy birthday hat, either. It was a floppy one with a yellow daisy and it covered my head all the way down to my ears.

I blinked. *Whoa. I think I remember this hat…the daisy…*I got in trouble for yanking off the flower and putting it in a vase with water. Seeing this hat jolted my memory and images came flooding back. Suddenly I could picture a hat rack attached to the wall in my room. All those hats, and I couldn't stand wearing any of them.

Mom tried to make a game out of it—anything to get me to keep a hat on my head. But they were too hot or too itchy or too big, and I always took them off

I felt unsteady as another memory surfaced. This time,

it was Mom and me in front of the mirror, battling over a hat. I struggled and she held my wrists down, which made me cry. *"Just wear your hat, Cassie,"* she begged. *"You want to look pretty, don't you?"* I'd finally stopped resisting and Mom had said, *"There, see how pretty you look?"* I sucked in a gasp and could almost *taste* my tears from that day.

In my mind, I replayed what Mom had said to me that first day, when I showed her the towel covered with hair: *"Just cover it up. No one has to know."* For Mom, if anything was less than perfect, it had to be hidden.

I continued going through the pictures, and in the next one, the hat was off. I'm smiling and clapping and had just blown out the birthday candle. And only a few tufts of hair were left on my head.

Suddenly, I wasn't alone. "What are you doing?" Mom asked.

I was startled back to the present, where Mom and Dad stood in the doorway. They could see that boxes and containers from Mom's closet had been moved, and I was standing there with the photos in my hand.

I didn't answer her. I was too stunned by what I held in my hands—the missing pieces of the family photo puzzle.

How could she have done this? It was like she'd edited me out of the family—out of her perfect world—just because of how I looked: like a bald little girl.

I stared hard at Mom as all those fragmented memories swirled in my head. *Pretty* was all that mattered. It was what she'd emphasized over and over, then and now.

"You hid these," I said, showing her what I'd found. "And you hid *me*! That's exactly what you were doing when you took me out of school back then. You were trying to hide me because I wasn't perfect enough for you!"

"That is not true!" Mom said.

"Nice try, Mom, but I'm holding the proof."

"You have it all wrong. I-I- kept you home to protect you. Kids can be so cruel." She held out her hand. "Why don't you give me those—?"

"Sorry I didn't turn out to be your clone, Mom—another little Miss Perfect," I told her. "Too bad you ended up with a defective kid and couldn't handle it. Obviously, you still can't."

My words hung in the air as Mom looked to Dad for support but he didn't react.

I was getting angrier by the minute and couldn't hold back. "I'm not four anymore, Mom. Now it's my secret, not yours," I said. "And trust me. No one's ever going to hear about this from me."

My parents looked at me like they didn't recognize me, as if they'd come upon a stranger in their bedroom. And at that moment, I wasn't quite sure who I was either, or what I might say next. All I knew was, I needed out of there, and fast.

Still gripping the photos, I bolted to the bedroom door but Dad blocked me.

"Hold on," he said.

"Nothing is ever good enough for her," I shouted.

Mom reacted as if I'd slapped her in the mouth. Her eyes seemed to ask, *How can you say that?*

Then a grenade went off in my head and I lost it. "It's true!" I said. "She criticizes my clothes, my friends—even track! And now my hair! Just leave me alone!"

I pushed harder, trying to get past Dad, but he caught me in a bear hug. I kept struggling to get away and the pictures went flying.

"Did you hear her, Victoria?" Dad said as he continued trying to restrain me. "Don't you see it? You're doing the same thing to Cassie that *your* mother did to you."

Writhing, I tried to pry his arms off me and said, "Let…Me…Go!"

"Chet," Mom pleaded. "Let her go."

Dad said, "This is ending right now. Cass, come on. Settle down."

I threw my weight to one side, then the other. But his arms were like a vice. I was flailing, kicking, and hitting, all at the same time and getting nowhere.

"It's her fault!" I screamed. "This shit disease came from *her* gene pool!"

Mom's face was streaked with horror at my words.

Dad tried to calm me. "Just listen a minute, Cass. Please."

My heel made contact with Dad's shin and he still hung onto me. Damn, he was so strong,

I shouted, "Let me go!" But it was no use. I couldn't break free. I was weakening against his grip. I settled down a bit, feeling that it was all too much effort.

I gritted my teeth, thinking, *Fine. Enough!* Panting, the back of my neck moist with sweat, I took a minute to catch my breath. And when Dad realized I'd stopped fighting, he finally let me go; he was out of breath, too.

"What does Gramma have to do with anything?" I asked, changing the subject a bit, hoping they'd let me go.

Mom stood up straight and smoothed her hands over her hips. I could tell that everything I'd said had struck a nerve, and whatever was coming must be big. But somehow her internal switch flicked on and she once again became a pillar of composure. Suddenly she turned her anger toward Dad.

"I don't know what you're talking about regarding my mother," she said. "And I haven't done anything wrong here. I've only ever tried to protect our daughter. Is that some kind of crime?"

"Okay, maybe not, but—" Dad said, like he was using his last ounce of patience, "—it's the *way* you go about things."

"Look, honey," Mom said to me. "I tucked those pictures away because—" she gestured toward them where they lay on the floor, "—well, see? Look how upset they made you?"

I was all out of patience so I asked, "Can I go now?"

Mom raised an eyebrow at Dad, who moved out of the doorway.

I flew to my room, thinking, *I hate her. I hate them all.* I locked my door and crumpled onto the floor, hugging my knees.

Then came the inevitable knock on my door.

"Go away!" I moaned. Then I put my head down and covered my ears.

"Cassie?" It was Dad. "Can I come in?"

"Leave me alone."

And after a long silence, he was gone.

I stared at the picture I was still gripping. Even though it was from forever ago, I felt like I was peeking through a keyhole into the future.

And I wondered, *what did it mean for Tommy and me?* I wanted to believe that I'd be okay and that eventually the medicine would work—it had to. But the more I thought about it, a sinking feeling hit me in the gut. My mom was right: you can't be bald *and* pretty. Who'd want to go out with a bald girl? I mean, if it were the other way around, would I want to date a bald guy? Even Tommy? It killed me that I was so shallow, but I knew it was probably the truth.

I shook my head and dragged myself off the floor. Then I smoothed the creases on the picture and tucked it into my jewelry box. It made me sick to realize I was no better than Mom, because looks mattered to me, too.

It was late when I remembered the composition I was supposed to write for school the next day. But I wanted to get ready for bed before tackling it so I changed into pj's, and when I was sure nobody was around, I headed to the bathroom to wash my face. I wanted to apply more medicine, too. But when I took down my ponytail, out came a continuous stream of hair from the scrunchie.

124

No. No. This can't be happening! I thought. *This scrunchie shouldn't have pulled out more hair.* It was my softest, and I thought—safest.

I shook the hair off and into the toilet, then watched, terrified, as it floated like a web. I covered my mouth to muffle the sound of my gulping breaths when Kyle, oblivious as ever, barged in.

He peered into the toilet, his eyes bugging. "Holy shit!" he said.

I flushed quickly and we watched my hair get sucked down the drain.

"Mom!" he yelled.

"Get away!" I said, pushing past him so roughly that he flew backward and hit his head against the wall.

I ran to my room with the bottle of medicine and shut the door, shaking.

"Dad! Mom!" Kyle shouted.

They were at my door seconds later.

"Come on, honey, open up," Dad said. "Let me help you."

"Why did more hair have to fall out?" I sobbed from my bed. "Forget it. There's nothing you can do."

"We'll make another appointment with Dr. Barnett," Mom said.

"Whatever. Just leave me alone."

All the good things in my life were slipping away already. I'd only been with Tommy for a few weeks. It was so unfair. My pillow was wet with tears before I finally sat up and felt around on my scalp to find the new bald spot. I sniffed and went through the motions of applying the useless medicine that hadn't grown back one freaking hair. *Why do I even bother?* I wondered. Finally, when I saw that a ponytail would still cover the holes, I climbed into bed and pulled the covers over my head.

My life totally sucked.

Thirteen

The next morning, Mom was in the kitchen making Kyle's lunch and even in the dull light from over the sink, I could see the creases around her eyes. Kyle was at the table, cramming a bagel into his mouth and giving me the death stare. He was still mad at me from almost sending him through the wall the night before.

I toasted half an English muffin for myself.

Dad came down a few minutes later and poured a cup of coffee, giving Mom one sideways glance after another. Some kind of eerie silence hung between them and she wouldn't meet his eyes.

A muscle in Dad's jaw flexed, but then I noticed something else: a scratch on his cheek.

Did I do that? Oh, God. My heart deflated. It seemed like no matter what went on in this house, my dad always got stuck between Mom and me. I didn't want him to be mad at me and I was all set to apologize when he lifted his keys off the hook.

"Early meeting," he said to no one specifically. "See you tonight." And he was gone.

I choked down the muffin and a mouthful of juice.

"Listen, Cassie," Mom sounded exhausted. She sat across from me, both hands wrapped around her coffee mug.

"I don't want to be late," I warned and stood up. I was glad Dad wasn't around; otherwise, he might've made me stay. I left the table, scooped up my backpack, and rushed out the door. I was so early, I was the first one at the bus stop. I didn't even shower, which grossed me out, but I didn't want to risk touching my hair any more than I had to for fear more would come out.

At school, Tara wasn't in the cafeteria, so I started toward my locker where Tommy was slipping a note into the vent. *A kiss and run? Not today.* I ducked behind a few people but it was too late—he was headed straight toward me.

He plucked the hat off his head and plunked it down on mine, punctuated with a minty kiss. Any time but now, I'd want an even bigger taste of those lips.

"So I'll see you later," he said, tapping the brim of the hat. Obviously, he meant that time and location of the kiss-and-run would be in the note.

"I can't," I said, desperate to get away. "I have a test."

"What period?"

Shit. I should've waited to read the note.

"Every period."

"You're kidding."

"I'm sorry, Tommy. It's not a good day. I'm totally swamped."

Just at that moment, Tara walked up to us.

128

"Geez, Cassie," she said. "I wait for *you* in the cafeteria every day. You couldn't wait for me just once?" Then she said, "Hey, Tommy."

"Listen," I said to Tommy, removing his hat and handing it back to him. "Tara and I have to go. Right, T?" The mental telepathy I had going on with Tara at that point could bend a steel beam. She nodded on cue, but Tommy gave me a quizzical look, almost like I'd slapped him in the face.

"It's a chick thing," Tara said, which seemed enough of an explanation.

"Okay. Whatever," he said. "Catch up with you later. Not today, though. Don't worry." He put on his hat and took off, but it was obvious he wasn't a happy camper.

I looked back. "God, I wish I didn't blow him off like that. He didn't do anything wrong, but I don't think I can handle being with him today."

"Why? What's with you, anyway?" Tara asked.

"I'm literally unraveling here. I had a major blowout with my parents last night. And then right before bed, more hair came out."

"What? Oh, my God."

"Why is this happening to me?"

"Take it easy. Let me see."

No one's supposed to see. But this is Tara so I made an exception. We slipped into a smoky but otherwise empty bathroom and I showed her where the patches were forming into one.

"It's not that bad," she said. "Want me to French braid it?"

I was so afraid to touch it myself that I hesitated. But Tara persisted.

"I'll be really gentle," she said. "I promise."

Maybe I could relax if Tara braided it for me.

"I didn't even shower this morning—too scared to lose more," I said.

"That's okay. Where's your comb?"

I sat on the radiator as she gently combed and divided my hair into three sections at the top. She's explained how she does it, trying to teach me, but this time I could feel each step.

Tara smoothed the sides and gathered sections of hair from one side, then the other, and a pleasant wave of chills spread over my arms and up my back as she worked. Braiding downward, she picked up more sections of hair from each side.

I reached up, asking, "Is it covering?"

"Yes. Move your hand," she told me.

"The medicine I'm using isn't doing jack," I said.

Tara stopped braiding.

"Done?" I asked, reaching up again to feel the braid. But it was loose and slipping out.

"Oh, Cassie, I'm so sorry. I'm sorry. I'm sorry. I'm sorry," she whispered.

I turned around to see Tara backing away from me looking horrified. She was holding her arms out stiffly in front of her with her fingers caught in a net of my fallen hair.

"I'm sooo sorry," she said again, staring down at her shaking, hair-covered hands. Her eyes were filling with tears when I stepped over and pulled the hair off her fingers. She lowered her arms, then broke down and sobbed, still apologizing between gulping breaths.

"It's okay, Tara. You didn't do it. It just came out. It's okay, really." I rubbed her back and put my arm around her shoulders and kept saying, "It's okay. It's okay."

She was so shaken up, and I felt awful.

"I didn't mean to—"

"I know. It's okay."

When she finally calmed down, I realized that this was the first time it'd happened when *I* hadn't cried.

The last warning bell rang and I said, "Go out and get a drink of water. I'm all right."

When she left, I quickly smoothed my hair back and gathered it together. Strands fell from my comb and I felt around for any exposed skin on my head. I kicked at the hair on the floor to spread out what looked like the remains of a major girl-fight, then dashed out the door.

I scrambled to my locker, grabbed and read Tommy's note on the way to homeroom. *Roses are red, Frogs are green. The boiler room at 11:15.* That would be during French class. I'd saved all of his notes so far, and practically everything he's touched. This kiss-and-run made four.

In French, Monsieur Haus left plenty of time for free conversation. *Great.* Robin and I looked at each other as the rest of the class began the standard rehearsed conversations. I knew she expected me to start as usual, but I was thinking about Tara and couldn't be bothered making small talk with Robin only to have her respond with her typical response of 'Je ne sais pas.' Suddenly I remembered my

English composition. Crap—I never even started it last night in all the commotion. I opened to a clear page in my notebook, figuring I could chip away at it before seventh period. I didn't much care what I wrote, as long as I had something to hand in.

I got down my name and the date, then got stuck. I wiggled my pen and felt Robin's eyes on me. Nervous, I casually patted the back of my head and was relieved that my secret was safe. When the time for meeting Tommy came and went, I was so dejected, I practically had to scrape my heart off the floor. Then, still ignoring Robin, I flipped through a folder of loose papers, pretending to search for something important. I hoped to coast through the rest of the period without having to talk to her, but she had other plans.

"Qu'elle heure est il?" she asked.

Even though I knew there were only four minutes left until the end of class, I said, "Je ne sais pas," with the same blank expression Robin had whenever she said this to me. The look of surprise on her face was priceless, and that cheered me up a little.

Before seventh period, I waited outside our English classroom as Tara approached.

"You okay?" I asked.

"I feel terrible, Cass. I can't believe I did that to you," she said.

"It's not your fault, Tara—far from it. Please don't worry about it."

She nodded and we went into class.

Just my luck, the first thing Miss Troy asked for was

last night's assignment. Everyone passed their essays forward. Since I only got as far as my name and the date and couldn't plead writer's block on a long-term assignment, I landed a big fat zero for myself. Frustrated, I lay my head on my desk. I just couldn't seem to catch a break.

When I got off the bus after school, Mom was unloading groceries from the car. Even with everything going on, stupid things like grocery shopping and compositions still had to get done. I came up the driveway, not sure if I was ready to deal with her. Blaming her for my hair had been an evil thing to say, but I was still pissed. Still, I lifted the last bag out of the trunk and followed Mom inside. And just like robots, we put everything neatly away.

"Cass, do you think we could talk?" Mom asked.

I pressed my lips tight together, but I didn't say no.

"About last night," she said, leaning against the counter. "Cassie, you're my daughter and I never set out to hurt you." She started twisting her rings. "No one hands you a how-to manual when you have a kid…" she said, trying to joke. "I just hope it's not too late to fix things between us."

I shrugged almost imperceptibly.

"Does that mean we can try?"

I narrowed my eyes and said, "What did Gramma *do*?"

"That's not important, really. This is about you and me."

So there was something. Last night, she flat out denied it. I just shrugged again.

Mom opened her arms to me, but I remained anchored in place. She waited awkwardly, her expression uncertain.

She'd done most of the talking up to now, and after the lousy day I'd had, I really could've used a hug.

I realized that I *did* want to fix things between us, but by that point I'd left her hanging too long. Embarrassed, she folded her arms, like she was warming herself after my freeze-out. Then she nodded to herself and blotted the corner of eye with her pinky.

"Fair enough," she said, then sat down at the table.

Treating Mom this way didn't make me feel any better. If she was going to try and make amends, the least I could do was give her a chance. So I sat down, too. She seemed surprised but pleased that I'd decided to stick around.

"I made another dermatologist appointment for you," Mom said. "Next Thursday, after school."

"But that's our first track practice," I said.

"I think the doctor wants to try a different treatment."

"I read about injections on the Internet," I told her.

Mom shifted in her seat. "I guess there's nothing you can't find out about online. You're still using the liquid medicine, right?"

"It's not helping at all," I blurted out, panic rising in my throat.

"Oh, honey." Mom reached for my hand. "For now, I think the best thing is to try and stay positive."

"That's not going to make any difference, Mom. I didn't want to tell you, but I lost more hair today."

Fear flashed in her eyes, even though she tried to hide it. "Maybe the doctor'll—"

"*Maybe* isn't going to cut it. Besides, that's a whole week away—who knows if I can even last *that* long."

"Let's try not to think like that."

"That's all I *can* think about. Nothing's growing back, and I need *someone* to tell me this is all a mistake, that I'll somehow live happily ever after."

Mom's expression was pained. Her eyes searched the ceiling for an answer, but we both knew she couldn't tell me what I so desperately wanted to hear. Instead, she got up from her chair, came over and wrapped her arms around me and pulled me close, our heads touching.

My throat knotted up and I gulped in breaths, then surrendered to Mom's embrace. But no matter how good it felt, it wasn't going to be enough to end this nightmare.

Fourteen

I thought I heard my phone ringing in my room, but before I got to it, the call went to voice mail. When I checked the phone, it was a missed call from Tommy. I punched in my password for voice mail and listened.

"Hey, Cassie. It's me. Just wondering when we can get together. Maybe we can hitch a ride with Eric and Dina for a movie this Saturday. Give me call."

I dialed Tommy's number. There was no way I could face him after last night and what happened today with Tara. I'd have to avoid him at least until I saw Dr. Barnett again.

"Hi, Tommy. This weekend isn't good. I have to baby-sit." *Lie.*

"How about Sunday? We can hang around the mall or get a slice of pizza."

"No, we're spending the day at my grandparents'." *Another lie.*

"Maybe Sunday night when you get home we can catch—"

"*No!* Um, yeah, I don't know."

136

"Okay. Whatever." He sounded hurt. *Damn.*

"I wish this weekend wasn't so booked. And right now I have a mountain of homework and some power cramming to do for tomorrow…you know how things get."

"We can chill, then."

"You're the best. I'll talk to you, okay?"

I hated lying to Tommy, but I wasn't ready to supply the gory details yet. Why freak him out for no reason if Dr. Barnett has a real solution this time? He still didn't know anything about my hair and I wanted to keep it that way.

At least the homework part was true, not that I was getting anywhere with it. I'd been reading the same paragraph in my World Cultures book for the kajillionth time when Kyle came home. He charged up the stairs and passed my door, and I gave up, tossed the book off to the side and went after him.

Kyle scowled at me standing in his doorway. "What do you want?" he said, then dumped the contents of his backpack on the floor, picked up a loose Twizzler and took a bite. "Need my head for a punching bag or something?"

"I didn't mean to push you so hard last night. I was totally freaking out."

"Exactly. I thought you needed help," he said.

"I'm sorry," I told him. I felt like a piece of crap.

"How sorry?" he asked with that all-too-familiar glint of mischief in his eyes.

"You still owe me the ten bucks," I said. "Actually, it's more like eighteen if you count the rest you borrowed."

"Damn," he said, shoving the rest of the Twizzler in his mouth.

"Nice try, though. But you know you didn't hit your head *that* hard."

He changed the subject. "Hey, wanna see my new comic?"

"Sure," I said. He handed me the *Incredible Hulk vs. Abomination*. "Is this how you spend my hard-earned baby-sitting money?" I leafed through it, and mused that last night, I practically *was* the Hulk—I did everything but turn green.

It was so weird. I'd never thrown a tantrum in my life, and it was a little scary that I could totally lose control like that. And after all that screaming, I didn't feel that much better.

At least today things were better with Mom—that was a real start. But there was still that something Mom didn't say—whatever it was that Dad already knew that she's not telling me.

Later, Dad came home with Chinese food and I met him at the front door.

"I'm sorry about last night," I told him.

"I know, babe—and it's okay. Really. It was a rough night for everyone." Dad frowned and glanced toward the kitchen—where he'd left Mom this morning without really speaking to her. "Your mother and I will do everything we can to help, Cass. You know that, don't you?"

I looked at the scratch on his face with embarrassment and nodded, even though I felt lower than crap cubed.

"Mom and I talked a little," I offered. That seemed to be enough to relax the crease between Dad's eyes, and I hoped it would help ease things between my parents, too. I wanted to show him I could be grown up, that I wasn't really a crazed maniac.

In the kitchen, Dad hoisted the bags onto the counter.

"Mmm, China Kitchen," Kyle said. He vaulted over the couch from the family room and started digging in a bag for barbecued spare ribs.

"Nice to see you too, Kyle," Dad said.

"Oh, hey, Dad." They bumped fists.

"Must you climb over the furniture like that?" Mom asked. She put down her decorating magazine and demonstrated the proper way to exit the family room.

He shrugged and shot Mom a Kyle-smile.

"Mom made another dermatologist appointment for me next week," I said in my most upbeat voice. "Let's hope this will be the last one."

"Atta girl," Dad said, giving Mom an appreciative nod.

We finished unloading the food containers and sat down to eat.

"Track starts Thursday," I said to Dad, "and I was thinking maybe I can get a little time in at practice before we go to the doctor."

"Thursday?" Dad asked. "That was the earliest appointment?"

Mom nodded.

He shook his head. "I'm locked in—I'll be in Texas. I'm running the training program for our new account."

I wanted to ask if he *had* to go, but how babyish would that be? I knew he had to do his job.

"We'll be just fine," Mom said to me. "Right, honey?"

The last thing he needed was to go away thinking he

was leaving behind a basket case of a daughter who couldn't survive without him.

"Oh, yeah," I chirped. "Totally."

Bravo! What a performance. We were no longer the twisted, dysfunctional family from last night's reality TV show. If this kept up, we were destined for Emmy Awards for our performances.

"How long you going for?" Kyle asked. "Can you get me a ten-gallon hat?"

"It'll be two weeks, and I'll see what they have in a few quarts for you," he teased.

Whoa, two weeks with just Mom and me? I watched the condensation on my water glass drip onto the table and thought *Mom and doctor visits don't mesh.* We all knew that.

"But when I'm out of town, if there's anything you need," Dad said, looking at me, "I'm only a phone call away."

"Thanks, Dad. I'm good."

After dinner I checked in with Tara.

"We're all going bowling Saturday night," she said.

"I don't feel like going out," I told her.

"Girls against the boys, and we are going to kick a-s-s. It's all set up, so don't even attempt to weasel out of it," she said.

"What guys?"

"Tommy, Glen and Jason."

"I can't," I said. "I already told Tommy I have to baby-sit."

"Tell him they canceled. You're coming!" That was Tara. She wasn't going to tolerate any of this moping around business.

A night out might keep my mind occupied, because waiting alone at home until my doctor's appointment wasn't going to make it happen any faster. And if we're playing girls against the boys, I should be able to keep a safe enough distance from Tommy so that he wouldn't see anything weird going on with my hair. Not that I'd be able to stand it for long—I totally hated the idea of avoiding him.

"What time are we meeting?" I asked, weakly.

V-Bowl was a dark cavern warmed with soft neon lights. And as far as I was concerned, the darker the better. The crash of pins echoed from the far side of the alleys where a mixed league was going at it.

Two of our friends, Monique and Amy, had joined a teen winter league here and were proud to be the only ones who didn't need yucky rental shoes. I gave the shoe rental kid one of my sneakers and he handed over a semi-flattened pair of shoes.

"I'm going to burn my socks when I get home," I said.

"Not these babies." Tara showed me her bowling pin socks. "Now quit complaining and let's find a good ball."

The ball racks were loaded with hundred-pound balls each with finger holes the size of wishing wells. That didn't leave me with a lot of options, and I ended up lugging an ugly black-and-red marbled ball over to our lane and placed it in the ball return, right next to Monique's and Amy's pretty, personalized ones.

Obviously, V-Bowl with seven other people wasn't the most romantic date, but it was just fine with me. I was glad I'd fought the urge to back out at the last minute and loved being close to Tommy, especially the little things like sitting with his leg against mine or holding hands. We had no real personal space boundaries, but still, I was worried about being so close to him, worried that my hair would betray me at any moment, so to stay calm, I spent most of the time sitting in the scorekeeper's chair with one of the girls, where Tommy couldn't get too close.

Four frames in, I had to go check my head. So I said, "I'm going to get some fries. Be right back."

"Can you get me an orange soda?" Amy asked, handing me some money.

"And an order of nachos for me?" Ginny said.

"I can go for a slice of pizza," someone else said.

"T, how about a hand?" I said. But it fell on deaf ears. She was too busy flirting with Glen to even notice I was talking to her. Good for her—she was recovering nicely from the Adam/Robin matchup.

Noticing the situation, Tommy said, "I'll take a walk with you."

We sat at the snack bar and waited for our order, which by that point had grown to include another order of nachos, a hot pretzel, and four more sodas. Tommy tried to put his arm around me, but I swiveled around on my stool. Then he started playing with my ponytail, and that's when I lost it.

"Stop that!" I told him.

"What's with you lately?" Tommy said, obviously surprised. He blinked, waiting.

Maybe it is time he knows. I can't keep shutting him down or treating him like he's some kind of leper. He's sweet—he'll understand. But my fears over saying the words and living with his reaction had me in a choke hold. I had to change the subject, and quick.

I noticed a burly construction worker–type hunched over the bar and he was wearing plastic bag booties over his shoes.

"What's that all about?" I nodded toward him and asked, praying Tommy'd excuse my latest Jekyll and Hyde episode.

"To keep your shoes dry, and so you don't track anything onto the alleys," he explained, then slipped his hand over my fist.

"Cassie, you'd tell me if something was wrong, wouldn't you?" he said.

Slowly I fanned out my fingers, accepting his touch, knowing he'd interpret this to mean *yes*, but of course it was a lie.

When our order was ready we carried the snacks to the alley.

"We bowled your turns for you," Tara told us, picking at my fries.

Everyone started munching and reaching for their drinks. Tommy moved a few bags and jackets to sit next to me.

"After all that, I forgot my soda," he said.

I skooched forward as he rested his arm on the back of

my seat. He sniffed his armpits with a grin in response, then eased me closer to him, nuzzled against my face and stole a quick kiss and a French fry.

"How about a sip of your soda?" he asked.

"Just take it," I said, then jumped up and ducked into the ladies' room.

Great plan, Cass. Now what? I kicked one of the stall doors. *I'm such an idiot.*

"Someone's in here," a tiny voice said. The lock clicked open and a little girl darted out, trying to fasten her suspenders.

Oh, no! Poor thing.

The water trickling out of the faucet formed a rust ring around the drain. That's exactly where I was headed with Tommy if I didn't stop losing it like that. Soon he'd be telling people, *Yes, I'd like you to meet my schizoid girlfriend who scares little girls right off the toilet."*

I had to cut myself a break. Even the criminal justice system gives inmates time off for good behavior. I reasoned with my reflection: *No one knows, so just act normal.* But I couldn't help worrying. *What if my hair gets worse? Just put it out of your mind—at least for tonight. Oh, yeah, that's me—a total schizoid.*

Back at the lanes, it was Glen's turn and his first roll left him with the bowler's nightmare—an impossible seven/ten split.

"Pick a pin. Any pin," Monique said, laughing.

I smoothed in next to Tommy and he patted my knee.

"Watch this," he said. "I've seen him make this shot."

Glen's powerful curveball sent the seven-pin spinning

like a helicopter toward the ten-pin and we held our breath as it blasted its target, picking up the spare. The guys cheered; the girls groaned.

"I saved you some soda," Tommy said. He picked up the cup and tipped the straw to my lips. I grinned and took a sip.

"It's your turn, Cassie," Amy said. "Get a strike. They're killing us."

"No problemo," I said, sarcastically.

The worst part of this game was having my back toward everyone, and the alley wasn't quite dark enough for the bowler to appear as a silhouette. I got up slowly, wondering. What did I watch when someone else bowled? Just their approach, swing, and the release of the ball. After that, I focused only on the ball on its way to the pins. And that's what my friends would be looking at—the pins, not the back of my head! Okay, maybe Tommy would be checking out my butt, too, but I was willing to live with that.

I took my ball and lined up with the marks on the floor. After moving a few times, trying to get in the right spot, I approached the line, released the ball and *bang. Uh, oh.* It was off course. I waved at the ball, trying to coax it back to the center of the alley, and it headed for the corner pin.

"Hang on. Hang on," the girls chanted.

But, no. Thunk—a spectacular gutter ball! Everyone cracked up, including me.

Fifteen

Next week at school, I wanted to play it safe as I counted down to Thursday's doctor appointment. I navigated the halls, flying way below Tommy's radar as much as I could. I blew him off three days in a row for kiss-and-runs, and on Wednesday, he offered about ten different choices when to meet, to try and make it easy for me. I just played it ditzy, like I had track practice on the brain and nothing else. And after school I made excuses. I even told him I had to help Kyle paint the garage. To fill the time after school, I went on long runs, promising myself I'd explain everything to Tommy after seeing Dr. Barnett.

On Thursday morning, my eyes snapped open at four forty-six a.m., which gave me a little time to see Dad before he left on his two-week trip. I tied my hair back and felt my way down the stairs in the dark, not wanting to wake up Kyle by turning on the light. I followed the glow of the morning news on the TV in the family room, then curled up on the couch and snuggled under Mom's chenille throw.

"Morning," Dad said. "Up early, huh?"

"Too early."

"Today's your appointment with Dr. Barnett," Dad said.

I twisted a tassel around my finger. "She may want to try injections," I told him. Injections into my scalp; I'd been thinking about how that'd go. It sounded painful, since there's no meat between the skin and my skull—no buffer. I imagined I'd feel everything. I pictured an inch-long needle that she'd have to jab in sideways to get the medicine in there.

"The doctor didn't recommend injections for a three-year-old," Dad said, "but at your age, it might be an option now, so discuss it with her. It may be the thing that helps."

I'd much rather take a pill instead of a shot, but I could handle needles if they'd help me keep my hair.

"I wish you were coming," I told my father.

"Me too, honey. But Mom'll be there for you."

Yeah, but only because she has no choice.

Dad kissed the top of my head and brushed my cheek with the back of his hand. "I have to go," he said. "You'll be fine today. See if you can fall back to sleep for a while before school."

I closed my eyes. I didn't want to get my hopes up *too* high, because even if the next treatment worked, I'd have to wait a long time for the new hair to get back to the length I'd been wearing. I sighed. It would be great not to obsess about this 24/7, and to be with Tommy and my friends again—like a regular, non-diseased person.

I didn't go back to sleep, and before long, Mom and Kyle trudged into the kitchen. I stretched my legs and, wow, they were tight. I'd been hitting the pavement a lot lately to decompress, so it made sense. I'd probably run ten to fifteen miles in the previous few days. But I figured it was better to have a few sore muscles than walk around with knots in my stomach.

"Mom, what time are we leaving for the appointment later?" I asked.

"Right after you get off the bus after school." Mom poured a cup of coffee and took cold cuts out of the fridge for Kyle's lunch.

"Could you write me a note for the coach since I have to miss practice?"

Mom nodded, then penned a few words on her lilac stationery. "Here you go."

I took it from her. Even her penmanship was perfect.

At school, Tara and I made the usual rounds.

"I want to bring this to the office for Coach McCaffrey," I said, holding the note. I folded it and wrote her name on it. "It's about missing practice. I don't want her to think I'm blowing it off."

"You won't be missing anything," Tara said. "Sprints, laps, bleachers, and remember my personal favorite, high-knee warm-ups, the real downside to hurdles." We jokingly called them hiney warm-ups because we'd have to jog around lifting our knees high up in front of us, and at one practice, Coach McCaffrey was shouting, 'Let's see it ladies! High knees! High knees! High knees! Get 'em up! Let's go!'

"You're such a moaner," I told her as I popped the note into the coach's mailbox.

Homeroom announcements started with a reminder

about track practice. I was bummed that I had to miss the first one, then smiled when I thought of Tara, sitting there in homeroom, bummed about going to practice. She hates it; she's all about the meets.

During sixth period, we had a mandatory assembly on violence in the schools and I had to miss lunch to go to it. We all herded ourselves to the Driscoll gym, clogging the halls all the way back to the main office. We funneled in through four sets of double doors, and among the shuffling bodies, I found my friend Monique. We climbed the bleachers together and sat near the bottom, like most of the other freshmen. In our school, upperclassmen got the higher seats.

"I can't believe I have to miss lunch," I complained.

"Here, you can have these," Monique said and handed me half a pack of LifeSavers. Then she said, "You never wear your hair down anymore, Cassie—" She scanned the bleachers for Amy and added, "—not that it looks bad or anything. Amy happened to notice and pointed it out to me."

I shrugged. "It stays neater all day when it's pulled back and out of the way."

"Gym class is a killer for me, too."

After a rippling wave of shushes, Mr. Rayner, the principal, spoke from the podium on the gym floor. "In light of recent incidents of high school violence in surrounding towns and across the country, the Board of Education has invited Officer Ben Kessler from our own local police force to explain how this impacts on our school."

I wondered where Tommy was among all the faces.

My brain was battling a tug-o-war, wanting to see him, yet also hoping I didn't.

"Darlington High has not had any problems that have required police attention," Officer Kessler began. A few cheers rose from the audience, then he went on. "Our goal is to keep it that way and a zero tolerance policy is now in effect. This means that even the *threat* of violence against any individual or against the student body or faculty, such as a bomb scare, will become a police matter."

Suddenly a knee poked into my back and I turned around.

"Excuse me," a girl said as I looked up at the crowd. All those rows of bleachers behind me were packed, and the highest level of seats were about even with the basketball hoop. That meant all those kids were high up enough to see the top of my head. And it meant that during track meets, spectators would also have a bird's-eye view of my head.

I was nervous enough before a race without the hair situation. But I wouldn't be able to stand it if the crowd only came to gawk at the balding weirdo sprinting down the field. With that thought, my mind took off like a runaway train, imagining what they'd say: *Hey, it's the girl with the bald head disease.* They'd be pointing, staring, laughing. *This is what I'm setting myself up for? No way. I'll quit first,* I told myself, clutching the bleachers and bracing myself for the humiliation. But wait a second—I had to chill out. Maybe today's treatment would be the key to getting my life back to normal. Gradually, I took a breath to calm down and loosened my grip on the bleachers.

Having missed almost everything said at the assembly, I tuned back in time to hear the announcement to report to our seventh-period classes. But instead of going to English, I detoured to Hot Topic, the cosmetic store across the street. An arsenal of hair accessories covered the back wall, from the floor to the ceiling. There were claw clips, headbands, barrettes, combs, chopsticks, and scrunchies made out of hair. Now that would be perfect! I grabbed one and saw from the package that it wrapped around a ponytail, the extra hair would fluff out close to the head, and that might be just what I needed. I also wanted something that would hold the hair in place where I wanted it, even if I had to go against the grain a little to hide a patch. I needed something that wouldn't slip out or tug at the roots—I didn't want to lose any extra hair if I could avoid it.

I started with a pack of little tortoiseshell hair clips, neutral enough not to draw too much attention. I thought they'd work with a ponytail holder, and I figured I could get away with wearing them in a random pattern the way I saw other girls wearing them. I also got a pair of wide stretchy-fabric headbands for maximum coverage.

Now it was time to get creative. Next aisle, eye make-up. I drew on the back of my hand with eyebrow pencil testers to match up my hair color—Tawny Mist, to help tone down the white spots on my head. And I'd have it if I needed it to make eyebrows—shit, I didn't even want to think about that!

I picked out a small mirror from one of the bins near the register and paid for everything, along with a diet soda for the walk back. If I started using some of this stuff now, it won't look like I was trying to cover up anything later on, if things get worse.

Tara was waiting for me outside the art room.

"Where were you last period?"

"Hot Topic."

"You *cut*?"

I shrugged and opened the bag for Tara to see. "I got all this—for camouflage."

We set up our easels and Tara began to work on her painting. I swished my brush in a cup of water and zoned out, preoccupied with Dr. Barnett and the possible needles ahead.

By the time class was almost over, I hadn't even dipped my brush into the paint.

"I think I'm getting some shots today," I told Tara.

"Into the bare spots, right?" she whispered. "I read about it online."

"It'll be worth it, if it stops this whole thing." My voice sounded shakier than I'd expected.

"I have something for you," Tara said and unzipped her purse.

She handed me an envelope made out of wrapping paper and I opened it.

"A bracelet!" I said. I'd seen hemp bracelets and jewelry made of thick twine. I'd tried to make one myself once, but it turned out nothing like the one Tara had just given me, which had silky threads in shades of honey brown and gold. It sparkled with glass bugle beads and seed beads woven into the pattern, and each knot was a perfect link in a braided chain.

"I made it," she told me with pride.

"Really?"

"This is tiger's eye," she explained. "It's supposed to be a power bead—for courage. That's what I read, anyway. It made me think of you and I wanted you to have it."

I rolled one of the beads between my fingers and light seemed to shimmer from inside it.

"See," she said, "it's pretty...from the inside out—like you."

"It's awesome," I said and held out my wrist so Tara could fasten the catch. I twisted my wrist over and back, admiring it. Hours of work must've gone into making it. Courage—with my appointment less than an hour away, and a needle waiting with my name on it, a little extra courage sure couldn't hurt.

I bumped my shoulder into hers and said, "Thanks, girlie."

Sixteen

There were no outside windows in Dr. Barnett's waiting room; only a mirror disguised as one. The silk plants in front of it added to the illusion. We sat down and Mom nodded encouragingly and gave my arm a little squeeze. It was like we were in this together and not to worry—she'd take care of everything—and I really needed that. I relaxed a little as Mom thumbed through a *Better Homes* magazine, and I glanced at the clock behind the receptionist. By now the team would be done stretching and the coach was probably barking out which drills to run. I bet Tara got stuck with the hiney warm-ups she likes so much; I felt myself grin thinking about it.

I crossed my legs, then uncrossed them, fidgity as I thought about my first visit to Dr. Barnett. She'd wanted to start with the least aggressive treatment—a liquid, which didn't hurt like needles would—if that's what I'd be getting next. *I don't care how you put it, needles suck.* My heartbeat kicked up a notch or two just thinking about it. But whatever was going to happen in there, it better work.

A tall guy wearing a baseball cap skulked in and gave his name to the receptionist, followed by a lady who sat down with him, probably his mother. I tried not to stare, but the poor kid's face was covered with angry red welts so bad, they had to hurt. He slumped in his seat, no doubt wishing he could disappear, but there was no hiding it.

He caught me looking. *Shoot—I didn't want to make eye contact.* He was checking me out, most likely trying to figure out why I was there. I hid behind a magazine, but nobody could tell what my problem was by looking at me, at least not from where he was sitting. He probably settled on warts or ringworm, or something equally appealing.

Finally, the assistant called my name, Mom patted my leg, and we got up together. And I realized I was actually glad she was there. The assistant led us to Dr. Barnett's office and we sat down. The only thing going through my mind was, *please, let today bring the answer*.

Dr. Barnett came in, shook our hands, leaned on the corner of her desk, and looked into my eyes.

"Your Mom told me you've lost more hair," she said.

I nodded.

"May I see?"

I carefully loosened my ponytail holder and slid it off, feeling as embarrassed as if I were taking off my clothes. Even though she was a doctor, I didn't want anyone to see those bald spots. Dr. Barnett walked around behind me and I pointed to the holes as best I could. As Mom watched, she began twisting her rings—never a good sign.

"So, you've been using the prescription," Dr. Barnett asked.

I nodded and told her, "Nothing's grown back yet."

Dr. Barnett flipped through my chart. "When you experienced hair loss at age three, there were no good treatment options for young children. So we hoped that your hair would grow back on its own, and it did."

"And now?" I asked.

"Since the minoxidil didn't give you good results, I'd like to try cortisone injections next." Dr. Barnett shifted her attention to Mom, telling her, "Cassie's mild form of alopecia may respond."

Mild? Sure, your *hair's not falling out.* But I was ready to try something else, especially if it worked.

"I use a tiny needle to give multiple injections in and around the bare skin patches," the doctor explained.

"Like how many? Two or three?" I asked.

"It's hard to say until I get started," she said. "The largest of the patches may take five or six injections."

Four patches times six. *Yikes! That's twenty-four shots.* My stomach bottomed out at the prospect and my face must've given me away.

"I know it sounds like a lot," she said, sympathetically. "But it's very tolerable. The worst you might feel is some slight discomfort."

Slight. As if.

"One thing I want to be clear about: this treatment won't stop more hair from falling out. It only addresses the hair we're trying to re-grow. I've had success with a number of patients using the cortisone shots. So, do either of you have any questions?"

I cleared my throat. "Is there anything I should be

doing to keep more hair from falling out? Or to try and slow it down? Because it'll take a long time to get back to this length again."

"I'm sorry, no," the doctor said. "There's no known preventative."

"Does it usually happen fast, when people's hair is falling out?" I asked. "Or does it take a while before...?" My voice trailed off and I couldn't bring myself to finish the sentence with "before it's all gone."

"Unfortunately, we can't predict the rate at which an individual's hair may fall out. Every case is different, and so is the way each patient responds to treatment."

That must have been her sneaky way of saying that I may end up completely bald. I kept praying that didn't have to happen, that somehow I could avoid it. But all the arrows kept pointing me to the same place: bald. A lump formed in my throat and I had no more questions.

"Are these injections safe?" Mom asked, like she was running the show now—something I didn't expect.

"Yes, it's a safe procedure."

"How often will Cassie need to come in for the cortisone shots?"

"Once a month," Dr. Barnett said.

"And how long before we know if it's working?"

Wow, Mom was right in there again.

"New hair growth should become visible in about four weeks."

Should become visible. I hated the way this doctor said things like "*may* respond" and "successful with *a number of* patients." What good was she and all her useless diplomas? She should have been a lawyer instead, considering that you couldn't get a straight answer out of her. The whole thing made me want to run out the door screaming.

Mom glanced at me, then started twisting her rings again and said, "Cassie, what do you think?"

Two dozen needles? Forget it. There were no guarantees. Just get me out of here. I'm not even supposed to be here. I should be at practice like everyone else.

Then I ran my finger over Tara's bracelet.

No guarantees.

I picked at one of the tiger's eye beads that Tara said symbolized courage.

They were waiting.

So I said, "I think I should try."

"Good," Dr. Barnett said. "Then come with me."

Whew, things were moving fast.

Dr. Barnett motioned to the assistant in the hallway and said, "Liz, please prep Cassie for cortisone injections."

As I stood up, Mom leaned forward in her seat, clutching the arms of the chair. Then she seemed to freeze there and turned pale.

Oh, no. She was bailing on me! Not now—don't tell me she's too embarrassed or afraid. Please! I don't want to do this alone.

"Mom?"

Then she blinked and stood up awkwardly with a half smile. *Thank God—all she'd needed was a little jump-start.* I swallowed hard as we followed Liz to the examining room.

"Have a seat," Liz said to Mom as she pointed to a

chair across from the exam table. She motioned to me to hop up onto the table, then began sterilizing the bare patches on my head. I counted four spots as she swabbed each one with a cotton ball. The biggest one was now the size of a quarter.

Then Dr. Barnett came in and thanked the assistant, who then left.

"How long does this take?" Mom asked, still looking pale.

"Not long," the doctor told her. "Maybe ten, fifteen minutes."

"We can handle it," I told my mom.

She nodded, looking relieved that I was staying calm.

Dr. Barnett pulled on latex gloves from a box on the counter, then unwrapped a needle and placed it on a sterilized tray. It wasn't nearly so big as I'd feared.

"Okay," Dr. Barnett said. "I need you to lie on your side and we'll start. Are you comfortable? Please try to relax—that way it won't hurt."

"You're about to stab me in the head with a bunch of needles," I quipped, trying to lighten the situation. I slipped my arm under my neck to prop up my head, then added with a laugh, "Sure, I'm totally comfortable."

Dr. Barnett smiled. "Great. And let's try this so your head's cushioned a bit more." She rolled up a white cloth and slipped it under my neck. Then she walked around behind me and had barely touched me when I jumped.

"Didn't mean to sneak up on you, Cassie. Please try to relax." She touched my head again and pressed.

"Okay. Here's the first injection." The needle went in

with a pinch. Then came the next and the next. A cortisone hornet was stinging me over and over and I couldn't even swat it.

Slight discomfort, my ass! Who was she trying to kid? It hurt like a bitch!

Then I felt an icy sensation spreading under my scalp. "Feels cold," I said.

"That's the Kenalog—the steroid I'm using. It's cold because it's stored in the refrigerator. You doing okay otherwise?"

"Mm, hm."

Four, five pinpricks; more tingling and coolness, then on to the next patch.

"The cortisone should stimulate the hair follicles to produce hair again," the doctor explained. Then came more needles, until one must have hit a nerve.

"Ow!" I said and my hand jerked up, pushing her away. That made the needle drag across my scalp, scratching me. "Ouch! That hurt!" I said and jolted upright.

"Cass!?" Mom cried out and was on her feet.

"I'm very sorry," Dr. Barnett said.

But Mom laced into her. "I thought you said you've *done* this before."

"Dozens of times, Mrs. Donovan," she told Mom. "I assure you. This has never happened before. Again, I apologize."

I touched my head and looked at my fingers, rubbing a drop of blood between them, and Mom wasn't exactly helping the situation by pacing back and forth.

Chill out, I willed myself. *Chill out and don't cry! Think of something else—think about running. Let your mind run. Suck it up and tough it out. You won't have to come back for a month.*

Dr. Barnett gave me a minute, then said, "Let me see that scratch. It's okay, so I'd like to clean it up and then continue if you're up for it."

I wasn't, not really, but I'd come too far to turn back now. I nodded to Mom and we continued. I lay back down and adjusted the neck roll, then stared hard at a cabinet knob as Dr. Barnett blotted the scratch. It stung!

I wished I could be just about anywhere else as every nerve in my body braced for the next round of stabs. I willed myself to stay calm, and then I felt something warm and unexpected—and good: Mom had taken my hand in hers. We squeezed them together, each of us drawing strength from the other.

"I'm going to continue with the injections now. So please, Cassie, try not to move."

I said, "Okay. We're ready."

Then came more needles, pinching and stinging. I took a deep breath and told myself *I could do this.*

As she worked, Dr. Barnett rested one hand on my head, with her fingers sweeping back and forth to move my hair away from the patches. I could feel her soft breath on my skin.

"You're doing great, Cassie," she said. "Just a few more minutes and we'll be done."

At last she said, "All set," and squeezed my shoulder.

"Good job." A slight tingle on my head marked where my hair was supposed to grow back. It also reminded me that with this disease, there were no guarantees.

But I'd done it! I'd survived round one. I sat up and Dr. Barnett told me I could wash my hair as usual that night.

After making some notes in my folder, she tucked it under her arm and said, "I'm hoping for the best for you, Cassie, and some of my patients have had very good results. So let's plan on seeing you again in a month. Don't worry if you feel indentations in your scalp at the injection sites—it's normal. But call if anything else changes or you have questions." Then she said goodbye and left, closing the door behind her.

Still sitting on the table, I looked at Mom as I gathered my hair back into a ponytail. The color had returned to her cheeks and she was smiling at me.

She'd made good on her promise, that she'd try to fix things. We'd gotten through the appointment—*together.*

Seventeen

When we got to the car, Mom said, "You did a good job in there."

"So you think this'll work?" I asked.

She considered her answer as we got into the car. What I wanted was a big, giant, undisputable *yes!* They hadn't tried injections when I was three and all of my hair fell out. At least this time, there was a solid plan of attack.

"There's no reason why it shouldn't work," she said, with a tiny spark of optimism as she drove out of the parking lot.

"You were great back there, too, Mom," I said. "It didn't occur to me that it might not be safe so I didn't ask about it. I'm glad you did."

"Side effects can be worse than the original problem, so I had to make sure before I could agree to the shots."

I wondered what I'd be willing to risk if I knew a drug would, *without question*, make my hair grow back. I thought of those drug commercials on TV, with their hurried list of reactions like dry mouth, headaches, dizziness, or internal bleeding. No matter what, I was sure I'd take whatever they dished out, as long as it worked and I had hair when it was over.

"Mom, I know it's not your fault that I have this," I said. "It was a rotten thing for me to say. I mean, I get genetics. It's not like you had any control over it. I was just so upset—"

"I know, honey. It's okay."

"I really *don't* blame you. I swear."

Mom stopped for a red light and said, "I really appreciate that." Still staring ahead, she smiled sadly, then added, "Gramma wasn't a bad person, Cass. I don't want you to think that."

Stunned by that little tidbit about someone she barely ever mentioned, I finally found my voice.

"I didn't really know Gramma," I whispered, as if we were still at her funeral.

"I think she meant well," Mom said, as if trying to convince herself. "And how she adored you! She called you her 'perfect, pink, puff-a-lump.'"

There it was again—that word: *perfect.* It felt like lemon juice in a paper cut. "I'm sure not perfect anymore," I said.

Mom's shoulders sagged. "But who is?" she muttered, a bitter edge in her voice.

I asked again, gently, "Mom, what did Gramma do to you?"

To my surprise, Mom's eyes filled with tears. I waited.

Mom took a deep breath. "I wasn't very good in school. I really tried, but it was so hard for me. My mother

164

used to say, 'You're no genius, Vicky, that's for sure. But lucky for you, a pretty face still opens doors in this world. So all is not lost.'" Mom sniffed and looked at me. "And dope that I was, I believed her."

Geez. Gramma had totally screwed with her head. How could she say something like that to her own kid?

"It wasn't until the other night when your father and you—" Mom was shaking her head. "I'm so sorry. I didn't realize I was doing the same thing to you. I'm really sorry, Cassie."

I thought about Mom and me. It suddenly all made sense, but I didn't have to be treated the same way Mom was. I mean, it was inexcusable and I wanted to tell her so. But she knew that firsthand—nobody deserved to feel like their only value comes from their looks.

The light changed and a car behind us tapped the horn. Mom acknowledged the guy with a wave and said, "I guess we should get home."

❦

As Mom pulled into the driveway, Tommy cruised up on his bike wearing that cute Sinatra hat and stopped next to my window. *What lousy timing.* I gave him a weak smile and got out of the car; Mom just said hello and went inside.

"What are you doing here?" I asked.

"Hey, nice to see you, too," he said with a grin. "I haven't seen you all week, so I stayed after school to sur-prise you on your first day of practice and you weren't there." He got off the bike and asked, "Where were you?"

I crossed my arms and half shrugged.

"Anyway, Tara said she didn't know where you were either, so I waited around for a while. When you were a no show…well, here I am."

Being near Tommy had me all twisted up inside. I wished he already knew about my hair so I could jump into his arms and have him hug me and kiss me, and tell me that it didn't matter. But at the same time, I felt diseased and disgusting, and totally not good enough for a great guy like him.

"I have to go in now," I said.

"What's with you, Cassie? I blew off rehearsal today just to see you. My brother was pretty pissed off about it, but I thought at least you'd be happy to see me."

"No one said you had to show up at my practice."

"I have no idea what your problem is," he said, getting back on the bike. "Just forget it. And by the way, nice paint job on the garage."

Agh. Busted. I'd forgotten that I'd told him I'd had to paint it and couldn't see him.

Tommy rode off, rapidly widening the distance between us. As I watched him get smaller in the distance, I gripped the front porch railing to keep from falling over. When he was finally out of sight, I slumped down to the bottom step and dissolved in tears.

My hair was destroying my life! Tommy was already getting tired of being jerked around. So what did I go and do? I pushed him away again, this time to the point where he got so pissed—*Omigod. Did he just break up with me?*

My head was reeling and I tried to blink away the tears. How could I have screwed this up so badly?

Eventually I dragged myself inside and up to my room and called Tara.

"How was practice?" I asked, my voice raspy.

"Tommy stopped by looking for you," she said.

"I know. He left here a minute ago and I'm pretty sure we broke up."

"Oh, no! What happened?"

"It totally sucks, T. I didn't feel comfortable around him anymore. I kept waiting for a wad of hair to come out in his hands the way it did when you braided it. It was just too intense, ya know? And it's my fault we broke up—I'd been giving him the big runaround lately. But I like him so much! It's killing me that I can't make it work."

"Maybe if you told him what's going on, you wouldn't feel so bad."

Tears were threatening to fall again and I sniffed. "I wish I could tell him, T. But I just can't."

"Want *me* to talk to him for you?"

"No! Please don't say anything. Besides, by the way he tore out of here, I'd say it's already too late." I felt drained and empty, but I knew I had to ask how her day went. "So tell me what happened at practice."

"It was good, and I got a copy of the meet schedule for you." I was glad Tara let me drop the Tommy subject. "Coach McCaffrey started with a big pep talk—you know, like we have a real shot at a winning season based on what we did last fall. But she said we have to really dig in and work for it, give a 110 percent. She got us all pretty pumped. Oh—and here's the best part. At least once a week, we'll be training with varsity. The word is Coach Minnelli wants to be able to keep his eye on the freshman team!"

"That's awesome," I said, trying to scrape up some enthusiasm.

"Now tell me, what happened at the doctor's. Any good news this time?"

"Not really, but I did get those shots, though."

"A-a-a-nd?"

"It was pretty weird. All of a sudden I was a human pincushion or something."

"Damn."

"But at least it's over—for now," I said, touching the back of my head. "Hey, thanks again for the bracelet. C'est tres magnifique. It helped when I was getting the shots." We said goodbye and ended the call.

When I got downstairs, I stopped for a second. From where I stood, I could see Mom's hands on the armrest of the chair in the family room. She was holding a mug and dipping a tea bag up and down.

"Mom? I just talked to Tara. We have track practice every day now."

She sipped her tea and nodded. "Would you like a cup?"

This was the first time she'd ever offered me tea. And it was another opportunity to talk. I said okay and she put the kettle on the stove.

"Tommy didn't stay very long," she said. "Everything all right?"

It hurt too much to go there, so all I told her was, "He had to get to rehearsal."

Mom poured the hot water into my cup. "Let it steep for a minute or so."

I added a teaspoon of honey and the spoon clinked softly as I stirred. Mom sat across from me with her perfect posture. I watched as she absently rubbed her mug with her finger.

"Did you ever worry that alopecia could happen to you?" I asked.

Mom blinked and let out a shaky breath. "I suppose it's haunted me since you were little, once they told us what it was. It can happen to your brother, too. So yes, I've worried about it—for all three of us."

I took a sip of my tea and, strange as it was, I started to feel sorry for Mom. All this time, she'd been living in fear of alopecia, especially growing up the way she did, with a hyper-critical mom. That had to be *almost* as bad as being blindsided by the damn disease and having to live with it. *Agh.*

"Cass, I wish there was something I could do," Mom said. "Maybe down the road we can take a look at some wigs if you need one."

"Wigs?" I jumped up so fast, my tea splashed all over the table. "Do you think all those shots were for *nothing*?"

"No, honey. That's not it." Mom stood up, too. "It's just something we may need to think about."

"No way! That is *never* going to happen. How can you even *say* that?" I ran back to my room and slammed the door. Obviously, nothing had changed between us, no matter what I'd thought. It was *still* all about how I looked.

I changed into running clothes and stretched out to prepare for my run. Then I was ready to go. Mom called to me as I opened the front door.

"I'm going for a run," I said as I left.

Before I got to the end of the block, I saw Mrs. Vetrone lifting Nick out of the car.

She waved me over as she bounced him, asleep on her shoulder, then asked, "Can you sit with Nick three weeks from this Saturday? It's our fifth anniversary."

I peeked at his drooly face, patted his back, and said, "Sure." I could use the cash. Kyle was bleeding me dry. I waved goodbye and took off running.

Seeing Mrs. Vetrone set me off. I thought about New Year's day...hair all over my pillow. *Alopecia*—such an ugly word. I wished I'd never heard of it. It made me hurt Tommy's feelings and got me dumped.

Thinking about it, I realized I'd made him do the dirty work. I got him mad at me before he even knew about my horrible ugly bald spots. Being such a bitch to Tommy wasn't like me and it was the worst thing I'd ever done to anyone—pushing him away like that! And to make things even worse, I didn't know how much longer I'd be able to keep my secret.

But Tommy was so sweet. I wondered if I still had any kind of chance with him.

Enough! My mind was going in circles so I picked up my pace, but my brain chatter wouldn't stop. I pushed faster still, and a gust of wind challenged me. I leaned forward and pushed even harder, forcing myself to run faster still, trying to silence my thoughts.

☙

Later, after my run, I showered and carefully combed my hair. A few strands came out—nothing to panic about, but still, I'd never get used to it. I touched the bare spots to take inventory—no dents. If the cortisone was going to work, it would be at least a month before *something* grew back. I'd end up with fuzz or stubble at best, not the long hair I'd had before. I realized I might never be able to wear my hair hanging down again.

That night, Kyle and I were in the family room, watching our favorite show. Every guy was a total hunk, and all the girls were knockouts. Suddenly I noticed that every female actress had gorgeous hair and it struck my last raw nerve. I stood up in a rush, startling my brother.

"Where you going?" Kyle asked. "Don't you want to watch this?"

"It's a rerun."

"No it's not—it's a brand-new episode."

"Whatever," I said. "I'm going upstairs."

In my room, I opened my jewelry box, where I kept my personal treasures. I cleared a compartment for my new bracelet. Next to it were the butterfly barrettes from Dad and a dozen other keepsakes, especially the ticket stubs from the jazz concert and movies with Tommy. All his notes were there, too. *If I had the chance, could I smooth things over with him?*

171

I looked inside the satin pocket at the bald picture of me from my fourth birthday.

If this happens to me now, I'm never gonna make it, I thought. *There's no way.*

Eighteen

On Friday, the screech of tires peeling out of the parking lot echoed down to the gym locker room. Everyone was going home but the track team. Dressed for practice, I inspected the back of my head from every possible angle. It looked normal so far. Maybe when I got out on the track, I'd feel halfway normal, too. Tara took a look and gave me the final okay, then we headed for the equipment room.

We each carried two sets of starting blocks to the bleachers on the visitors' side of the football field. The boys lugged out two-feet thick monster mats that were for pole vaulting and the high jump, and set them up in front of the home bleachers.

No real spectators came to the practices, except for a pair of girls wandering from field to field, scoping out hot guys. I pictured Tommy showing up here yesterday, hoping to see me. I couldn't believe I acted like such a jerk after he came all the way to my house. But the timing was totally wrong after all those needles and not knowing if I had dents in my head, let alone whether they'd work—and worse, not knowing if I'd lose more hair.

I was so afraid of his reaction if he knew the truth about me. I knew I couldn't take it if he got grossed out and told me to take a hike.

I knew Tommy was probably still pissed, and maybe even kind of hurt. But what if he could flip a switch and totally stop liking me? Then what? Agh! My head hurt thinking about it—but I couldn't stop those thoughts swirling around in my brain.

We dropped our starting blocks and Tara nudged me. "Check out Ron Sperling," she said. "What's with the tank top?"

I rubbed my hands together and blew on them for warmth as Ron heaved a shot put from his shoulder. With the tank top, we could see he was sporting a dragon tattoo on his upper arm.

"Guess he couldn't wait until it warmed up to show it off," Tara said. "Can you imagine all those needles?"

I gave Tara the look and suddenly she looked embarrassed. She'd obviously forgotten about my appointment yesterday. I let it go with a shrug.

Since I missed the first practice, I wondered if Coach McCaffrey made you run penalty laps like last fall—even *with* an excuse note. It wasn't the best way to start off the season, but if that's how it played out, so be it. I'd take whatever she dished out.

Tara and I hung with the rest of the team, waiting for Coach McCaffrey, when Coach Minnelli, the varsity coach, trotted toward us.

"Freshman team, listen up." He wasn't especially tall, but his deep voice, squared-off shoulders, and scruffy jawline created an illusion of a much larger man. "Coach Mc-Caffrey is out today and won't be here at all next week. So until she returns, you'll be training with varsity."

We jogged to their end of the field—a prime location and much closer to the hot varsity guys. The other coach was talking to some of the girls and I recognized most of the faces from the fall.

Suddenly Tara gasped. "Look, Cass—there's Adam. Don't you love that dimple he gets when he smiles?"

"Better take a number," I said as Robin sauntered over and parked herself next to Adam and the entire boys' team. She straddled in the grass and leaned forward until her chest hit the ground. *Lucky her, with those boobs, she didn't have to stretch as far as I did to accomplish the same thing.*

We gathered around Coach Minnelli, who stood before us with his arms crossed, tapping his side with the clipboard.

"Listen up," he said. "Wagner, Lakewood, get everyone stretched out. Then give me eight laps, nice and easy, to warm up. Then we'll work on getting off the blocks. It looked too sloppy yesterday."

"Okay," Lauren said, tying her sneaker.

"Where's Lakewood?" Coach asked.

We all looked over toward the spot where she sat with the boys' varsity.

"Lakewood!" Minnelli's voice was a bullhorn. "Move your butt! Let's go!"

Robin turned her head and calmly looked at him. Anyone else would've bolted across the field in fear, but not Robin. She got up and crossed the center of the football field, nonchalantly swinging her hips as she strolled over to us.

I watched the guys watching her and she certainly gave them something to look at. She was mesmerizing in a way, like one of those gorgeous Japanese fighting fish. It was hard to look away, even though everyone knew that getting too close could be dangerous.

But Adam, I noticed, kept his head down and didn't even glance her way. I wondered what was up with that.

"Lakewood, if you want to do some extra training chasing the guys, that's your business. But do it on your own time or we'll get another co-captain." Then he clapped and said, "Let's go people. Gimme eight!"

"Doesn't this guy ever smile?" Tara asked in a whisper.

"Tough love," I said.

As Robin and Lauren led the runners around the track, the usual gab-fest began: homework, guys, shopping, guys, part-time jobs, guys. But varsity had placed first last fall and you could tell these girls meant business. Their pace was quick for a warm-up, and by the sixth lap, the pack of runners had divided into two groups, and the conversations had dwindled to three-word sentences and one-grunt responses.

Tara started losing steam and fell behind, but I managed to keep up with the front runners the entire time. It felt great.

I was hoping that if I trained with varsity, it'd give me an edge when I raced for the freshman team. Then I'd really shake things up out there. Dad would be in his glory if he ever came across *my* stats in the sports section of our local paper, and I wanted to soak up everything I could from Coach Minnelli for however long we were with him.

After the last lap, we gathered by the coach and sat down to wait for the stragglers. Sitting there, I noticed that every girl had her hair pulled back into a ponytail, whether they were short, stubby ones or wild bushy ones, to foot-long, braided ropes. Compared with all of those girls and their thick, healthy hair, I felt like damaged goods. I squeezed my ponytail and gently ran my hand down the length of it. Then I bargained with who- or whatever might be listening. *If I could just keep the hair that I still have, I think I can be okay—even if nothing ever grows back.* I wasn't asking for the moon.

And maybe it wouldn't be too much to ask for another chance with Tommy. I had to figure out a way to talk to him again and set things straight.

Tara wiped her forehead with the back of her sleeve and looked at me. "You're not even winded," she said.

"Two miles isn't that bad," I said. "You'll build up to it again pretty fast."

"So, how far have you run on your own?"

"I clocked my long route with Kyle's odometer. I can do 5.2 miles, no problem."

"Sweet."

Minutes later, the coach had us up on our feet, with Lauren and Robin leading us through a grueling set of bleacher exercises, but with a new twist. Metal thundered as we *hopped* up the bleacher steps single file. If you couldn't keep up, you'd end up caught in a human logjam.

We stampeded across the top to the next flight down, snaking over and up again, the stairs and handrails vibrating along with my eardrums. The clatter finally faded as we rumbled back down onto the track.

"Nice job," Coach Minnelli said. "We're going to break up by events now. Sprinters stay here with Coach Litowsky to work on starts. Hurdlers, follow me."

Tara mouthed the words, "Hiney warm-ups," and wiggled her fingers goodbye.

Coach Litowsky wasn't much older than we were and he was hot. A chemistry teacher, he'd raced for Darlington only about five years ago and his warm-up suit hugged his tall, well-built frame so perfectly that some of the senior girls were about to spontaneously combust.

"Set up your blocks—next pair be ready," he told us.

I adjusted my blocks and tried them out a couple times as the coach stood by the next pair of runners, checking their form and balance, foot positions, and power off the blocks. Then he made minor adjustments for each of them.

It was at last my turn. I pressed the balls of my feet against the blocks, balancing on my toes, and planted my fingers inside the starting line.

"Set," said the coach.

I lifted my hips.

"Go!"

I pushed off and ran about five steps.

"Nice. Let's see it again."

After the rest of the girls each had their turn, the coach called a few names for those needing extra practice off the blocks. This gave me a chance to watch the team practice for the other events.

Under the goal post, the pole-vaulters took turns. Adam was up next. He approached, planted the pole and his body was an arrow, straight and clean, as it flew upward. With his waist even with the bar, he pushed higher, then released the pole. He floated, suspended for what seemed like a full minute in a graceful arc over the bar, then dropped to the mat. It was an incredible effort.

I also loved watching the hurdlers, especially Tara. She had it all: speed, power, and precision. She leaped with the grace of a dancer with perfect form and her landings were fluid, continuous motions back into the sprint. She was as natural to the sport as a wild horse to an open plain.

We were the mighty Falcons—the perfect team name. That's because track events were as close as we could ever get to flying.

❧

Coach Minnelli blew the whistle again and motioned to Coach Litowsky, spinning his finger in the air to round us up. The hurdlers followed the coach to where we stood, then he told us to grab the blocks and we all walked to the far end of the track.

"How you holding up?" Tara asked.

"Pretty well. How about you?"

"I'm totally sucking wind. I took down two hurdles out there."

Oops, I must've missed that.

We heard two sharp blasts from the whistle and Coach Minnelli yelled, "Line up for sprints!" Tara stuck out her tongue, pretending to barf.

"Let's go, ladies," Minnelli said. "We have two weeks to get it together. Let's set up the blocks, five across."

I hated to admit it, but Robin was right. This guy was brutal.

Coach Litowsky called the names for the first two heats, mixing together freshmen and varsity sprinters. When they were ready, he signaled Coach Minnelli, who was waiting at the other end of the football field at the hundred-meter mark. Then the first two groups ran.

Geez, these varsity girls were real speed-demons. It was no wonder that Darlington had been state champs for the last two years. And, of course, Robin took off like a shot in her heat and nailed her race, no problem.

At last it was my heat. I had the middle spot between Lauren and Melissa, both seniors—just the tiniest bit intimidating. But I shook out my arms and legs, then took a few deep breaths. As adrenaline sped up my heart rate, I prayed to get through the race without screwing up and embarrassing myself.

Then it was *ready, set, go!* and the coach blasted the whistle.

We charged down the track side by side, with no clear leader. By some miracle, I was in the game. I tried to kick in some extra power, but sprints are short and all I could do was keep up with the other runners. At the last second, Lauren squeaked ahead and won.

"Nice race," Coach Minnelli said, looking at me, arms folded over his clipboard. "What's your name?"

"Donovan," I said, feeling like a soldier reporting for duty. He didn't seem to use first names.

"Donovan," he mumbled and jotted something on his clipboard.

"Great run, Cassie," Lauren said.

I was surprised the varsity captain knew my name.

"You really hung in there with us," she said. "The heat we ran had every top sprinter on the team except Robin. And it looks like Minnelli has his eye on you for varsity."

Meanwhile, Robin leaned against the fence, watching the guys. She didn't turn around, but I was sure she'd heard what Lauren had told me. I shook my head and dismissed the idea with a backhand motion as we walked back to the starting line.

Varsity? Wow. No added pressure there.

Then it was the last race. But this time, Robin and I were in the same heat. I exploded off the blocks and in a few steps was out in front—with nothing ahead of me but the finish line. As I tore down the track, I pushed even harder, stretching my legs, making every step count. And then I was there, crossing the finish line—all alone. I threw back my shoulders and arched my back, turning to look behind me. No one was even close—not even Robin.

I walked it out, hands on my hips, sucking in deep breaths. I squeezed under my ribs to massage a cramp, then looped back toward the varsity coach who remained at the finish line.

"Don't open up until you're *over* the line," Coach Minnelli said. "You need to stay tight and focused, and I want you to lean into the finish. You don't ever want to pull back," he told me.

I nodded, too nervous to speak, then moved off to the side and began my cool-down stretches. Some of the other sprinters came over to me.

"There was no catching you," Melissa said.

"You were on fire," Suzanne said.

Then a man's voice said, "Donovan."

I looked up at Coach Minnelli.

"Nice run."

I wasn't positive, but I think I saw him cracking a smile.

"You almost had her, Robin," Lauren said, giving her a friendly nudge.

"Yeah, right—as if I was even trying," she said.

Shit. I'd just splashed into her fishbowl and she clearly wasn't happy about it.

"That's it for me," Robin said. "I'm outta here." She sashayed toward the guys, shouting and clapping, "Let's go, Adam!"

Lauren came over to me again. "You were like a bullet from the get-go. Bet you're even faster when you haven't had Minnelli cracking the whip over you all afternoon. But I think Coach Minnelli's right," she said, surveying the team. "We have a real shot at State Champs again this year, and as a senior, I'd love to go out on top. He'll start timings next week—you know, give us the weekend to rest up. Starting Monday, he'll run us like dogs, so take my advice and rest up while you can."

"Thanks, I will," I said.

I watched as Lauren took the clip out of her long hair and held it between her teeth, twisted her hair back in place and re-clipped it. Seeing her perform this simple task, I felt my back go rigid. But I couldn't escape my hair problem and it would be pointless to keep obsessing about it on the track.

While I was here, I had to be here totally—mind and body. And when I'm running, something amazing happens to me, something powerful, like I'm living in a Nike commercial and sweating Gatorade. If I wanted to analyze it, I'd have to say it's the feeling of being in total control. And I needed that right now, considering everything else that was messed up in my life.

Before Lauren walked away to join her friends who'd just finished, she added, "Hey, remember what I said about Minnelli recruiting you for varsity. Keep doing what you're doing—you never know."

Varsity. It was like Lauren had handed me a tiny gold box with a poufy red bow on top. She was great and I could see why she was team captain. She had a way of reminding everyone we were racing as part of a team, not just for ourselves.

❧

Tara ran in the last heat and I cheered her on, but I could see that her heart wasn't in it. She finished fourth.

The whistle blew, and Coach Minnelli clapped his hands. "Listen up, folks. That was much better today. But there's plenty of work to be done. Freshman team, nice work." He checked his watch. "Okay, give me one lap around to cool down, and don't forget about the equipment. Make sure all the hurdles and blocks get put away." He clapped again, said, "That's it, folks. I'll see you on Monday," and he and Coach Litowsky jogged away across the field.

"Thank God that's over," Tara said.

We shuffled around the track, but I felt like I wanted to run another twenty laps—that's how charged up I was that Coach Minnelli might actually consider me for varsity. I wouldn't dare say it out loud to Tara, though. The part about running extra laps would've made her crazy. But the truth was, I couldn't wait for Monday.

Nineteen

Mrs. Spez dropped me off at home after practice, and when I got inside, Mom had dinner going. She was thawing a frozen block of spaghetti sauce in a pot, then checked the clock and lowered the flame under a pot of boiling water. A box of bow tie pasta sat waiting on the counter.

Kyle was at the table doing homework.

I picked an olive and a cucumber chunk out of the salad and popped them into my mouth.

"Could I sleep over Tara's tonight?" I asked.

"That's fine with me," Mom said. "Are you eating dinner here?"

I nodded and took out three plates, forks, and napkins, then went back for the glasses. Kyle moved to Dad's seat and continued working.

"Get this," I said. "I didn't know it at the time, but today I had to race some of the best sprinters on varsity—we practiced with them today. We were really cranking out there, and I hung on as long as I could. Then this girl squeaked ahead of me and won by a nose."

"You mean, she won by a beak," Kyle said.

"Ha—I get it. Falcon, beak. Very funny, Kyle. Anyway, then, in the last race, I won! Can you believe it?"

"Not too shabby," Kyle said.

"That's really great," Mom said as she finished refilling the soap dispenser. "Your father will be happy to hear about it."

"And, Mom, it gets better. The coach might be looking at me for varsity."

"*Really?* That's a pretty big deal, for a freshman to be picked for the varsity team, right?" And she grinned and nodded, one eyebrow arched high. "Not too shabby, Cass."

Wow. She seemed genuinely psyched. And for the first time, she didn't try to push tennis or cheerleading on me. Finally there was something Mom could be excited about *with* me. I knew getting picked for varsity was far from a done deal, but I didn't want to ruin the moment by reminding her that it was only a possibility.

"When's dinner?" I asked.

"About half an hour." She tapped the brick of sauce in the pot with a wooden spoon.

"I'll run upstairs for a shower. Will you take me to Tara's later?"

"Right after you and your brother clean up."

On my way upstairs, my phone rang. My heart bottomed out when I saw it was Tommy. I bobbled my cell back and forth between my hands, nearly dropping it as I frantically tried to answer it. When I finally got it open, I didn't give him a chance to speak. I just blurted out, "Tommy, I'm so glad you called. Listen, I'm really sorry

186

about the way I acted yesterday. I didn't mean to be so rude."

"Me, too. I wasn't exactly Prince Charming, either. It took me a while, but then I figured something important was up, because otherwise you wouldn't have missed your first practice. And that maybe it was something *not so good*."

"I just have a lot to deal with right now. It doesn't have anything to do with you—I promise. It's things at home."

"I hear ya. If there's anything I can do..."

"I'll be all right."

"Maybe I can cheer you up. There's something I've been working on. Listen."

It sounded like he put the phone down, and then a warm melody drifted from Tommy's saxophone to my ear, sad and sweet. I listened, picturing his dancing fingers and puffed-up cheeks, and those too-long bangs. And I imagined my head leaning on his shoulder. I closed my eyes and breathed the notes as he played a private concert for me, and it was so, so wonderful.

"Cassie?"

"Wow. You wrote that, didn't you?" I knew it was hard for him to share something so personal, so packed with emotion. "It was amazing."

"Needs more work, but thanks. It's kind of the way I feel about…us. So anyway, whaddya say? Are we good?"

I so totally wanted to get back together. He trusted me with his music, and now it was my turn; I had to trust him, too. I'd tell him soon.

"Yeah, we're good," I said. I told him I had to get cleaned up for dinner and that I was going to Tara's later.

"So maybe we can do something this weekend?" he said.

"I promise."

I rushed into the shower and washed my hair, but in my excitement after patching things up with Tommy, I scrubbed the bald patches too hard as I shampooed. Yeoch! I must've torn off the scab from where that needle had scraped me the day before. But I'd live. Then I rinsed and loaded on the conditioner.

I stepped out and draped a towel over my head like a hood, folding it under my hair in the back. I never twisted it into a turban anymore for fear I'd pull out more hair. I used a puff of mousse the size of a tennis ball to cut down on the knots, and it made combing pretty easy.

Despite having less of it, it took my hair forever to dry. That's because I'd switched the blow dryer to the lowest setting—another anti-knot tactic I'd developed. The low setting probably was about as slow as if I'd used a paper fan to dry it.

When it was dry, I brushed my hair gently in long, careful strokes. Suddenly I felt a draft on my scalp in a new place—over my right ear. I pulled the brush away and a thick ribbon of hair came with it. It was too much—way too much hair.

Then I just couldn't stop. Like a robot, I kept on brushing. But this time it was like I'd left my body and was hovering, watching the massacre. Harder and faster I brushed, scraping my head and stripping away my hair. How much more would come out? I kept brushing. *How much more!?* Hair kept melting away and the spot kept growing.

Stop it! I told myself, but I kept brushing and brushing. There was my hair, all over the floor as the bristles bit into my scalp.

Stop. Please, no more. Please.

Finally, my hair-brushing frenzy was over. My fingertips tingled as I dangled the brush in my hand, long strands of thickly wadded hair still clinging to it.

My hair.

I suddenly felt like I'd throw up. I was dizzy as I teetered a few steps and dropped the brush in the wastebasket. It almost looked like a dead animal covered with all that hair.

What have I done? I wondered. *They're going to lock me up and throw away the key.* I tipped my head to the side to check the damage in the mirror. And there it was: a gaping hole, almost as big as my palm. It was pink and sore from my frantic brushing. This was the most that had ever fallen out at one time, and it was way too close to the front.

I felt sick and my legs turned to liquid as I collapsed on the toilet seat cover. I hid my face with a towel and, eyes squeezed shut and rocking, I screamed and screamed into the towel.

More lost hair. Why is this happening to me?

Why am I being punished?

I screamed my throat raw, until I had nothing left. Until I felt nothing.

At last I took away the towel, and when the room came into focus, I had to struggle to breathe. Hair was everywhere, like on the floor of a busy hair salon, but instead, all of the hair was *mine*.

Frantic, I wet some wadded-up toilet paper and got down on my hands and knees to sweep it all up. Then I dropped it into the garbage, completely burying my hairy brush.

Not knowing what else to do, I opted for camouflage. With a shaky hand, I colored in each hole with eyebrow pencil and needed to adjust the hair at my right temple and over that eyebrow, and managed to cover the bare skin with a thin layer of hair to hide the damage I'd done. I spritzed on hair spray to hold it in place, then compared the two sides. Ugh—the right side of my head was flatter and my ponytail thinner than before. Panicky by that point, I fumbled through the vanity drawer for a wide terrycloth headband and tried it on. At least it covered things pretty well.

Then Kyle yelled from the bottom of the stairs. "Cassie! Supper!"

In a daze, I mechanically went back to my room and got dressed.

Downstairs I slumped at the table. Food was the last thing on my mind as Mom brought the pasta bowl to the table. It'd been hours since lunch, and I'd had that hard workout at track practice, and I knew I should eat, but I wasn't sure I could keep anything down.

I took a sip of water that burned my throat. The next sip was soothing and my stomach rumbled, insisting on a full meal.

"Oh, no," Mom said the instant she sat down at the table. She could see what had happened with one glance.

I turned my face away. It took a few seconds to gather myself to keep the tears from falling and my voice came out in a raspy plea, "I don't want to talk about it."

I took two scoops of pasta and ladled on the sauce. Although the food had no flavor for me, at least my stomach was quieting down.

It was amazing how quicky everything can change. Two hours ago I was connecting with Mom about track, and Tommy and I had made up. It was the happiest I'd been since all of this crap started. But *nooooooo*, the minute I was actually getting a grip, starting to deal and thinking I might function like a normal human being, I was handed this rotten break. I got tasered by this stupid disease. I could almost picture it sneering at me, saying, *Not so fast there, missy. You can't run around just being happy. Well, at least not for too long anyway.*

I was barely holding it together and seriously didn't know how much more I could take.

Then Kyle said, "So, sleeping over Tara's tonight?"

"What do you care?" I snapped.

"What's your problem?" he said.

Now it was Kyle's turn to get back at me. With each mouthful he took, he clamped his teeth down on his fork and dragged it through them with an annoying scrape. I cringed and shot him a sideways look and he did it again, knowing how much I hated it. After the third time, I'd had enough. I slammed down my fork and spaghetti sauce splashed in every direction.

"What are you looking at?" I said to him.

"Not much," he said.

"That's e-nough." Mom's chair scraped against the floor as she jumped up to wipe the sauce that had spattered onto the table.

I didn't say another word as I ate my salad and most of my pasta. Kyle blathered on about video games and the new video machine at his favorite comic book store. He demolished his plate of seconds, gabbing the whole time and I wondered how he didn't keel over from a lack of oxygen to the brain.

"Whose turn is it to do the dishes?" Mom asked.

"Hers," he said pointing at me, the corners of his mouth curving down.

"How is it my turn?!" My voice came in dry hollow bursts as I got right in his face. "I'm so sick of you, you little shit!" I sputtered. "It's your turn! You don't do anything around here, you lazy sack of—"

"I said e-nough!" Mom was up on her feet again.

"Fine," he said with eyes narrowed. "Let's not throw a hairy fit about it."

"Kyle!" Mom shrieked.

I hate him. I wished his hair was falling out, not mine. I pressed the soft terrycloth against the side of my head and then my Einstein of a brother finally caught on.

"Yeah, whatever. It's my turn," he said, quietly.

Mom stayed calm after my little hissy fit and asked, "You still want to go to Tara's?"

I shrugged. Maybe it'd be better if I got out of here for a while.

"Go get your things together and I'll take you over."

On the ride to Tara's, Mom said, "I saw the upstairs bathroom."

My insides bottomed out as the vision of the scene in the bathroom and the floor covered with my hair flashed into my mind. I turned my face to the window, pressed my lips tight together, and prayed I could forget.

"Maybe next time, you can come to me or your father, and maybe we can talk or something. But I know the last suggestion I made really set you off." She was talking about the idea of getting a wig. She hadn't even given the shots a chance to work—I'd only started with them the day before.

"I do want to help," she said, "even though I don't have any answers, or answers you want to hear. I think that'd be better than dumping on your brother like you did at dinner."

I didn't say a word in response. I just got out of the car and turned away.

From her window, Mom called out, "Listen, honey, try and have a good time."

When I rang the bell, Tara opened the front door and I walked inside, then said hello to Mr. and Mrs. Spez in their family room.

Mr. Spez nodded and aimed the remote at the TV and pressed mute, then said, "Tara tells us you can travel on the track at the speed of light."

"Not quite," I said and quickly turned on my all-is-right-with-the-world attitude.

"You're faster than Robin Lakewood," Tara said.

I smiled a little. "Yeah, but who knows what's going to

happen Monday. I don't think she's going to let me pass her up so easily at a meet."

"You guys should've seen it. Cassie dusted her. Totally blew her away. Robin was picking gravel out of her teeth when it was over."

Mr. and Mrs. Spez laughed as Tara led the way out of the room. I shouldered my backpack and followed her.

Tara's room was fully equipped with a flat-screen TV, a DVD player, and a laptop. All she needed was a fridge and she'd never have to leave. But for now, we had to rough it by going all the way to the kitchen to get frozen yogurt for dessert.

I'd brought back the last novel I'd borrowed from Tara and wedged it into the basket next to her bed. She kept her reading material fanned out in rows that reminded me of a peacock's tail: magazines in the back, hard covers next, and an amazing assortment of paperbacks. In front she kept the mini gift books I gave her for Christmas.

Tara opened the drawer on her night table and took out a bottle of nail polish remover and a bag of cotton balls and got to work on her left hand. Then she glanced over and caught me checking myself out in the mirror. I couldn't help myself—I lifted the edge of the headband and it was just as bad as I'd thought. I let the headband fall back into place, careful not to mess with the hair-sprayed arrangement I'd hidden under there.

"You look fine," Tara said. "Really."

I totally wanted to believe her.

"Will you do my right hand when I'm done?" she asked.

"Sure. Whenever you're ready." I examined my own nails. "I need a nail file."

I rummaged around in the night table under pens, lip gloss, barrettes, hair scrunchies, two clear vials with the leftover beads from my bracelet, and some bottles of nail polish.

"Yuck," I said, holding up a bottle of hideous orange nail polish. "What are you doing with this one?"

"Don't you remember Halloween, when I did my nails like candy corn? While you're in there, can you find my Wicked Winefrost for me?"

I found the polish and a pair of nail clippers. I started working on my nails with the clippers, then filed them until there was hardly any white left.

Tara waved her left hand back and forth and blew on her nails. "Okay, I'm ready."

We leaned over her hand as I polished her nails, working on top of a magazine with our heads almost touching.

Tara'd been so great. But how long would she put up with a whiney friend who had some weird disease? I knew how that would end up. Before long, people would start looking at her funny, just for hanging with me.

I dipped the brush, wiped off the excess polish on the rim of the bottle, then painted her pinky.

"Tommy called," I said.

"No way! What'd he say?"

I stopped polishing and looked up at her. "He wants to get back together."

"Aaaand?"

I shook my head and polished her ring finger.

"He called before it happened again," I told her and polished her middle fingernail. But I couldn't stop the brush from shaking. "I'm really scared," I whispered, afraid to say it out loud.

Tara sat back on her seat and looked at me.

"I have to show you something," I told her.

I unzipped the outer pocket of my backpack, where I'd tucked my 4th birthday picture. Then I handed it to her, and as soon as I did, I wished I hadn't. What was she supposed to say?

Tara's face tensed, as if she were holding a picture of a puppy with four bandaged legs. But then her expression softened.

"You were such a cute kid" was all she said.

Twenty

"Everything's going to be okay." Tara's voice echoed her hopeful expression. "The shots are going to help. You'll see."

I shook my head. "The shots can't keep up. It's falling out faster than it can regrow—if it even does."

"You have to give it a little more time, Cass."

"I just lost a massive amount of hair less than two hours ago. Even you noticed the difference. And it'll take over a month before my hair grows back where I got the shots. And then how long before it gets to this length? We're talking years, here. That's if it ever grows back at all. What if it doesn't?"

"Don't say that," Tara pleaded.

"What if I'm one of those people who's immune to treatment? I know this is totally happening to me." I searched Tara's face, framed in all those curls. "I'm going to lose all my hair."

I'd tried so hard not to cry, but I could feel my throat closing and tears welling up, waiting to spill. I could barely breathe when I broke from Tara's terrified gaze and covered my face. She wrapped her arms around me, and then it all poured out. I clung to her like a life jacket. And she was crying, too.

There was no way I had a chance of any kind of a normal life with this going on.

❧

When I was all cried out, we cleaned ourselves up and Tara went to the kitchen to get us each a bottle of water. She also brought back a cookie-dough log and two spoons, then peeled back the plastic wrap, dug a spoon in and presented it to me. She clinked her spoon to mine and said, "Eat."

I nipped at a chocolate chip and noticed that Tara's eyes were a little puffy. I imagined mine looked even worse. As we chewed mouthfuls of sweet pasty dough, I thought about Mom's *suggestion*. I didn't have a better plan, that was for sure. Then we put the spoons aside and I held my stomach.

"I'm going to buy a wig," I announced, more to myself than to Tara.

"That's probably a good idea." She licked her lips and took a drink of water.

"Or maybe a raccoon skin hat."

"Or maybe one of those 1960's beehive jobs that'd go up to here." She held her hand high over her head. "I bet I'd look good in a wig like that." Then she balanced her stuffed panda, Oreo, on her head. "Or one like Martha

Washington wore, or ohhhh, how about Rasta dreadlocks? That'd be awesome."

I laughed, then choked on more tears. I kept laughing and crying, sputtering like a defective lawn sprinkler and I couldn't believe I had any more tears left. Eventually I managed a weak smile as Tara sat there with Oreo perched on her head, looking worried that all the kidding around had backfired. I pointed to Oreo and shook my head with a little smile.

"It's probably good to laugh a little, Cass," Tara said.

"Oh, yeah. It's a laugh a minute." I sniffed, dabbing my eyes with a tissue. "God, this totally sucks. But I figure a wig'll be less conspicuous than a panda."

Tara dropped Oreo into my lap and I hugged him tightly.

"I'll go shopping with you," she said. "And I promise I won't let you go home with any animal skins on your head. Not even if you beg me."

I nodded and buried my nose in Oreo's fake fur. He smelled just like Tara's perfume.

"Tommy's still clueless about all this. What do you think he's going to say when I tell him?"

"He really likes you. I'm sure he'll be okay with it."

"How can you be sure?"

"Well, you trust him, don't you? You know, like when you're alone together? I guess the only thing you can do is trust him with this, too."

"Just for the record, we haven't progressed real far in the 'alone together' department. Not that he hasn't tried, but he does back off when I ask. So you're right—I do trust him in *that* way. But still, my hair is a whole different situation. What if he gets all grossed out?

"And what if he doesn't? Cass, you have to at least give him a chance. You'd want him to tell *you* if the situation was reversed, wouldn't you?"

"Totally."

"Well then?"

℮

That night, after we turned off the lights, I lay awake for a long time listening to Tara's nose whistle as I tried to figure out how to tell Tommy what was happening. What were the right words? I had to choose them carefully and rehearsed them in my mind.

So, Tommy, how do you feel about bald chicks? Or, when I was three I had this strange condition. I can't use the word disease. *Or, remember that time at the movies when I was kidding around about shedding like a dog? Well, it's no joke.*

By the time I got sleepy, I wasn't any closer to knowing what I was going to say.

℮

The next morning, I slipped out of bed and adjusted my headband before Tara woke up. I checked under the covers and around the pillow for any signs of fallout, and thank goodness I didn't find any hair.

200

I headed to the kitchen, where the Spezes were chatting quietly in the basket-filled room. Mrs. Spez was crazy about them and they were everywhere; there was one filled with fruit on the counter, another with catalogs and mail waiting to be opened, others brimming with silk plants sat above the cabinets, and one on the table that held napkins. She even coordinated them with the seasons.

At the stove, Mr. Spez had ham and cheese omelets going in two frying pans; they were his specialty and the best I'd ever eaten anywhere.

Mrs. Spez sat at the table browsing through grocery store fliers and clipping coupons.

"Smells awesome in here," I said.

"The secret is fresh scallions." He tells me this every single time. He shook both pans, and then, with a flick of the wrist, tossed each omelet into the air and caught it effortlessly. "Haven't dropped one yet," he told me.

"I guess that's not counting the one that you tossed so hard it got stuck under the range hood, right, Dad?" Tara said as she joined us.

Mrs. Spez rolled her eyes and grinned. I'd heard this story before—Tara and her mom always teased Mr. Spez about his culinary expertise and they all had the same sense of humor.

"Clearly you've missed the point," Mr. Spez said.

"What point was that? And what a joy *that* was to clean up," Mrs. Spez said.

After breakfast, Mr. Spez left to run errands and the three of us cleaned up the kitchen.

I was always comfortable at Tara's. Mrs. Spez even

knew about my hair, but I didn't mind because Tara told her mother everything. They were really close, like friends kind of close. And when I was here, Mrs. Spez made me feel like part of the gang. She even referred to me as her second daughter sometimes.

Tara and I hung out in her room for most of the morning, listening to CDs and Googling. I found a cute hairstyle online and gave it a try. I didn't comb hard, but I had to remember to regulate the pressure in the bare spots. The one from last night was still tender.

I touched up the white skin again with eye pencil and swept my hair into a sideways-messy-on-purpose twist and anchored it with a clip and some bobby pins. Tara misted on a layer of her mom's wind tunnel-tested hairs pray, then we compared it to the model on the Internet. Yikes—there was no comparison.

"Think I can pull it off?" I asked.

"Sure," she said, "especially if you're trying to rock the whole shih-tzu look."

"'Zackly what I thought. Oh, well," I said and undid the twist. "Ponytail it is."

Before lunch, I called Mom for a ride and she seemed especially chipper when she picked me up.

"Cassie, I spoke to your father last night and told him all about you being on the varsity team. He's thrilled and itching to get to a match."

"Meet," I said.

"About twenty years ago, a boy who graduated from your school went on to the Olympics," Mom continued. "Did you know that?"

"So I've heard." I smiled to myself. *You'd have to be blind not to notice the Darren McBride banner hanging in the gym or the list of his school, regional, and state records on the engraved brass plates hanging on the wall by the Phys. Ed. office.*

"But I'm not on varsity yet. I mean, it *might* happen." I flicked the zipper on my backpack. "I just thought it was pretty cool that the coach might be considering me."

"Well, there's no reason that you shouldn't be on the team, right? I'm sure it'll just be a matter of time."

I bristled. For any other mother, being on the freshman team would probably be enough. But with her, there's always another hurdle, so to speak. *And what if she turns into one of those insane sport moms who get so crazed that the coach has to call for a restraining order?*

But I shrugged it off for now because, duh, varsity's what I wanted, too.

When we got home I checked my e-mail. Tommy sent one last night, late, about the same time I was lying awake thinking of him, too. I printed the e-mail before deleting it:

roses are red. tubas are big.
guess who landed a paying gig?
call me

This was one of the things I liked about him. He wasn't afraid to be jerky or wear a Sinatra hat, or play jazz sax instead of a guitar or drums. Tommy couldn't care less about what someone else might think—he was a "no worries" kind of guy. In that way, we weren't alike. Here I was, either preoccupied with hiding my secret and pretending that everything's great, or else I'm mopping up after a total meltdown.

I guess opposites really do attract.

But lately I'd been about as cuddly to Tommy as broken glass. Tara was right—it was time he knew what was going on.

I'll tell him face to face. That's it. I'll march over to his house right now and knock on the door, then spill it....Or...maybe I could tell him Monday at school...Or the next time we're alone later in the week. That's a much better idea. This isn't the sort of announcement you make in front of a crowd. I'll just slip a note into his locker for a kiss-and-run.

I rehearsed the conversation in my head and imagined Tommy saying, *"Is that what you were so worried about? You should've said something sooner."* And him plunking his Sinatra hat on my head and tapping it down over my eyes for being such a dummy.

But then doubt stung my cheeks like a wicked sunburn. No—not in person—I didn't want to see the expression on his face if it's bad. I'll tell him over the phone—*now*. I punched in his number and Tommy picked up.

"Cassie, you're not going to believe this!" he said.

"Eric sent out a million of our demo CDs—okay, maybe thirty—and one finally hit. We're playing at Once Upon a Time, the bookstore in the mall."

"That's so awesome. I love that place! But it's pretty small. Where are they going to put you?"

"Who cares? We'll play on top of the bookcases if they want! We'll play in the men's room!"

"The men's room?"

"Don't you sing in the shower? The acoustics are awesome in there."

I caught a glimpse of myself in the mirror and turned away. Tommy was so pumped about his gig, I didn't want to ruin it with my downer news.

"Eric's a maniac," he continued, his excitement pouring into my ear. "Besides rehearsing every day after school, he wants everyone to come back after dinner. I don't know when we're going to see each other this week—unless you want to sit in on a rehearsal."

"I wish I could, but I have track, and after dinner is tough with homework and all."

"That sucks! And Friday night is out, too. My brother's a total slave driver. Last night we were jamming until midnight."

"It's cool, though, Tommy. Do what ya gotta do."

"We're playing this Saturday, from eleven to four. So come and bring Tara and the rest of your friends—anyone you can think of. Jason and Glen are rounding up a gang, too. The bigger the draw, the better it looks for us."

"Well, there *is* a book I've been wanting to pick up," I said.

"Book?" he said in mock horror. "You're a piece of work, Cassie. Oh, and my mother is inviting the band and a few people back here Saturday night to celebrate, so don't make any other plans."

"Tommy?" I tried to interrupt. *I can't keep postponing the inevitable.*

"I am so stoked. This is going to be awesome," he said. "So you'll be there, right?"

Agh. What I called to say would have to wait a little bit longer.

"I wouldn't miss it for anything," I told him.

Twenty-One

Meanwhile, I didn't stop shedding. Every day that following week, more hair was gone. By that point, what had been small white circles of skin had become bigger, shiny patches all over my head. And the thickest patches of hair that remained were thinning out. The eyeliner helped blend the white patches under what hair was left, which I cemented in place with hair spray and covered most of the mess with two stretchy headbands. But people noticed.

On my way to lunch, the Goth queens were hanging by the window, talking. Someone in the crowded hallway accidentally knocked my lunch bag out of my hand, and when I leaned over to pick it up, I could tell that the Goths were totally checking me out. I could almost read their minds: *Like, what's wrong with this picture?* I wondered if they felt that way when people stared at their pierced lips, tongues, or eyebrows. But it wasn't the same thing. They'd *chosen* to look different; I didn't.

In the cafeteria, I choked down a few bites of my sandwich, trying to pretend that I didn't notice all the sideways glances coming my way. Humiliated, I threw away the rest of my lunch and dashed upstairs to try and hide out in the library for the rest of the period. But as I swung open the door at the top of the stairs, I barreled straight into Tommy.

"Whoa," he said, catching me by the shoulders. "That's one way to knock a guy off his feet. I was just coming to find you. I have a sub this period, so I snuck out for a few minutes and—Cassie, what happened to your hair?"

Omigod. He can see it. I shook my head and stared at the floor. None of the words I'd rehearsed would come out.

He put a finger under my chin and peered at me from under his hat. "Are you okay?"

"I'm fine," I said as I tried to step around him. But he took my hand.

"Are you sure?"

"I can't talk about it right now." I tried to wriggle my fingers free, and said, "I have to do some research in the library."

But he just squeezed my hand tighter. His eyes, concerned, were locked on mine. "No problem. You don't have to talk. I'll walk you there, and then I'll go back to class."

At the library doors, he tucked his hands in his pockets and leaned against the wall. "I'll be around all night if you want to give me a call—even during rehearsal."

I nodded. He was being so nice. He didn't deserve a brush-off, but I just couldn't help it. I was too embarrassed to tell him anything, especially now that he'd noticed something was wrong.

He strode away, turned the corner, and was gone.

I never called. Not that night or the ones that followed. By Thursday, I was losing it. I jumped down Kyle's throat for no good reason, and Mom went all ostrich on me, like she was afraid to talk about it. What I was hiding.

At school, I could barely pay attention in class. The only good thing I had was track practice, and that was turning into a disaster, too. I couldn't get off the blocks right, my pacing was all screwed up, and I didn't win a single race all week. I just couldn't concentrate. So much for "being there" when I was on the track.

By Friday, I couldn't manage to camouflage my hair loss anymore; nothing worked—not mousse, or hair spray, or headbands. I couldn't go around school looking like a molting parakeet, so I snagged one of Kyle's baseball caps. The natural hairline behind my ears had already receded and vanished beneath the cap's edges and I threaded a scraggly ponytail through the strap in the back.

I wasn't sure if I was going to make it through the day. As it was, I could barely keep myself from getting hysterical before I even left for school.

In homeroom when we stood for the flag salute, I wondered what to do about my hat. Boys are supposed to remove their hats during the national anthem. Did it apply to girls, too? Mr. Marsh glanced in my direction—he was a stickler for stuff like that. But no way—that hat was staying put. I ignored the teacher's eyes and focused on the eagle on top of the flagpole, shifting my weight back and forth until it finally was over and I could shrink back into my seat.

Later, in French class, Robin got right down to business. "Tough week at practice, huh?"

We both knew she didn't mean how the coach was running things. She'd smoked up the track all week and no one saw anything but her back. She was on top again, and she was loving every minute.

She fixed me with a fake expression of concern and said, "Are you okay?"

I didn't trust her and I wasn't going to tell her, of all people, anything.

"I mean, your hair," she added. "Is something wrong?"

Robin was all too happy to bring up the subject. Most people were at least trying to be polite, like not pointing out a zit on the tip of your nose or mentioning that you're cross-eyed or missing a leg. They'd all sneak a peek when they thought I wasn't paying attention, but not Robin. She got off on making me want to crawl out of my skin and evaporate.

"Allergic reaction," I said. Even my explanation made me feel stupid.

"To what?" she persisted.

"French class."

With that, the class began.

"Bonjour, mes eleves," Monsieur Haus said. He opened his briefcase and told us we were having a test: "Testez aujourd'hui. Effacez vos bureaux, s'il vous plait." He repeated the last part, then, using exaggerated motions, pretended to place his things on the floor. If the French teacher thing doesn't work out, Monsieur Haus had a real future as a street mime.

As books dropped to the floor, he counted off enough papers for each row and handed them out. It didn't look too bad: translating sentences from French to English and English to French, some verb conjugations, and using vocabulary words in sentences.

I got through the translations okay and ran down the list of vocabulary words, most of which included colors, animals, and body parts. I was doing great until I came to *cheveux*—hair—near the end of the list. It came directly after *belle*, or beautiful.

Beautiful hair. That was it. I couldn't write another word. When Monsieur Haus called time, the bottom half of my test was as blank as it started out.

The rest of the day went the same way, and most of the time I was on some other planet.

But when we were changing for gym, the girl whose locker was next to mine seemed to be keeping a safe distance away from me. When I realized what was happening, a stinging case of hives spread over my chest. I was horrified to think I'd creeped her out so much. I wanted to tell her, *It's not my fault!*

In gym class, I stayed away from everyone, which made me the most useless player on our floor hockey team. Even the girlie-girls were mixing it up as the squeak of sneakers and the clap of hockey sticks echoed in the air. I was hanging way back when I heard two girls whispering about me on the sideline.

"It might be cancer," one said.

"Oh—so that's why she's losing her hair? Poor thing," the other girl replied.

I glanced over at them and they gave me one of those "it's-such-a-shame" sort of smiles, and that made me feel even worse.

I wasn't fooling anyone with this hat. And why the hell did they think it was okay to talk about me like I wasn't in the room? It made me wonder: *Were they all talking about me?* I wasn't imagining their quizzical expressions.

Smack in the middle of the game, when I couldn't take it anymore, I headed toward those girls sitting on the sideline and stood over them.

My voice cracked a little when I said, "Can I borrow your phone?" Mine was back in my main locker, and I knew the one girl kept her cell on her at all times, even gym class, being a total text-oholic.

"Um—" She was staring at the bare skin that was now visible under the hat, probably wondering if she could catch something from me if I used her phone.

"Look," I whispered and glanced over my shoulders. "I don't have cancer or anything contagious. You'd really be helping me out if I could just borrow your phone for a second."

I felt like a complete idiot begging like that, but after a nudge from her buddy, the girl reluctantly handed me her phone. Then I ducked into the locker room and dialed Dad's number.

"Hello?"

"Hi, Daddy."

"Hey, how's my girl?"

I leaned my forehead against the painted cinder block wall. I was falling apart.

"I bombed my French test today," I told him, trying not to cry.

"That's okay, Cass. It's just one test."

I heard voices in the background near Dad, and someone said, "Chet, they're ready to start."

"Start without me," Dad told them.

"But *you're* giving the presentation."

"Then they'll have to wait, won't they?" Dad was clearly annoyed by the interruption.

"Honey, you still there?" he asked.

"Sorry if this is a bad time, Daddy."

"Talk to me, Cass. Are you okay? How are you?"

"Not so good." I smeared away the tears and told him, "I can't take it. I look horrible now and everything is spinning out of control."

"Okay, so when you feel this way, you have to start small. Try to grab a hold of one thing right now, something that makes you happy, and concentrate on that."

"Like what? I can't think of anything that's good anymore."

"How about track practice? Think about how good it feels to stretch and loosen up. What about that adrenaline rush you get at the start of a race. And think about how much fun it'll be with Tara and your friends on the new team, Miss *Varsity* Track. Congratulations, babe!"

Right now I couldn't deal with explaining that it hadn't happened yet, so all I said was, "I borrowed one of your bandanas to wear for practice."

"Good girl. Cass, you're going to pull through this. I promise."

"Okay…I'll try."

"Honey, I know it's hard. But we can't always control what happens to us. The only thing we *can* control is how we react to the situation. You're going to be all right, Cassie. I know it."

I wiped away another tear and wished I had the same confidence in myself as Dad had in me.

We said goodbye and I went to my locker, blowing off the rest of gym. I'd return the phone to the girl later. I changed back into my clothes and checked out my hair and hat in private—without grossing anyone out. I smeared more eyeliner on the bare patch that was visible behind my ear; it looked more like a bruise when I was done, but that was better than showing shiny white skin.

I shut the locker door and spun the lock; in a few periods, I'd be right back here, getting ready for track. I sat down on the hard bench and debated whether I could even get through a whole practice after the crappy day I'd already had. I didn't know which end was up any more.

But what if I was approaching it all wrong? What if practice was the key to pulling myself back together?

Okay, so I'd start small. Get it together on the track.

Maybe then everything else would follow.

Twenty-Two

All through art class, I tried to psych myself up for practice, just like Dad had suggested. I needed to be in control again—of something.

I tried to remember that feeling of a great run, or how I felt when I crossed the finish line, or the rush that time I caught Minnelli cracking a smile, and how great it was when the other girls high-fived me. I tried to recall how, at that moment, nothing else in the whole world mattered.

Then Tara and I cut out of art class a few minutes early. We waited in the locker room until the last of the gym classes had cleared out and changed into our workout gear before the others came in.

I knew that the baseball cap wasn't going to cut it if I wanted to turn it on full throttle out on the track—I could just see it flying off and screwing up my run. So for days, I'd been experimenting with hair spray, clips, headbands, and Dad's bandana.

"I think I have a way to keep this mess hidden," I told Tara. I held up Dad's large Yankee bandana and folded it into a triangle, then draped it over my head like a kerchief and pulled it forward to just above my eyebrows. "It covers a lot if you tie the two side pieces over the flap in the back."

"Let me help you," Tara said. "Hold it in place."

"Tie it as tight as you can," I told her. When she was done, I shook my head and jumped up and down. "Feels good. How does it look?"

"Stylin'."

Yeah, right. I knew that from the back, my ponytail trailed out from under the bandana like a dying vine. But no matter what, Tara never seemed the least bit grossed out by anything that had to do with my hair. She was the absolute best about the whole mess.

Once we were all outside on the track, we ran a half-mile warm-up. Until now, I'd always felt the bounce of my ponytail, but now there was hardly anything. And naturally, I was worried about the bandana; with every step I took, for two entire laps, I focused on it. But there was no slipping. It didn't feel loose and it didn't budge. So far, so good.

Coach McCaffrey had returned and she called me over after the warm-up.

"Cassie, you made quite an impression on Coach Minnelli. He said your times were a little off this week, but he wants to work with you and see how things go. So how about it?"

"Seriously? I mean, definitely. This is incredible!"

A whistle blew on the other side of the field and she said, "Well? What are you waiting for?"

On my way, I swung past Tara to quickly give her the scoop.

"I'm training with varsity."

"You go, girl," she said.

"Okay, folks, stretch it out," Coach Minnelli said. "Sprinters, get ready for the four hundred. I want to see your best out there. We're closing in on the first meet, so let's see what ya got."

"How many per heat, Coach?" Robin asked.

"Four at a time. Wagner, I want you in the first heat. Lakewood, take the last heat."

He jogged a few yards ahead of the farthest starting position, with his clipboard and stopwatch in hand. The four hundred meter was one full lap around the track that ends where the inside lane runner starts, and Coach Litowsky stood near the inside lane starting blocks. He'd take away the blocks after the first group started.

The rest of us waited in the grass as Lauren and three other runners set up their blocks, staggered. I liked the inside lane for the four hundred—it gave me a chance to check out the competition. Starting behind the pack might seem like a disadvantage, but it all evens out at the first turn. That's why it's such a rush when I catch up and blow past the runners in the outside lanes. Robin, on the other hand, gravitated toward the outside lane; she started out in front and usually stayed there.

"Ready?" Suzanne asked.

"Melissa has the inside lane," I told her. "I'll wait for the next heat." Meanwhile, I pulled off my warm-up pants and unzipped my sweatshirt to cut down on drag time. A great run for the four hundred is around sixty seconds and I wanted to try and hit it.

Next heat, I slipped into the inside lane and adjusted

the blocks up one notch for my back leg. I shook out my arms and legs and jumped up and down a few times. My bandana still felt secure. As the three other lanes filled in, I kept telling myself, *Don't think about your hair. Just run the race—that's why you're here.*

Coach Minnelli motioned that he was ready for us.

"See ya in a minute," said Suzanne.

I nodded and kept my focus. I took a deep breath, my feet in position.

Set, Go!

I thrust off the blocks, gaining instantly on the outside lane runners. I led the pack out of the turn and then the other runners disappeared from my peripheral vision. I poured it on, lengthening my stride. My groin burned down the straightaway and I leaned in to cross the finish line, clean and tight. I reached up to the bandana—still there. *Yes, I nailed it.*

Robin's group ran next, and, of course, she finished first. Coach Minnelli let everyone catch their breath before he told us the results.

"Best time out there was fifty-eight point eight. Very nice—that's the time to beat."

Robin nodded; she was so smug, so confident. How did she know that was *her* time? Maybe it was Lauren's.

"At the high end was a minute, twelve seconds. That has to change if we're going all the way. The number we're shooting for is a minute four, minute five, tops."

"So who had the fifty-eight eight?" Melissa asked.

"Yeah, Coach," Robin said. "Who had it?"

"Donovan," Minnelli said.

I don't know who was more shocked, Robin or me. Whoa—if looks could kill! I just couldn't get the smile off my face. And the fact that she was so ticked made it that much more delicious. But I did make it a point to stay out of her way for the rest of the afternoon.

That night, I was totally flying high. It was the weekend; I had no homework and I'd finally pulled myself together, thanks to Dad's advice. I danced around in my room singing: "Fifty-eight point eight, not too shabby. Fifty-eight point eight makes Robin crabby."

I knew that if I worked at it, I had a good shot at getting my time down to fifty-eight seconds, even. *Let that smug Robin Lakewood try and beat that!*

Dad was right. I could do this. And if I could refocus, forget about stuff for a while and make varsity, how sweet would that be?

I took the picture of myself with no hair out of my jewelry box and told myself, *Yeah, I just gotta hang in there.* I slipped it into my back pocket. Maybe after that triumph on the track, I'd be able to work up the nerve to tell Tommy everything. Then he'd understand why I'd been acting like a schizo. I cranked a CD, shut my door, and danced around my room lip-syncing. After I'd worked up an appetite, I tied on another of Dad's bandanas and headed downstairs.

In the kitchen, I rinsed a big bowl of grapes, then headed out and plopped in front of the TV with Kyle. We sat through one beauty product commercial after another as I thumbed through one of Mom's magazines, which also had almost nothing but ads. Bored, I shoved grapes into my mouth, put the magazine aside, and looked up at the TV again, only to see a drop-dead gorgeous blonde stroll into the room, complaining on and on until I couldn't stand it anymore and clicked off the TV.

"Hey, turn it back on," Kyle said.

"No!"

"What's your problem, Cass?"

I just stared at the blank screen, disgusted.

"Gimme the remote," Kyle demanded.

I didn't answer and he said, "Put it back on!"

Hearing us, Mom walked into the room in time to see Kyle snatch the remote out of my hand.

Then he said, "You've been busting my chops non-stop. It's not my fault you're going bald."

"Kyle!" Mom said. "Your sister is not going—" then she choked, unable to finish her sentence. She knew it would have been a total lie.

I pulled the picture out of my pocket and waved it in her face.

"Do you see this, Mom? It's happening." My eyes blurred with tears as I shouted, "It's really happening."

The earth had shifted and I felt like I was sliding away. There was no way to stop it, and nothing to hold onto. And I didn't even care. I just wanted to be gone, to fade out of existence, and never have to see my own hideous reflection ever again.

I crushed the picture in my fist and tossed it away. I was ready to drift away in a current of my own tears.

Mom swooped in and wrapped her arm around me. "That's it!" she said. "I'm not waiting any longer for you to ask! Tomorrow we're going shopping for a wig. Just please try and hang in there one more night, okay, Cass?" She wiped my tears and rubbed my back soothingly, then said, "We can fix this, honey. Please let me do this for you."

I didn't have the strength to argue.

Twenty-Three

Saturday morning came and on my pillow lay the menacing reminder of why I was going wig shopping with Mom. I just couldn't catch a break. As I scraped up the strands from my bed and pillow, the tears fell as always. I was lucky my hair hadn't been short; then I'd never have been able to hide the patches for so long. But it wasn't much consolation.

Last night's shedding left me with two holes I could no longer hide. One was at the crown, the other between my left ear and the back of my neck. *Shit*. How much time before it was all gone? A couple weeks? Days?

I hate this! I smacked the mirror at my reflection. *This isn't me! This isn't fair! I don't deserve this. My real reflection is supposed to be there—not this ugly one.*

I opened my jewelry box and took out my bracelet from Tara. I rolled the tiger's eye beads between my fingers, then fastened it on. *Courage—that's a laugh.* I put on my baseball cap and tugged it down tight.

Mom agreed to let Tara come along, so we picked her up on the way. We were out early, so other than retirees in

walking groups or store employees, we were the first ac-
tual customers in the mall.

The store we headed for, Cutting Edge Wigs, wasn't a
destination for most people, and the only time anyone noticed the place was at Halloween, when they sold wacky
metallic wigs or puffy cotton candy numbers. Otherwise, it
blended in with everything else.

When we arrived, the store was empty except for the
staff; not that I expected a wig store to be a popular hang-
out, especially at that hour.

There were signs everywhere warning customers:
Please ask for assistance before trying on wigs. I felt itchy
just thinking about it and hoped my hives didn't start up.

"May I help you, Madam?" Tara asked, pretending to
be the salesperson.

"Yes." I played along.

Tara glided around the store, pointing to wigs with
both hands like a game show hostess. Mom and I watched
and enjoyed the show.

"How about the red-headed Cleopatra look?"

I turned up my nose.

"Dracula's daughter?"

"I'm thinking, no."

"Mrs. Logan, the gym teacher?"

"Ewww, no way."

"This one's nice," she said, turning back into her normal self.

"It is," I told her. "It's about the same color as mine,
maybe a little shorter. It might look like I just got a hair-
cut."

"Want to try it on?" Mom asked.

"Okay." But suddenly I looked up at the store's front window and felt like I was under a magnifying glass. I didn't want to be their display mannequin and said, "Maybe another time, Mom. Let's just get out of here."

Suddenly an older saleswoman in an ugly, flashy print dress waltzed in from the stockroom. She wasn't a walking ad for the place—her hair shot up in every direction—way too messy to be a wig.

"Welcome to the Cutting Edge!" she said and waved her hand with a flourish. She wore a triple-strand of clunky coral beads and matching lipstick that almost went with her dress.

"May I help you, dolly?" she asked Mom.

"Maybe," Mom said, hedging. Then she placed her hand on my back. "My daughter may want to try this one on."

The saleswoman lifted the wig off the Styrofoam head and draped it over the back of her hands, the way a pizza maker does before tossing the dough. She shook the wig a bit and said, "This is synthetic hair, very good quality." She stroked the hair and handed it to me.

I stroked it the way she did. It felt like hair and was soft enough. I let Mom and Tara feel it, too. I slid my fingers through a section of my own hair, then I did it to the wig. It felt a little waxy, but not bad. I wiggled my fingers through the hair to the cap, where I found plugged-in strands clumped together and glued to form a part in the center; it looked too fake, like Barbie doll hair.

"We also carry this," the saleswoman said, handing me another wig in my color. It was all one length, with a cleaner looking part. "See, dolly," she said. "It gives a more natural appearance of the scalp. My alopecia and chemotherapy clients find it works well for them; they're all people who've experienced total hair loss."

She said "alopecia" so matter-of-factly. For me, it'd been a secret word, something you'd never talk about with a stranger. But here it was an everyday word.

The saleswoman turned the wig inside out to show us where the hair was attached to rows of nylon ribbons between rows of meshy, pantyhose-like material. "It's made that way so the scalp can breathe," she said, then pointed out a plastic hook and some satin loops to adjust it to the right head size.

"Go ahead," Tara said. "Try it on."

I nodded and the saleswoman said, "Please follow me."

I was relieved when she led the three of us to a private dressing room. I sat on one of the stools in front of a mirrored wall and turned over the price tag attached to the wig, which sat on a stand. *Whoa. Two hundred eighty-nine bucks!*

"Use this to keep your own hair on top of your head," the saleswoman said, handing me a stretchy cap made out of the same pantyhose-like material. "We can anchor the wig to your hair if you like. Just line up the marks on the wig with your temples and it'll be on straight. Do you need any help?"

"No, thank you. We'll figure it out." She was nice and

all, but still, she was a stranger and I was too embarrassed to have her see the mess that was my head.

"I'll be right outside if you need me," she said before she left, closing the door behind her.

I sat there for a long time without taking off my cap. "This is harder than I thought it'd be." I looked down, then back up at Mom's reflection. I touched the ends of the hair on the wig sitting on the stand. "No one, beside Tara, has seen me with my hair down for months."

"Oh." Mom was visibly embarrassed, hurt even. "Um, if you'd feel more comfortable, I can wait outside."

"That's not what I meant," I said. *Damn.* "N-no—I want you to stay, Mom. I just hope you're…ready."

Mom nodded solemnly and said, "Whenever you are."

"So let's do this, girlie," Tara said, her tone encouraging.

After a deep breath, I took off my hat. I couldn't bear to look at myself in the mirror so I just focused on Mom and T.

Mom's eyes welled with tears. "All this time…" she whispered, shaking her head. "You're incredibly brave, honey. I didn't realize how far this had gone."

I gave her a weak smile and fingered the beads on my bracelet. I wasn't sure it counted as brave when you have no choice.

"Okay, dolly—" Tara said, mimicking the saleswoman. She stepped closer and said, "Let's get your hair up." Tara was amazing; even though I knew she was shocked by the latest round of fallout, she handled it without making me feel more self-conscious. She was like that about everything to do with my hair situation and warmth radiated from her, no matter how bad I looked.

Mom seemed okay with Tara helping me, to my relief. And a minute later, the wig was on.

"Wow" was all I could say. To see all that hair again, and feel it against my neck and shoulders—it felt incredible.

"Awesome!" Tara said.

"It's really great, Cassie. Just wonderful," Mom said, her eyes glassy, her expression—proud? She reached for the doorknob and said, "Shall we?"

Hand on her heart, the saleswoman gasped, "It looks fabulous, dolly!"

I stood in front of a mirror, shaking and bouncing my head up and down. It stayed put.

"Can I run with it? Will it stay on?" I asked the saleswoman.

"Sure. I'd use double-sided tape at the hairline to keep it secure during strenuous exercise. Meanwhile, how about a test drive? Take a walk around the mall and see how you like it."

"Go ahead, girls. I'll wait here," Mom said.

I checked myself out in every mirror we passed, and after a few stores I decided that it looked okay. It felt snug and comfortable, except for one scratchy spot at my temple, but I'd have worn it even if it had been lined with sandpaper. That's how relieved I was. Then we turned toward Macy's and heard plinking piano chords, the t-t-tst, t-t-tst of a cymbal, and the mellow voice of a saxophone.

Oh, no—Tommy's gig at the bookstore! I'd totally forgotten about it. Before I could pull a one-eighty, he saw us and waved us over.

"I still haven't told him yet," I said.

"You're kidding," Tara hissed. "Well, there's no time like the present."

"Wait—are you sure I look all right?"

Tara flounced some hair in front of my shoulder. "Totally."

"Are you positive? Swear?" Suddenly I didn't believe her or the mirrors.

"Get your butt over there and say 'hi' right now!"

The floor space outside Once Upon a Time was transformed into an outdoor café, and Silk City was set up opposite the umbrella-covered bistro tables. The band continued to warm up as Eric walked inside to speak with a lady wearing an employee badge.

"I didn't expect you this early," Tommy said. "Glad you made it."

"We came to wish you good luck," Tara said.

"Um, yeah, good luck," I told him.

He gave me a confused half-smile. "You look different. Good different—I mean. You get your hair cut?"

My cheeks stung with embarrassment. "Sort of," I said and tried to act nonchalant. *Big deal, so I'm wearing a wig.* I playfully pressed a button on his sax, but inside I was kicking myself for not telling him when it all started.

"So the whole mall gets to hear you today," I said, touching the side of my head. Duh, like I needed to draw more attention to my stupid hair.

"Yeah," he said. "Turns out we didn't all fit in the men's room."

"Well, um, we have to get going now," I said.

"Wait. Aren't you going to stick around?"

"We'll be back later," I said and whisked Tara away.

She gave me a look.

"I know. I know," I said. "I'll fill in the blanks tonight at the party."

She squinted at me, her eyes accusing me of lying.

"I swear! Okay?"

But Tara just shook her head.

℮

Back at Cutting Edge Wigs, I announced to the saleswoman, "I'll take it."

"Terrific—it's very natural looking. You won't be disappointed, dolly." She stepped behind the counter. "This is your first wig, yes? You'll want to wash it in the sink with a mild shampoo. Just swish it around and rinse it with warm water," she said while demonstrating a swish. "After that, don't use a blow dryer on it; just let it drip dry on the wig stand, then you can brush it back into shape when it's fully dry. Here's a roll of double-sided tape and a sheet with care instructions." She placed that and the foam head-shaped stand into a bag, then added, "Oh, and another thing, avoid any extreme heat."

"Like the beach?" I asked.

"No. Like the blast of heat you get when you open an

oven door, or around an outdoor grill. Because the hair will melt if you get too close."

"*Melt?* Oh, well. There goes my career as a master chef."

"Ah, yes. Such a shame," Tara said, rolling her eyes.

I shrugged at Mom and the saleswoman. "I even figured out how to burn Jell-O."

"Oh, my, sounds just like me! When I first got married," the saleswoman told us, "I took my husband by the hand and led him first to the kitchen and then to the bedroom. I said, 'I can only perform well in one of these rooms.' Did I mention what a fabulous cook my husband is?"

We all laughed but, omigod, that was way too much information.

"So, do you plan to wear your wig every day?" she asked.

Answering yes would have been admitting defeat. Besides, my hair grew back once before and I wanted to believe it could grow back again. So I answered with "For now."

The saleswoman said, "Then I'd recommend a second wig. It'll extend the life of the hairpieces."

"How long does one usually last?" Tara asked.

"If you wear it every day, only about three or four months."

"That's it?" I was surprised.

"I'm afraid so, dolly. The friction of the long hair against your clothes makes it fray on the ends and eventually it'll start to look fuzzy. For young people, I recommend having two wigs. It's good to have a back-up, anyway."

I turned to Mom. It was a lot of money for just one, let alone two.

"We'll take two, then," Mom said.

I couldn't control the sheer joy bubbling up inside me and I threw my arms around Mom.

"Thank you!" I said.

She hugged me back. "I'm so happy I can do this for you, Cassie."

"Hey, Cass, how about this one?" Tara said as she lifted up a foam head wearing some sort of hair helmet. She bounced it through the air, showing off the short, steel gray wig with flecks of white. It was awful.

"That's a man's hairpiece, dear," the saleswoman said.

"Is there a rule that all men's toupees have to be totally cheesy?" Tara asked.

She couldn't argue with that one, so she just shrugged.

I studied the saleswoman's hair, which had to be real. At least, that's how it looked to me.

"How about a different style for the second wig?" she asked.

"Like a dressy wig and an everyday wig?" I asked.

"Most certainly! Variety is the spice of life, dolly," she said as she fluffed the side of her hair and peeked in the mirror. "I like a change every now and then. And so does the hubby."

She *was* wearing a wig. And, omigod, she was totally into sex. I couldn't believe it for someone that age.

After pondering the idea of having two looks, I decided, "No—I really don't want anyone to notice anything more than they do already."

Mom nodded and said, "Okay, we'll take two of this style, please," and whipped out her credit card.

I thanked my mother again, not caring quite so much about who saw me in a wig store.

Twenty-Four

"Let's get going," Mom said and we left the store.

"We promised to go back and listen to Tommy's band," Tara reminded me with a not-so-gentle elbow to my ribs.

I was about to say forget it, but Mom agreed to a quick visit.

The whole scene with Mom in that store had been kind of intense, but she'd seen my ugly, patchy head and still held it together. I was grateful for that. And Tommy was next.

As I caught a glimpse of my reflection in a store window, I shook my head, thinking how I didn't want to mess this up with him. Tommy was such a great guy, and soon he'd know my secret. My heart was tapping out SOS as I pictured him getting pissed off at me for not telling him about it sooner, and even being turned off about me having this disease. I shook that image from my mind and prayed as we walked toward the bookstore, *Please, let things stay the same between us when he finds out.*

I couldn't help touching the long, thick strands of my

new hair, but I felt weird walking around with the wig store bag. It was like announcing to everyone in the mall that I was a wig owner in training—something I'd rather have kept to myself.

As we got closer to Once Upon a Time, jazz music drifted toward us through the mall. Then we heard a soft round of applause. We stopped behind a wall of flowers as Silk City played their next number and we could see Dina, Tommy's brother's girlfriend, sitting at one of the tables with two friends. Tommy's friends Jason and Glen were hanging out behind the band with some other guys from school, and after a few minutes, Tommy noticed me in the gathering crowd and gave me a smile and a nod.

"Do you want to sit down, Cass? There's an empty table," Mom said.

"It's fine back here," I said, recognizing the first few notes of the next song. It was Tommy's, the one he'd played on his sax for me over the phone; it sounded fantastic with the whole band joining him and the crowd was totally into it, including Mom. I bobbed my head in time to the music, my new hair lightly resting on my cheek and the Cutting Edge bag hidden behind me. After a few songs, Mom gave the "time to go" signal and I waved goodbye to Tommy. *Later*, I thought, *you'll know everything later.*

As we turned to leave, Mom unhooked the wig bag from my fingers and carried it out of the mall for me, to my relief. I could see that she really was making an effort to make me feel comfortable with my new wig.

On the ride home, we listened to the jazz station and talked about Tommy's band and what I'd wear to the party tonight. As for what I'd *say* to Tommy when I finally told him? *Agh*. That was still filed under C, for clueless.

When we dropped Tara off, she stood on the sidewalk, placed her hand on her heart, and said, "Your hair's just fabulous, dolly! And good luck tonight."

For the rest of the ride, while Mom kept her eyes on the road, I kept trying to catch glimpses of my reflection in the sideview mirror. When we turned onto our street she said, "You know, wearing a wig can be very glamorous. Look at all the singers on MTV, with dozens of costume changes per video. You can't tell me they aren't all wearing hair extensions and wigs."

Glamour was the last thing on my mind, but I loved the way Mom was able to put her own positive spin on the situation. But mostly I just wanted to feel normal again.

When Mom pulled into the driveway, Kyle and his buddy, Rob, were outside, tearing around the house commando-style, with camouflage face paint and wielding bazooka-sized toy electronic guns. "In-coming!" Rob shouted. "Take cover." And they dove behind the hedges.

Kyle poked his face through as I passed and said, "Check you out," and nodded approvingly.

That was about as close to a compliment as I'd ever get from him, so I took it. I walked into the house practicing how to toss my head with an air of confidence, making my new hair float over my shoulders.

Inside, Mom handed me the bag with my other wig— my spare hair.

"You chose a very flattering style," Mom said.

"And it debuts tonight at Tommy's party."

Mom's eyes glossed over. She touched my cheek, then stroked my new hair with a tender smile. "You'll be like a celebrity on the red carpet."

"Thanks, Mom."

Wearing my wig all day felt good—not glamorous by any stretch, but I felt protected in it, like being wrapped in a blanket on a stormy night. I practiced acting natural in the mirror, tucking the hair behind my ear and flipping it away without moving like a robot. And there was still that other little matter of obsessing over what I'd say to Tommy tonight.

That evening after dinner, I changed into a pale aqua top and beige khakis that went so well with the tiger's eye beads in my bracelet. I was combing the wig on the stand when Kyle popped into my room.

"Hey—you got two wigs? Can I try one on?"

I shrugged. "Go for it."

Kyle put on the wig and sashayed around my room, tossing his head, pausing here and there to strike a ridiculous pose with an even dopier smile.

He cracked me up and I said, "You make a really cute girl. I always wanted a little sister."

"Ha, ha. Next time you get mad at me, try not to 'wig out,'" he said and pulled the ends straight out to the sides.

"Take if off now, okay?" I told him. "I don't want you to mess it up."

Mom tapped on my open door. "Cassie, your father's on the phone."

I took it in Mom and Dad's room.

"Hey, babe. Mom told me about your new wig. So how're you doing?"

"Way better than the last time I called you, Dad."

"That's great. Good for you." He paused for a second. "Cass, your mother—I'm sorry if that made things harder on you. I didn't really know until that night what was going on, just how bad things were…I wish I'd figured it out sooner."

"She told me about Gramma."

Dad let out a long breath. "I think Mom always meant well."

Did that ever sound familiar…but I supposed it was natural to want to forgive someone you loved, even when they screwed up big-time.

"When are you coming home?"

"How about this?" he said. "I'll pick you up from practice Friday."

"Oh, and about varsity…"

"Yeah?"

"Things got a little exaggerated. I've been *training* with them, but technically, I'm still only on the freshman team."

"Don't say it like that. That's something to be proud of."

"I guess. Thanks, Dad. See you when you get back."

Just before it was time to leave for the party, Mom brought me her aquamarine stud earrings, a gift from Gramma before she passed away. "I thought you might like to borrow them," she said.

I put them on and looked in the mirror, then turned to Mom, my palms up. "Well?" I waited for something to be wrong, but instead, it was like she was seeing me for the first time.

"You're a beautiful girl, Cassie. And so strong, the way you've carried yourself all these weeks." Mom's gaze fell to the floor, then she looked up at me again and said, "I really admire that."

We weren't exactly the picture-perfect mother/daughter team, not by any stretch, but there we were, hugging for the second time that day.

As I inhaled the light clean scent of Mom's moisturizer while she pressed her cheek to mine, calloused bits of the past began to fall away, revealing a tiny pearl of trust building between us. And for the first time, it felt like we were finally going to be okay.

Twenty-Five

When I got to Tommy's, his mother invited me in and called him. "So nice to finally meet you, Cassie," Mrs. Sweeny said. "I'd love it if we could sit down and—" But then another group of guests arrived. She greeted them and said, "Tommy, bring Cassie inside. I'll catch up with you two in a bit."

Tommy whisked me into the house, introducing me to his aunts, uncles, and cousins as they bustled in, offering their congratulations on Silk City's first paying gig. Then the guests ushered themselves into the kitchen and no one gave me a second glance, much to my relief.

Black-and-white helium balloons with curling ribbons dangling from the ends rested against the ceiling and across one wall, a garland of metallic letters spelled out *Congratulations Silk City.* The other walls were dotted with large black musical notes, and their demo CD blared.

"Great decorations," I said to Mrs. Sweeny, as she came in carrying an armful of jackets.

"Oh, thank you, dear," she said.

"Let me take those for you, Ma," Tommy said.

"I've got it, kiddo," she said. "Why don't you get Cassie something to drink?"

The kitchen was packed with relatives as Tommy handed me a glass and smiled at me the same way as this morning at the bookstore, with that quizzical expression. My skin prickled as Tara's voice echoed in my head, *Just tell him.* But I'd already morphed into a bundle of raw nerves, and so, like a sphinx, I pressed my lips together into a tight smile.

Dina and Eric squeezed toward the freezer in a quest for more ice, while Jason and Glen loaded up on chips and dip from the table. Then Tommy slipped his arm around my waist and my heart went into hyper-drive.

How was I going to tell him? My hand shook as I brought the glass to my lips, took a tiny sip, and gulped.

"Congratulations on your big performance," I said. "You guys were great, and your song sounded awesome."

"I can't believe you remembered," he said, his smile huge. "I only played it for you once, and since then Eric helped me smooth things out on the bridge. He's got the ear, lemme tell ya. It's *so* much better now."

The warmth in his eyes made me believe I could trust him, so I decided to go for it, finally.

"Um, I guess you noticed there's something different about my hair, right?"

He nodded as the laughs and conversations grew louder.

"Is there somewhere we can talk for a few minutes? Alone?"

He nodded, then took my hand and led me down to the basement.

"I've been wanting to tell you something for a while now," I said. I fiddled with a button on my shirt, dreading what I had to do. "It's about why I've been less than friendly sometimes, if you know what I mean."

He hooked a finger on my belt loop and kissed me softly on the lips, then said, "You do get a little twitchy sometimes."

I breathed in his scent, then stepped back and summoned all my courage.

"It's my hair. See, I have this *thing*—sort of like an allergy—that makes my hair fall out a little and then grow back. But otherwise, I'm totally fine." My voice cracked a bit as I fed him the biggest lie I'd ever told. At the same time, my heart hammered in my ears as I searched his face for a glimmer of understanding and acceptance.

His mouth formed a tiny O and his brows knit together. He didn't say anything, but I had to keep going even though I dreaded it. I had to get it all out in the open, once and for all.

"I know it's a little strange that I'm wearing a wig, but it's only temporary."

He took a deep breath and shook his head, then said, "Whoa."

Then came a long, uncomfortable silence.

Yeah, it takes a while to process this one.

"Damn. That's gotta be tough. I mean, I'm really sorry," he said.

I smoothed the back of my hair. "Um, do you want to touch it? It feels pretty good—just like real hair." I attempted to demonstrate how natural it was, but it was like trying to coax a kid to pet a big, scary-looking dog.

Then somehow my bracelet got caught and I clutched at the top of my head.

"Are you all right?" he asked, eyes wide.

I yanked my wrist away, snapping the strand; the bracelet was free, but a bit of hair was attached.

Yeah, that went real well. I bit my bottom lip. Wasn't this where he was supposed to say it was okay? *Shit. Say something. Anything.*

At least he managed a sympathetic smile, which kept me from completely losing it

"You and Tara are the only ones who know," I told him, "so please don't tell anyone else."

"No, I won't say anything—don't worry. It's, uh, only temporary, right?" he said, shrugging it off like I'd just told him I'd dyed my hair green accidentally.

But I'd noticed that he'd latched onto the word *temporary.*

Soon we heard Glen's voice from upstairs, asking, "Where're Tommy and Cassie?"

"Well, we better get back to the party," Tommy said.

Back upstairs Tommy was great, but he kept excusing himself and going off to talk to other people. He was one of the guests of honor and I couldn't expect his undivided attention, so I hung with Amanda, who was much friendlier in a non-rehearsal venue. She introduced me to Natalya, Smoke's on-again-off-again girlfriend. I wondered if I should thank her for the DuValle ticket, but then thought better of it. I didn't want to dredge up any hard feelings between her and Smoke.

Eventually Tommy came back with his oldest brother, Richie, who grabbed Tommy in a playful headlock. "So, Cass. You keeping this guy in line?" he asked.

I nodded and Tommy rolled his eyes.

"Now that Silk City's hit the big time, I might pick up my sticks again," Richie said.

"Who said you were invited back?" Tommy teased.

Laughing, Richie mimed pulling a knife out of his stomach. Tommy's brothers had the same lean frames as Tommy, but he and Richie had amazingly similar features and the same to-die-for smile.

"Hey, Cassie, mind if I borrow this sorry excuse of a sax player for a few?" Richie said, then hooked his arm around Tommy's neck and led him away.

I sat in the living room with Elaine the drummer for quite a while; I found out she also played classical violin. Who'd have guessed? When I caught Tommy's eye from across the room, he only gave a quick nod, then pulled Eric away in the opposite direction. The next time we locked eyes, I didn't know what it was, but somehow Tommy was different. We were in the same house, but he was like a million miles away. A flash of shame stung my cheeks; now that he'd had some time to think, was he changing his mind about me?

Later, when I had Tommy to myself again, I twisted my finger around one of the curled ribbons dangling from a balloon hanging in front of me. He kept looking nervously toward the door and all I could do was wonder, *Did he want me to leave?*

"So," I finally said. "You're really okay with this?" and pointed to my wig.

"Um, yeah," he said, barely meeting my eyes. "Can you excuse me a minute?"

It was like he couldn't get away from me fast enough.

After that, the rest of the night dragged. Tommy had been MIA for an hour and the crowd was starting to thin. I was itching to go home and Mrs. Sweeny was thanking people for coming, when a strange man appeared at the door. He stood there and peered in, exchanged a few words with Mrs. Sweeny, and then she invited him in. He looked both ways when he entered, like he was crossing a busy street.

By now I wanted out, so I found Dina, my ride home, and told her I wanted to find Tommy and say goodbye. She nodded toward the kitchen and said she'd meet me out front.

In the kitchen, I found Tommy huddled in the corner with his brothers. *Was he telling them about my wig? Or did they already know?* Eric glanced over his shoulder, saw me, and tapped Tommy.

From the doorway, I mouthed, "I have to go."

Tommy nodded and managed a strained smile. Head down, he dug his hands into his pockets, glanced toward the living room and then back at his brothers. He walked over to me as carefully as if he thought he'd step on a land mine.

Not good. Not good at all.

"I guess it's late," he finally said. "Dina driving you home?"

I nodded.

"Um, okay, then," he said, edging toward the front door, his eyes still darting.

Was he worried what people would think if they knew about me? But he promised not to tell anyone, so nobody had to know.

He drew me into an awkward half hug, like I was his least favorite aunt, and "G'night," was all he said. That was it—no kiss.

Dina chatted as she drove us across town, but I don't think I processed a single word and wasn't sure I even remembered to thank her when I got out of her car. My mind was still reeling from what had happened at Tommy's.

Tommy'd said he was cool with the whole hair situation, but that scene when I left—I don't know—was it just easier for him to lie?

Before I changed for bed, I shot Tara a quick e-mail:

Subject: disaster
Tommy knows. Why did i think he'd understand?
SEND.

A minute later, Tommy signed on and IM'd me.

Saxologist: hi Cass
Cassie D: hi
Saxologist: glad you told me about ur hair

I held my breath.

Saxologist: something I want to tell u too. its crazy
Saxologist: rehearsals, track, homework
Saxologist: maybe we should chill as a couple. u no?
Saxologist: until we both have more time

I covered my mouth. *Oh, God—he dumped me.*

Saxologist: we can still be friends
My cursor blinked. There one second. Gone the next.
Saxologist: hello Cassie? r u there?

But I was already gone.

Twenty-Six

After that horrible IM exchange, I dragged myself to the couch and curled up.

I couldn't believe he dumped me *and* that I was so stupid to think that maybe he wouldn't. I replayed the entire evening in my head, especially his uneasy expression. By the end of the night, he could barely look at me. An ache spread through me, expanding in my chest. I lay on that couch awake for hours, waiting for the hurt to stop. But it didn't—it had no end.

The next morning, I woke to find Mom beside me; she'd covered me with her chenille throw. I reached up to make sure my hair hadn't shifted, then sat up, exhausted and glad the night was over.

"Didn't mean to wake you," she said.

"Who said I slept?" I told her.

I felt like crap and probably looked like it, too—I was still in my clothes from the party.

Mom brushed my hair back and over my shoulder with a concerned frown, then said, "Want to tell me what happened last night?"

"You were right." I swallowed the hurt rising in my throat. "Tommy fixed it so we can see other people now. My hair totally freaked him out and he broke up with me. It was just what you said would happen."

"Oh, honey, I'm sorry," Mom said and put her arm around me. "You don't know how much I wanted to be wrong. I wish it could have been different."

I rested my head on her shoulder and pulled the blanket up to my chin. The pendulum on the clock swung as the minute hand moved once and then again.

Mom said, "This may not seem like much now, but there will be other guys, Cass. And when it's the right guy, none of this will matter. It'll be different, and wonderful—I promise."

I tossed the blanket aside and stood up, fighting tears.

"There won't be *other* guys because I'm never going through this again!" Before she could debate the issue, I said, "I'm going up to my room, okay? I didn't get a lot of sleep last night."

My head barely hit the pillow when Tara phoned. "I just got home from church," she said. "What the heck happened last night?"

I gave Tara the blow-by-blow. "Like I believe that all of a sudden, he's so busy. Does he think I'm stupid?"

"That prick!" she shrieked, then proceeded to trash Tommy for the next half hour.

When Tara got going, she could jam more swear words into one sentence than anyone. But as much as she was trying to help, it wasn't working. That's because I wasn't angry—I was hurting.

"Forget him," she finally said. "He's not good enough for you anyway, the big dick wad."

"That's exactly what I'm going to do, T," I said. "Forget him." But even though saying it helped, I had a long way to go before I'd feel better. I was exhausted, so I told her, "Listen, T, I gotta take a nap. I didn't sleep all night and I'm totally shot."

"Maybe you shouldn't be alone. You want me to come over?"

"I'm just tired, T. Not suicidal."

"Well, um, call me if you need me. Um—" She wouldn't hang up.

"T, I promise that this wasn't a cry for help, okay?"

"So you're definitely not suicidal, right?"

"Agh. No, I'm not! I'll talk to you later."

I hit END, tossed the phone on the bed, and went to my jewelry box. I took off Mom's earrings and placed them in a velvet compartment, then I opened the skinny drawer on the bottom of the box—where I kept all my special mementos from Tommy. I leafed through his notes, our ticket stubs, and his printed e-mails. I'd saved practically everything he'd ever touched.

I'd trusted him.

A bolt of rage surged through me and I wadded up the notes and e-mails, crushing them until my fists hurt. I trashed them the way he'd trashed me, and then I dropped into bed and cried for a long time.

The rest of the day, I tried to convince myself I was better off without Tommy. I had to be! If he'd ever cared about me, he wouldn't have dumped me like this. It just hurt so much.

Last night had been a disaster, and tomorrow I somehow had to get through a whole day of school. But this time I'd be smart; this time, it was nobody's damn-freaking business. I checked my reflection in the mirror and my wig didn't look bad. I pressed my shoulders back and stood tall; I could wear a wig if I wanted. *I just wish I didn't have to.* I turned away from the mirror, blinking back a tear.

❧

The next morning at school, Tara was waiting for me when I stepped off the bus.

"Prick alert," she said, as Eric's car pulled into the parking lot. "What an immature jerk."

True, but what I didn't tell Tara was that before I left for school, I'd garbage-picked all of Tommy's rumpled notes and messages, smoothed them out, and put them away again. I just couldn't part with them, at least not yet. But I'd brought Tommy's DuValle CD with me to give to Jason to return. It was one small gesture of getting rid of Tommy's things, but it was better than nothing.

"Anyway," Tara said, "you look great."

"As long as I don't have to be the 'bald girl' at school, I'll be happy."

"You don't have to worry about that now." Tara made it sound so easy. But I knew she mostly was trying to distract me as Tommy shuffled along behind his brother, iPod plugged into his ears, on the way into the building.

I had to admit, though, that the wig was sort of working out. In school, I was blending in just as I'd hoped. People smiled at me the way they'd do when seeing someone for the first time with their braces off. They'd acknowledged a change, even if they couldn't put their finger on it. And, no longer feeling so conspicuous, I didn't scrunch down in my seat in class, trying to hide.

But it didn't last. In French class, Robin's eagle eye was on me as soon as I sat down. Suddenly I felt exposed and my insides squirmed, knowing she could swoop in for the kill whenever she wanted. Sure enough, during the usual free conversation time, she pounced.

"Is that a *wig*?" she asked.

"Yeah, so?" I replied. I'd never give her the satisfaction of knowing how she got to me.

"Why are you wearing a wig?"

"En Francais, mademoiselles," Monsieur Haus said.

Busted. But I couldn't answer in French, so I shrugged. But she just wouldn't let it go.

"Why are you wearing a wig, *mademoiselle*?" she said again.

"Until my allergies clear up, *mademoiselle*," I told her as the teacher scowled. That shut her up for now and she cracked her gum.

Between classes, I ran into Jason and said, "Can you give Tommy something for me?"

"Sure. And, hey, sorry about your hair. That's rough."

What? He told them?

"But it's cool, ya know. Uh—I don't mean *cool*. But you know what I mean." He drummed his rolled-up notebook against his leg and said, "Uh, what do you want me to give him?"

Besides a fat lip for running his mouth?

"Never mind—I'll give it to you tomorrow."

Jason shrugged and turned down the hall, and I ran to Tommy's locker, where I took the CD out of my purse and opened the case. I held it glistening in my hand.

He promised not to tell. I broke the CD in half. Snap. *Immature prick.* Another snap. *Jazz sucks anyway.* Snap. I shoved the shards through his locker vent.

After my next class people flooded the halls and somehow, coming straight toward me, was Tommy. It seemed he'd found my little present. But it didn't make me feel any better. That ache was back and it was filling up my chest.

Keep walking. Don't cry. Don't even give him the time of day, I told myself. But his eyes locked onto mine as he came toward me against the flow of traffic.

"Can we talk?" he said.

But I forged ahead.

Tommy got ahead of me and walked backward, facing me. "Cass, please. C'mon. I just want to talk."

I stopped in the middle of the crowded hall, my feet planted in a defiant stance, and with a hard look in my eyes. Everything about me shouted, *Why are you wasting my time?* But it didn't scare him off.

And to my frustration, I felt a pang of regret that things were over between us. I tried to shrug it off. How could I still feel something for the person who shit all over me not two days ago?

But my better judgment seemed to be on vacation and I said, "So talk."

"Here?"

"As you pointed out online the other night, neither one of us has a lot of spare time," I said.

I could tell from his expression that he'd gotten my point loud and clear. He dragged his hand over his mouth and looked hurt. Good.

"Can't we go somewhere and talk? We can sit in Eric's car."

Locker doors jangled open and slammed shut and the traffic in the hall began to thin out.

I stepped around him and said, "I'm going to be late for class."

"You're not going to make this easy, are you?" he called after me.

I turned to face him and said, "Why should I? This hasn't exactly been a freaking joy ride for me. But okay—everyone's gone and you have my undivided attention. So say what you have to say, and then leave me the hell alone!"

He stood there, regarding me with an odd kind of gaze.

"Stop it!" I said.

"Stop what?"

"Trying to figure out what I look like without my wig."

"That's not what I'm doing, Cassie! I'm trying to apologize here, if you'd just give me a minute."

"I trusted you, Tommy. How many times did you ask me what was wrong? And when I finally got up the nerve to tell you, you said everything was fine, but then you dumped me. Do you have any idea how that made me feel?"

He looked down at his feet and his expression was stone sober. "Yeah," he said. "I totally do."

I knew he meant his father, but I didn't care. I wanted him to be hurt the way I'd been.

"Why are you even bothering with me?" I said. Then I whispered, "Are you feeling guilty? Or is it that you can't face the fact that you're turning out like your father?"

His jaw flexed and he said, "Are you done?"

I looked into his eyes and kept quiet.

"Look, I didn't mean to hurt you," Tommy said. "But since *you* brought it up, here's a news flash: he's back. So I'm dealing with plenty of my own shit right now. Call it bad timing, being selfish, or whatever you want, but that's how it is." And he did look kind of beaten.

Then it came to me: the man at the party the other night—that was Tommy's father.

"I didn't mean it," I said, blinking back tears, wanting to comfort him and apologize for what I'd said. But the force field between us wouldn't let me touch him.

He half shrugged and said, "You can't un-ring a bell. Sucks, doesn't it?" Then he turned and walked away.

How could I know his father was back, or what that did to him? Judging by Tommy's face, there was a lot going on with that. Was that why he couldn't deal with me and my problems, too? Maybe things would've been different if his father hadn't shown up. But how could I be sure? I hugged my books in front of me as I stood there, alone in the empty hall. After what I'd said to him, I'd probably never find out.

Twenty-Seven

Track was about the only thing that kept my mind off the mess with Tommy—sort of. I kept wondering if he'd show up for practice and what I'd do if he did. I scanned the field for him every day, but it seemed he was getting on without me, "dealing with his own shit."

All week, Robin and I took turns beating each other's times by a second here and there, but I didn't touch the fifty-eight eight again. I lost time when I thought I felt my wig slipping, and that broke my concentration and stride. After only a few minutes of warm-ups, the wig got hot, itchy, and damp with sweat. *How long would the tape hold?*

On Friday Coach Minnelli cut practice short and called all of us to sit together on the bleachers.

"You really came through this week," he said, pacing as Coach Litowsky leaned on the railing. "And I guarantee you'll get back everything you put in. We can win this season. We have a lot of talent, a lot of speed. But you gotta want it."

Lauren shot me a knowing grin and a few people clapped and cheered.

"The Falcons can be the best!" the coach said. "Do you want it?!"

More of us cheered this time.

"I can't hear you!" shouted the coach.

We went wild, clapping and cheering and stamping our feet so hard that the bleachers vibrated. Caught up in my teammates' excitement, my desire to win resurfaced as I chanted "Fal-cons, Fal-cons!" and shook my fist in the air.

Coach Minnelli nodded, satisfied with the commotion he'd caused. When we quieted down, he went on with his speech.

"Okay, folks, our first meet is on Monday at Spring Valley. They've got a strong team with a lot of seniors, and they want to win. So victory won't fall into your lap. When you're out there on the field, you'll have to work hard. That means every race, every hurdle, every step. Got that?"

"Yesss!" echoed through the bleachers.

"Okay, then. Good. I'll see you on the bus Monday. Now get outta here."

I found Tara and walked toward the parking lot with her, keeping my voice down. "My times were off a little this week, but I think I can win on Monday if he puts me in. He said we can make it happen if we want it bad enough. Does that sound crazy or what?"

Tara snapped her fingers. "Nah, it's not crazy. Just run at the speed of light."

We grabbed our gym bags from our spot against the fence. Dad was waiting to take us home and greeted us when we got to the car. I slid into the front seat as Tara got in behind me, and I leaned over to kiss Dad's cheek. "Glad you're back," I told him.

"Let me take a look at you," he said. "Wow, you look great."

"Gross, Dad, I'm sweatin' like a pig. At least wait till I'm cleaned up. But check this out—I trained with varsity all this week and it really might happen. Can you believe it? Our first meet is next week."

"Are you ready?" Dad shifted the car into drive.

"Absolutely."

❧

That Monday, I was psyched for our first meet of the season against the Cougars. We piled into the team bus, our destination Spring Valley High School. The team captains took attendance and nobody was missing—no surprise, considering how the coach had gotten us so jazzed up the previous Friday. *Jazzed.* I sighed. I was going to have to stop using that word.

As we rode along, Tara unzipped her gym bag, which was loaded with oranges.

"Want one?"

I reached in. "T—ya think six'll be enough?"

"My mother said it's supposed to get hot today. We need to stay hydrated."

Mrs. Spez was right. The temperature blinked eighty degrees on the bank we passed. Tara and I had gotten stuck with the seats over the bus's tires, and it was like sitting on a furnace. Before we'd gone a few miles, two oranges were already history.

"Your parents coming today?" I asked.

"No, they can't take off from work."

"My father's stuck at his office, too, since he's been away," I explained. "But my parents promised to make the first home meet."

The bus slowed in front of Spring Valley High School and soon a pulsing rhythm from the back of the bus silenced the rest of the chatter. Our feet pounded the floor and the infectious beat spread through the bus. As we entered the Cougars' parking lot, our voices boomed, "WE WILL, WE WILL, BEAT YOU. DE-FEAT YOU!"

When the bus came to a stop and the doors opened, we filed off, everyone pumped up and ready as we headed for the Cougar locker room. I fumbled around inside my gym bag as we walked until I found what I was after—the wig tape. I tugged at my wig and the tape was holding well, so I tugged a bit harder—still good. Hidden underneath the wig were the seven remaining scraggly clumps of hair, each hanging on for dear life.

Out on the field, spectators trickled in as the teams warmed up. People from Spring Valley and our school filled the stands. I was determined not to let the pressure get to me, but the red blotches on my chest gave me away no matter how cool I pretended to be.

Coach Minnelli waited until just before the meet started to tell us who'd be competing in each event. He said he wanted us to work that much harder at practice to earn our shot at the meet, as not everyone could participate with only three runners being fielded per race. I held my breath as he ran down the roster until he called my name. I bounced up and down with excitement—I'd been picked for all three of my races, the same three as Robin. This was it—my first varsity track competition in high school.

The teams moved to their places on the field. Pole-vaulters, high jumpers, and long jumpers competed in the center of the field and the other events—javelin, shot put, and discus—were set up outside the track, where nobody could get hurt by flying objects. The schedule called for each running event to alternate between freshmen and varsity.

When the official called for varsity girls' two hundred meter, I jogged over with Melissa and Robin, the Spring Valley runners eying us as we approached. One of them had snagged the inside lane so I moved into the next one, then adjusted and tested my blocks. Robin took her usual place in the front outside lane.

"Runners ready," the official called out.

I pressed against my blocks.

"On your maaark. Set."

Crack! went the starter pistol.

I blasted off the blocks, fighting for every step. Spring Valley's runner on the inside lane got right on top of me and matched me stride for stride. I kicked in even harder coming out of the turn and had her by half a step. I dug in, keeping up the pace. Another fifty meters to go and I wanted it bad. Eyes focused dead ahead, I leaned into the finish line—but it was too close to tell.

"Runners, stay in your lanes," the official said, then he pointed me as the winner.

Thrilled, I trotted back toward the timekeepers at the finish line, my hair still locked in place. *I'd won. I'd actually won!* Tara jumped up and down as the crowd cheered.

"Donovan," Coach Minnelli said. "Twenty-seven point nine—beautiful. Lakewood, great run. You got us the points. Go stretch out and rest up for the hundred meter."

"Whatever," Robin said and stormed off.

"You did it!" Suzanne said. "Awesome race."

Robin, still scowling, kicked the fence.

"So she came in second," I said. "Big deal."

"Third," Suzanne said. "Spring Valley took second."

"Oh," I said.

I watched the boys' pole vault before my next event. The Spring Valley guy approached the bar with long calculated strides, then lifted up and over. But his ankle caught the bar; he twisted, trying to stop it, but the bar crashed down onto his shoulder. Ouch! Adam was up next, and off to the side I saw Robin. Was she flirting with a Spring Valley guy? Unbelievable—and right in front of her boyfriend.

"Next event, girls' hundred," Coach Litowsky called out. "Get ready, everyone."

My calves were a little tight so I loosened up with a face-down stretch. Suddenly I felt two quick steps behind me as someone shoved my face into the grass, clawed at my head—and yanked.

My hair!

Twenty-Eight

I could feel air and sunlight on my naked scalp, and my wig was in a heap in the grass nearby. I scrambled to grab it, half crawling as a piece of tape flapped against my ear. On my knees, I groped for my wig and pulled it on.

"Cassie! Are you okay?" Tara said, rushing toward me.

I couldn't move; the whole place had just had a front-row view of my freak show.

"Come on, Cassie. Get up!" Tara hooked her arm under mine and dragged me off the field, my eyes darting to the bleachers, the track, the goal post. People from our school stared, and people from the team stared. Then I heard the laughter. Tara heard it, too—Robin. As we left the field I could see her; behind her were a few guys, one of them wearing a Cougars T-shirt.

"Hey, a bald eagle is one thing," they snickered. "But who ever heard of a bald falcon?"

I shivered at the coldness of their voices.

"What a dirt bag," Tara growled as she led me through the parking lot and back to the bus. "Did you see who did it?"

261

"My head was down. It happened so fast. Oh, God," I said, shaking.

"I saw a guy run toward the Spring Valley side," Tara said. "But who'd do this?"

"I'm staying here," I told her.

"What?" Tara was surprised.

"Tell the coach I twisted my ankle or got my period. But forget it—I am *not* going back out there."

"Is that what you really want?" Tara asked.

"That's right—that's what I want," I snapped.

She started to walk away, then turned back to me and said, "But weren't you the one who told me that you didn't just want to be the bald girl? That you were going to win today?"

"Screw you, Tara. You expect me to act like nothing happened? They'll all be staring at me. No one just exposed *your* gross-looking head in front of everybody."

"Fine. I'll tell him." She started back to the field.

And she's supposed to be my best friend? She totally doesn't get it.

I remembered seeing Robin talking to the Spring Valley guys and the guy with the Cougars shirt laughing. That was the only way he could've known about my wig. That bitch put him up to it!

I hated myself for wussing out and paced the length of the bus, then kicked the tire. *If I back down now, she owns me.* I clenched my teeth and stared hard at the field. *Not today, Robin.*

I zigzagged through the parking lot to the visitor

bleachers. Coach Litowsky and the Cougars' coach were arguing at the long jump pit when I caught up to Tara.

"You talk to the coach?"

She shook her head.

"Good. Don't say anything. Did they call for the hundred yet?"

"I don't think so."

I had to move fast. I grabbed my gym bag and ducked behind the equipment shed and a pile of cardboard boxes. I squatted down, folded my bandana, and draped it over my knee.

I couldn't trust the wig. Pieces of tape were still half hanging onto my head. With no time for repairs, I positioned the bandana on my head and slipped off the wig in one motion. My wig dropped in the dirt as I tied the bandana good and tight.

Then I heard the bullhorn: "Varsity girls' hundred meter."

I shoved the wig into my gym bag and zipped it, catching some of the strands. *I'm gonna do this.* I tossed my bag into the bleachers and ran to the starting line. I landed in lane five, right next to Robin.

"Nice hairdo," she said with a smirk.

My legs almost buckled. *What am I doing? People aren't watching a race. They're watching a freak show. Run for cover! Get away and hide!*

I heard cheers and smatterings of applause that drifted down from the stands. *Calm down.* I squatted. *One hundred meters, and then it's over.*

"Runners ready."

Eyes were on me.

"Set."

I hadn't adjusted the blocks. My footing was all wrong.

Crack!

I pushed off, launching myself face first into the gravel. I wind-milled my arms, trying to recover, then struggled to catch up with the pack. But two Cougars runners blasted out in front and were long gone. I managed to catch Robin, though. Our arms pumped and grazed each other. But the Cougars had it. A few more pounding steps, and we were almost there.

"Bald, ugly bitch," Robin muttered.

Never again, I vowed as we crossed the finish line.

Even though I knew we were supposed to stay in our lanes, I just kept going—across the field, away from everyone, through a gap in the fence. I tore out along the front entrance of the school and into the street, where a car horn blared and brakes screeched. I ran behind a gas station, through a back lot of mangled cars and stacks of tires. I was sprinting and my lungs threatened to explode.

I plowed through a maze of identical brick apartment buildings and manicured shrubs, beyond the last numbered parking space, exiting Tulip Gardens onto Mountain Grove Street. Shooting pains sliced under my ribs when the road took a steep dive, but my momentum pushed me and I struggled to keep from wiping out. *Please, just a little farther, just until the road levels out.* I skidded at the bottom of the hill as pebbles sprayed out in front of me. But I'd made it.

Feet burning, I cut through a bank parking lot, past a school and a church, onto a trail that led away from the street, until finally I couldn't take another step somewhere behind a strip mall. As I leaned against a Dumpster, I breathed in the stench of rotting food.

Who am I kidding? I have no business racing. I belong in a circus sideshow. Robin wins. I quit.

I drew quick shallow breaths. Was I hyperventilating? My stomach lurched and up came the oranges I'd eaten on the bus with Tara. Then I fell away from the Dumpster and heaved again, this time coming up empty. I wiped my lips with my arm, tasting sweat and vomit.

It was bad enough about Robin. But Tara had a part in this, too. Because of my BFF, I'd made a first-class idiot of myself. Yes, I'd run off like a first-grader because somebody called me a name, but how could she throw that winning crap in my face? That was the reason I went back to the hundred-meter, when I wasn't ready or focused enough to compete.

And on top of all that, now I had to backtrack to Spring Valley. I must have run at least five miles from the track.

My feet sore from breaking in new running shoes, I limped to the front of the strip mall. A woman pulled into a parking space and got out, carrying an armful of suits and shirts into the cleaners, then emerged with her receipt. I'd moved past two storefronts, and by the time I was near her car, she rolled down the window.

"Are you a little lost?" she asked, raising her eyebrows at my uniform.

I asked her, "How far is Spring Valley High School?"

"It's a few miles. Are you running cross-country?"

"Kind of."

"When my younger brother ran cross-country for Spring Valley, he got separated from the pack at an away meet and got lost. We were all worried when he didn't turn up with the others and it took him a while to get back. Rather than go through all that, would you like a ride back to the school?"

She didn't look like a serial killer, although I was sure they use dry cleaners like everybody else. But by that point, the only things on my mind were my throbbing feet.

"How many miles is it back there?"

"Probably four or five," she said.

I winced.

"Come on, get in," she said. "You'll be there in a few minutes."

I knew there was no sense prolonging the inevitable, and it'd be worse if they had to come looking for me. She popped open the door lock and I got in the car.

Then I caught a glimpse of myself in her rearview mirror. A halo of sweat soaked the edge of my bandana, my face was blotchy and red, and I had a grass burn on my cheek. I kept my mouth closed, knowing I had to have dragon-breath—the taste in my mouth was so sour; I'd have given anything just for a Tic-Tac. Whatever had possessed this woman to offer me a ride? I was a total train-wreck. If it weren't for the track uniform, she'd probably not have looked twice. But a few minutes later, I was back in the Spring Valley parking lot. I thanked her and she drove off.

The team bus was empty when I got to it, and I could hide there until the meet was over. But first I had to let someone know that I was back. I eased off my sneakers and socks, and wiggled my toes; at last I could walk without limping. When I reached the edge of the field, my feet sank into a soggy patch of grass and cool brown water seeped between my toes. *Ahh.*

Coach Minnelli spotted me first. I wondered if he saw what had happened—if he knew.

"Donovan," he called.

I reached up to touch my bandana.

"You missed the four hundred. Where the hell were you? Spring Valley took first and second." He smacked his clipboard and sent a pencil flying. "And you made Spez miss her race, too." His mouth tightened.

I was too exhausted to attempt an apology and barely enough energy to remain standing while he chewed me out. Then he gave me a quick once-over as I stood there in a mud hole looking pathetic. He shook his head and grumbled, "Go sit down."

I sat on the footrest of the bottom row of bleachers, the gritty metal biting into the back of my legs. Head down, I pulled on my sneakers and guessed at how many more events were left, how much more humiliation before we could go home.

"When did you get back?" Tara asked, jogging toward me. "I looked everywhere for you—the bus, the locker room, all over the school and around the outside of the building."

"I need something to drink," I said.

Tara reached over and fished my gym bag from the pile. The zipper was caught and I forced it open, ripping out some hair from my wig. *Great.* I found my water bottle and squeezed a stream of water into my mouth, then swished and spit. Then I guzzled the rest.

"Ron Sperling overheard the whole thing between Robin and those guys on the other team," Tara told me.

"And?"

"Robin got the Spring Valley guy to do it."

"Who cares? I'm done. And don't give me that look. If it wasn't for you, I'd have been hiding on the bus until the meet was over, instead of going out there and messing up my race." I turned my back to her. Then she was gone.

Lauren came up to me, along with her mom, who had on last year's state championship T-shirt with her sunglasses hooked over the neckline.

"How 'bout a ride home, Cassie?" Mrs. Wagner had that 'concerned mom' look about her.

I nodded. I could hardly believe it: two guardian angels with cars in one day. What were the odds?

"Lauren, tell Coach Minnelli that Cassie's coming home with us," Mrs. Wagner said and Lauren left to deliver the message. "Do you have everything?" she asked me.

I nodded, grabbed my gym bag, and stood up.

We were out of the parking lot before the team was even on the bus. Mrs. Wagner asked me for my address and then said nothing more. I zoned out the entire ride, staring at the mud stains on the floor mat as the air conditioner circulated the scents of coconut and wet dog. As Mrs. Wagner

pulled into our driveway, she waved to Dad, who was dragging the garbage pails back from the curb, still in his suit.

"Thanks a lot, Mrs. Wagner," I said and got out of the
car.

"Hey, how'd it go today? Who dropped you off?" Dad
asked.

But I just rushed up the front steps.

"Cassie?" he called.

"I don't want to talk about it!" I told him and ran upstairs, slamming my bedroom door behind me. Dad's footsteps followed a minute later, then he knocked. He waited
and knocked again.

"Cassie, can I come in?"

I pulled off the bandana and a wad of hair with it, then
took inventory. The patch of hair over my left ear was
gone—more naked skin to hide. I peeled the pieces of tape
away from my scalp.

"Cass?" he called through the door.

I jammed on my baseball cap and said, "It's open."

By then, Mom was there, too, and she sat down next to
me on the bed.

"Oh, honey, what happened to your face?" She reached
for my cheek.

But I shrank from her touch, afraid something else
might fall off me. And then I totally lost it. "I can't do it
anymore. I'm not going back to school. I'm a freak! Please,
don't make me go back."

Without a word Mom threw her arms around me. I
curled up against her and sobbed.

"*Shhhh,*" she said, rocking me and patting my back. "*Shhhh.* It's okay. You don't have to go back, Cassie. We'll figure something out. *Shhhh.*"

Twenty-Nine

And then it was all gone. Overnight, I'd become a full-blown mutant.

My nose and lips seemed bigger, and my eyelashes and eyebrows were starting to disappear. Oh, God—not them, too. Eyebrows hold your face together, before your forehead starts. Now my forehead went on forever. I pulled on my wig and covered or hid every mirror in my room.

All week, I vegged out at home, wearing a wig. I even slept in it. I didn't tell *anyone* that I was completely bald now—not even Tara—as if keeping it secret made it less true. I hid in my room and plotted ways to never go back to school.

The previous year, a girl in my class had Mono. It kept her out of school for two months. That could get me through May. Then, I could have a relapse that'd take care of the rest of the school year. Better to admit to Mono than baldness—anything was preferable to that.

My parents were giving me plenty of space, but Mom made it a point to poke her head into my room every so often during the day. She'd smile, reminding me that she was there if I needed her, which actually felt really good.

Kyle popped in every day after school, trying to cheer me up; he'd ask me to play video games, go for a bike ride or just talk, but I never had much to say. That's when he'd resort to talking to one of my foam head-shaped wig stands, saying he'd have a better conversation that way. I knew he wanted to cheer me up; he even tried to pay back what he owed me—with three dollar bills and his prized state quarter collection.

I dropped the cash on my desk and told him, "Keep the quarters and we'll call it even."

But no matter what anyone did or said, I felt so alone, hiding my ugly secret. I knew I needed to tell them, so on that Friday night after dinner, I asked Kyle, Mom, and Dad to come into my room. As they stood there, I ran my hands over the wig I wore, then told it to them straight: "The rest of my hair's gone. There's nothing left under this wig."

"Oh, honey," Mom said, fighting back tears.

When I showed them, Mom totally lost it.

Dad put his arm around her and murmured something in her ear. I heard him say something about another doctor, but forget that. It was over; I'd read that treatments don't work when it's this bad. It's called Alopecia totalis, meaning all the hair on the head falls out.

"Sorry, Cass," Kyle said when Mom had calmed down. I knew he wanted to look at me but was trying not to stare.

"Your hair could grow back again," Dad said. "There's always that chance; it grew back last time, after all."

"That's right. That's something positive to hang on to,"

Mom said, trying to hold it together. "Who knows, maybe next week or—"

"I won't hold my breath," I told her.

"Your wig is lovely, Cassie," Mom said.

"I never knew you had a beauty mark," Kyle said. "It's right here." He pointed to the side of my head.

"I know. Too bad I had to end up like this to find it, huh?"

"It's always been there, Cass," Dad said and he leaned down to kiss my head.

I pulled back.

After that one time, I always kept the wig on my head.

That week, I didn't pick up or return any of Tara's phone calls. And even though no one asked her to, she brought my books and homework assignments to me the following Saturday morning. I heard her talking with Dad at the front door.

"Thanks for bringing all of this, Tara."

"Can I talk to Cassie?" she asked.

Before he could respond, I called out. "Dad? It's okay, Tara can come in."

A strange impulse made me slip off my wig and go into the hall as Tara lugged the stack of books up the stairs. She did a bit of a double-take, seeing her alien-looking friend, but she'd seen me at every stage before this, so I figured, why not? She just smiled cautiously at me and followed me into my room.

"Wow," she whispered. "I'm so sorry, Cass. Your hair, I mean, it's all—I mean, oh, crap. I'm so sorry this happened."

"I know. It sucks. And—thanks," I told her.

"I brought your homework so you won't fall behind," she said.

"Remember back in September, they told us not to share our locker combinations with anyone? Now I know why."

Tara rolled her eyes, then gave me a questioning look wondering where she could put her burden.

My room was crowded with piles of magazines and library books; I'd been living up there all week, and glasses and paper plates cluttered my desk. Clothes littered the floor, and forget the wreck of my bed. Finally I said, "Just dump it all on the chair."

"Think you'll be able to find them later?" Tara said with a genuine smile. She was great. Hair, no hair, wig or not; none of it mattered to her.

"It's good to see you," I said.

"When are you coming back to school?" she asked.

I slipped my wig on, then dropped onto my bed and lay back, my hands clasped behind my head.

"I don't know, Tara. I wish I could rewind to last year—this year so totally sucks. I know I have to go back eventually. Besides, what good is staying home if you're going to keep bringing in my homework?"

"I miss you at school and at practice. A lot of people have been asking about you, especially Suzanne, Melissa, and Lauren."

Robin?

"The coach, too."

"He'll figure it out soon enough."

"On the ride home from Spring Valley, they let the boys' and girls' teams mix. I was on the bus when Ron told Adam everything. Then Adam went up to Robin and totally slammed her. She didn't admit to it, but she didn't deny it either, and Adam got so riled he dumped her—right there on the bus, in front of everyone. Called her a 'pathetic loser.'"

I sat up. *Wow. That was something.* Revenge was sweet, but now everyone on that bus knew my business, and that kind of juicy gossip traveled at warp speed. And I'd flipped just because Tommy had told one of his best friends about my hair? *Crap—I'm never going back to school*, I thought.

"Everybody feels bad," Tara said. "No one on the team wanted you to quit."

"Except for Robin," I said.

"Whatever, but I thought you'd want to know."

As far as friends went, Tara always did the right thing. I'd worn her bracelet every day since she'd given it to me and it always helped when I touched it. She'd worried about me when I'd freaked out at the meet and took off, and then she missed her own race trying to find me. And here she was again, even after a week of the silent treatment; she still hung in there and didn't give up on me.

"You know, I looked up 'friend' in the dictionary," I said. "And guess what? There was a tiny little picture of you, right next to the definition." I squinted and held my thumb and index finger a half-inch apart.

"What? They were supposed to use the eight by ten!" she shot back.

"I can't believe how lucky I am to have you...even after the crap I gave you," I told her.

"Like it or not, you're stuck with me. Besides, being best friends works both ways." She wagged her finger at me. "So take that as fair warning, girlie."

We hugged, and I couldn't help thinking of Tommy. He'd said he wanted to apologize, but I never even gave him a chance. I wondered what the statute of limitations was on that sort of thing. *Should I call him?*

Tara stayed for the rest of the day, and after dinner, we cleaned up the kitchen. Every time she loaded a plate into the dishwasher, she'd bump her hip into me as I scrubbed the pots.

"I'm going to complain to that Webster guy," Tara said. "They better get a much bigger picture of me in the next edition."

"Absolutely," I said and flicked soap bubbles in her face.

The phone rang. Kyle answered it and held the receiver out to me.

"It's Mrs. Vetrone," he said.

Shit. Twenty after seven. Saturday night. I was supposed to be there twenty minutes ago. I took the phone and said hello.

"Hi, Cassie," Mrs. Vetrone said. "Is everything all right?"

"I'm on my way over right now," I told her and hung up. "Omigod—I totally forgot—I told her I'd babysit a couple weeks ago."

"Duh," Kyle said.

"I'm sorry, T. I totally spaced—I gotta get out of here. Talk to you tomorrow."

Mom unhooked my keys and jangled them in front of me, then I dashed down the street. Mr. Vetrone was waiting in the driveway with the car door open and a couple was sitting in the back seat. "Sorry I'm late," I said and whizzed past him. Mrs. Vetrone was holding the front door open and I slipped in, offering a weak "Happy Anniversary." She'd put her hair up and was wearing a killer cocktail dress cut above the knee. *Go, Mrs. Vetrone.*

"Nicky, Cassie's here," she told her little boy.

He ran to the door to see me and I picked him up. "Hey, little guy."

"Give Mommy a kiss," she said and backed out of the door giving me final instructions. "You can put him to bed anytime after eight-thirty. We'll be back around ten."

Then they were gone and somehow my wig was on the floor. Nick must've somehow gotten his fingers caught, and since I hadn't had time to tape it down, it didn't take much to pull it off.

Poor kid—was he ever surprised. I watched as he digested the whole situation. He leaned over in my arms to look at my wig sprawled on the floor, then he looked back to my head, and then back to the floor.

"No hair," he said, looking at me gravely.

"No hair," I repeated.

He reached up to touch my scalp—and I let him. His hand was warm and a little sticky as he swept it from my ear to the back of my head. Then he touched his own hair, then my scalp again. And then he laughed.

"Soft," he said.

I closed my eyes and tried it myself. He was right.

"Nice," he said.

"Nice?" *Hmm, nice.* That was a new take on things.

I plunked him down and picked up my wig, then said, "How about a snack?" I set the wig back in place.

"Cookie. Please and thank you," Nicky said.

I poured milk and placed a cookie on the table, then held the glass as he dipped his entire hand in it with the cookie. *I am the coolest babysitter ever.* When he was done, I wiped his hands with a wet paper towel.

"Go find a book," I said.

He peeled out of the kitchen saying, "Truck book, truck book."

As I cleaned up after Nicky's snack, I noticed my blurry reflection in the oven door. Although I couldn't make out much, what I saw looked familiar and okay. That led me to the mirror hanging in the foyer, where I could get a better look at myself. I saw thinning eyebrows—but they were *my* thinning eyebrows, along with my eyes—only with fewer eyelashes. I crinkled my nose and stuck out my tongue; still me, not some monster, not an alien. I slipped off my wig, took a deep breath, and smiled. Hair or not, no matter what anyone else might think, I was still me.

Thirty

Sunday morning, I made my bed and cleared the disaster area that used to be my desk. Then, for the rest of the day, I worked nonstop to get up to speed on last week's assignments. I'd made a decision: tomorrow I was going back.

That night at dinner, I had a nervous feeling in my stomach.

"Did you get all your homework done?" Dad asked as he passed the bowl of shredded lettuce, then took a pinch of cheese and added it to his fajita.

"Most of it," I told him.

"Are you sure you want to go back?" Mom asked.

"You trying to talk me out of it?" I said.

"No," Mom said. "Not at all."

"We're proud of you, Cass," Dad said. "But you can take as much time as you need."

"No—I'm ready. I can't hide out forever. I mean, there's nothing wrong with me, right?"

Mom nodded, and I could see she was convinced.

"I decided no more excuses. I have to just suck it up and go back."

Monday morning at the bus stop, I shifted the weight of my books from one hip to the other. In my mind, I pictured a strong wind carrying my wig away, and me chasing it as it flew off, just inches from my reach as people stared. Maybe it was too soon to go back.

If the bus is late, I'll take it as a sign to turn around and go back inside. I shifted from foot to foot for another minute, then decided to call it quits. But just as I turned to go, the bus swung around the corner. *Okay, fine.*

I settled into a seat, then my teammates Scott and Suzanne got on at their stop. Scott shuffled past me to the back of the bus, but Suzanne balanced on the edge of my seat next to my overstuffed backpack.

"Hey, Cassie, you're back! You coming to practice today?"

"No." I could've made up a lame excuse, but all I said was "I quit."

She nodded like she understood and felt sorry for me.

But I didn't want sympathy; I just wanted to be left alone to finish freshman year off everyone's radar. But as luck would have it, the first person I saw when I stepped off the bus was Robin. *Bald and ugly, she'd said.*

Distracted as I thought about her viciousness, I lost my grip on the unzipped backpack and books spewed all over the sidewalk. Robin didn't notice the line of kids waiting to get off the bus as Suzanne and I scraped my things into my pack—so much for staying off the radar.

Tara and I met up in the cafeteria as usual, and I heaved

my backpack onto a table and sorted out my papers while we waited for the bell to ring for homeroom. When we got to my locker, I fumbled with the combination.

"Allow me," she said.

I bowed and said, "Be my guest."

Tara opened it, first try. I needed books for my first three classes, Bio, Algebra, and—no, I wasn't ready for French just yet. I stuck the French book back into my locker and slammed the door. Not a good beginning—it was my first day back in a week, and I'd already decided to cut French.

Mr. Marsh mumbled through attendance in homeroom. He seemed about to breeze over my name as absent but glanced in my direction to be sure, and then his eyebrows perked up as he acknowledged my return.

I looked out the window during the flag salute and national anthem; a jock strap was new to the courtyard décor and the bushes were dotted with green leaves. Announcements came over the speaker. "Tickets to the senior production of *Godspell* go on sale this week. You can still order your yearbook, so get your deposit in. Baseball game will be away, at Teaneck. Track meet is home tomorrow, against Skylar High." Just hearing it, my chest tightened.

Then Mr. Marsh handed me a note. Coach Minnelli wanted to see me at the beginning of second period, but the note was from last week. He probably wanted the uniform back; I'd bring it in tomorrow.

Biology flew by as I played catch-up, taking notes and trying to copy last week's lab notes in between. We were having a test tomorrow—geez, gimme a break. But soon

the bell was ringing and books were being slapped shut as I scribbled down the last of the lab notes. When I got out in the hall, I glanced in the direction of my next class and pondered: Algebra or Coach Minnelli?

I had a good handle on the current unit in Algebra, so I started toward the gym. The stained glass of the Falcon Window splashed puddles of color over the floor. All the team yearbook pictures were taken in front of that window, and the track team's had been shot before Christmas. I pushed open the door marked Athletic Department, which led to a small hallway of offices. I peeked through the window on the Coach's door—empty.

Then I heard my name; Coach Minnelli was standing behind me, holding a cup of coffee in one hand and two bagels in the other. His clipboard was slipping out from under his arm, so I opened the door and the clipboard made it to his desk, then landed with a thud. A framed poster of a rock climber hung behind his desk. The climber was miles above the earth and still nowhere near the summit. The slogan said, *The body says stop, The spirit says never.*

We sat down, and the coach sipped his coffee, then nodded like he was trying to figure out what I was doing here.

"It's my first day back," I said.

"Thanks for coming down, Cassie; I thought we could talk. I heard about what happened and I'm sorry, especially for the way I came down on you."

I looked down at my lap and nodded.

"I want you to know that I didn't ask you here to convince you to come back or to give you the 'you have a responsibility to the team' speech. Could we win without you? Probably. Would it be easier with you? Definitely."

"It's funny," he went on, "No matter what you do or what you have, there'll always be a Pat McIntyre, trying to take it away from you."

"I'm sorry, who?"

"That's the guy who stole my girlfriend when I was a sophomore in college. I didn't think I'd ever get over it. Then he graduated and dumped her, but it was already over between us. Then, junior year, there was another Pat McIntyre. He beat me out for first-string basketball and got the last starting position. And my senior year Pat came along when we were applying for internships, and it came down to the two of us. After three grueling interviews, I got the job."

Yeah, yeah, I get it already.

"Cassie, you don't have to come back."

Sure, what did he care? He could afford to lose me. He still had Robin and Lauren. Bottom line, he'd built a winning team, and I was nothing to him but an expendable crybaby.

"As far as Lakewood goes," he shook his head and continued. "I've met with her and Ron Sperling—that Sperling's a decent kid. Anyway, she denies having anything to do with—you know—your hair, so it puts me in a difficult position. I'd like to slap her with unsportsmanlike conduct and bench her, but she didn't actually touch you so I don't think that's going to fly." He let out an exasperated sigh. "As her parents pointed out, it's a case of 'he said, she said.'"

I crossed my arms. *This is the strangest pep talk I've ever heard.*

"Out on the track, you might beat Lakewood or you might not. But, if you don't at least get out there, she wins automatically, doesn't she?"

He bit into his bagel, signaling the end of the discussion.

"I need a late pass for Algebra."

He scratched on a pad of passes, the same kind as Tommy's. "I'll tell you what I'm going to do, Cassie. The season's short." He tore off the pass and handed it to me. "So I'm leaving the door open. It's totally up to you."

"Thanks for the pass," I said and left his office. I stopped in front of the trophy case; most were for track and had little golden runners balanced on top of marble towers. One read, "ALBERT MINNELLI, COACH OF THE YEAR, PRESENTED BY THE DARLINGTON HIGH SCHOOL HOME SCHOOL ASSOCIATION." Plaques were mounted with gold plates engraved with rows of student names and their records. Girls' field hockey had a winning season two years ago.

I decided I could afford to miss the entire Algebra class, so I drifted down to the cafeteria, bought a soggy pretzel and a carton of iced tea, then sat down. I licked a piece of salt off my finger and remembered sitting in this exact spot with Tommy the night of Battle of the Bands. I shook my head. Before I could begin to get over him, I needed to talk to him and find out what his father did the night of his party and why he was there. I had to find out what Tommy had wanted to say to me that day in the hall, before I totally shut him down. I slipped Minnelli's pass from my pocket and looked at it carefully. Maybe I could change this one around a little and drop it off in Tommy's locker.

I didn't get far in my first attempt at forgery; I was interrupted by the fire alarm. I followed a small parade outside, to join the growing crowd in the parking lot, where to my dismay I ended up not two feet away from Monsieur Haus, my French teacher. *Crap!*

"Bonjour, Madamoiselle," he said.

Agh—I was busted in advance, my perfect plan ruined. I'd already sort of cut Algebra, so I couldn't *not* show up for French, too. I listened to him speaking French to someone in his second-period class. I finished my pretzel wondering if he spoke in French to the other teachers, too.

When it was safe to go back inside, I detoured back to my locker for my French book, then headed to class. I froze in the doorway and plucked at the spiral binding on my notebook and stared at my empty seat waiting next to Robin. I hated the power she had over me, but I forced myself through the door and into the classroom to the opposite side of the room, where I claimed a new seat for myself— an unprecedented move so late in the school year. But I didn't care; I half-smiled at Christina and Maggie, who smiled back, tacitly agreeing to a conversational trio. During class, instead of doing the worksheet the teacher handed out, I tore out a page from my notebook and wrote:

Dear Tommy,
I'd like to talk if it's okay with you.
Can you meet me at my locker today after 8th period?
Cassie

After class, I slipped the note into his locker vent. I was pretty sure he'd see it before the end of the day. Now the question was, would he show?

The next three classes were fine, but then it was time for gym. In the locker room as we got changed, a couple of girls nearby were whispering to each other; I knew they could've been talking about anything and not necessarily me, but it made me uncomfortable enough to get dressed in a bathroom stall after gym.

For eighth period, Tara and I headed for the art wing. It was T-minus forty minutes until I'd see Tommy. Then I thought about my note. If he *didnt't* show, it could mean either of two things: he was definitely blowing me off *or* he'd never gotten the note. *Shit. Why did I write him a note?* I caught a glimpse of my reflection in a display case and wondered what I'd do if he was a no-show.

"You seem a little zoned out," Tara said.

"Nah, I'm good." I tried to shake off the thought of standing alone, waiting in vain at my locker, as we approached three people were sketching a design for a mural on a humongous sheet of paper taped up in the hallway. It showed a falcon swooping down on the words 'Crush Cranford.' That meet would be at home in two weeks and it promised to be the biggest draw of the season against our rival school. Coach Minnelli had wanted me for varsity, thinking I'd be an asset to the team. For a while there, I'd believed he might be right.

"Hey, you coming tomorrow?" Tara asked.

"Oh, I don't know. I don't think so."

"I thought maybe you could hang out and cheer us on," she said.

I shrugged as we turned into the art room. Last week, they'd started a new assignment, one unfamiliar to me.

"What's this?" I asked.

"Linoleum carvings," Tara said. "Get a practice board and a handle for the linoleum knife. We can share the knife tips, and I'll show you how to screw them in without getting cut."

Alex held up a bandaged middle finger. "Three stitches," he said.

"Any excuse to flip someone off, huh, Alex?" I said.

His face lit up and he waggled his eyebrows. "You gotta seize the moment."

After Tara showed me the technique, I guided the knife over the practice board, gouging it without any bloodshed.

When I told Tara about the note, she stabbed her knife tip into her linoleum block and said, "He had his chance and he blew it."

I reminded her that she'd given me a second chance, and how it bothered me that I'd never let him apologize. Then her attitude softened a bit.

"Okay, then. Do what you gotta do. I really hope it all works out."

"That's if he even shows."

The bell rang and we headed our separate ways; I was halfway to my locker when I turned the corner to find Tommy leaning against the wall, one knee bent, listening to his iPod. I let out a shaky breath of relief as he plucked out the earbuds and straightened up. I hugged my books in front of me and said, "You got my note." I looked at him, trying to get a read on his mood.

"I can't hang too long." He nodded toward the parking lot. "My brother's waiting."

I stepped closer, not wanting to shout above the noise of departing students and caught a whiff of his clean scent—I'd almost forgotten how good he always smelled. I took a deep breath and started talking.

"Listen, I didn't mean to go off on you like that a couple weeks ago. I said some nasty things and I'm really sorry."

"No—I'm the one who should apologize." He dug his hands into his pockets. "Breaking up was the last thing on my mind that night. Yeah, what you told me threw me for a loop. But that's not what I'm about. I was going out with *you*, not your hair. I care about you, Cassie, really."

Then what happened? I wondered.

He seemed to read my mind and shifted his weight from one leg to the other. "So that night, my father showed up with barely any warning, and after everyone left, he dumped some pretty heavy shit on us. It kills me what he does to my mom. She actually thought he was going to tell us he wanted to come home." Tommy shook his head. A sour expression crept across his face. "And she would've taken him back in a heartbeat."

The hallway was almost empty and Tommy hesitated, searching the ceiling for the right words. "His big announcement was that he has a daughter. She's three. Which means my father was screwing around long before he packed his bags and took off."

"Oh, Tommy," I said, as impulse made me reach out to him and I rested my hand on his arm. He didn't seem to mind, but he glanced in the direction of the parking lot.

"Eric'll wait for you," I said.

"The kicker of this whole mess is that he wants his kid's big brothers to be a part of her life. I mean, how do I deal with that? This baby—my half-sister—is a major part of the reason he left. And now I have to go make nice with the enemy?"

"That's awful, Tommy. And this isn't even her fault; she's just a baby."

"I know, I know. That's the point. *I'm a big brother now.*" He exaggerated the importance of this with air-quotes. "So much came crashing down on me that night," he added. "And my mother's a wreck—she's really hurt, especially by this latest bit of news."

He let out a breath and said, "Turns out, I really needed you that weekend, and you really needed me, but I screwed up big-time. That's what I wanted to tell you that day in the hall. I never meant to hurt you—it was the last thing I wanted to do."

I believed him, and I felt that we could try again if he was willing.

"So now what?" I asked.

"We try and deal with all of it?" he asked, running a finger along my chin.

"Yes. Let's do exactly that—together." I said.

℮⌒

The next day after school, Tommy and I walked outside holding hands and headed toward the spot where the track team was gathering on the field.

"You sure about this?" he asked.

"I want to be at the meet for Tara," I told him.

He knew about what had happened to me at the away meet; my fifteen minutes of miserable fame had spread through school just as I'd expected. We'd talked for hours on the phone after school, piecing together the details from our two weeks apart. I confessed what it'd been like for me, trying to hide my condition all those months, and how afraid I'd been to tell him. I felt better now that we'd gotten everything out in the open, and I felt stronger just holding his hand.

When we got to the field, Tara was stretching with Melissa and Ginny; I waved, but we were too far away to get her attention. We found a spot in the bleachers behind a few of the moms at the finish line. Christina and Maggie from French class sat down next to us.

"What are you doing up here?" Christina asked.

"I got hurt," I said. *Geez, that's the understatement of the century.*

"I thought you're supposed to sit with the team," Maggie said. "That's what the football players do. Why aren't you down there?"

Good question. The only thing hurt was my feelings. I really *wanted* to run. I guess that was the real reason I was there: I belonged on the track. Skylar High's bus lumbered in and hissed to a halt in the parking lot, and the team got off and strode to the field.

The freshman boys' two hundred meter race was first; Darlington took first and second, and the crowd roared. Varsity girls' two hundred was next, and there was Robin, outside lane on the other side of the football field. The starter pistol cracked. They peeled around the bend, with Robin out in front. Christina and Maggie cheered and clapped. The Skylar High runners poured it on, but Robin shot away from the pack. They couldn't catch her. Darlington picked up first, with the spotlight on Robin. Coach Minnelli clapped against his clipboard and gave her a fist bump as she jogged in front of him.

I must have been crazy, thinking I could race. No way could I handle being on the same track again with Robin, never mind running against her. I'd made it as far as these bleachers, but even that wasn't going to work.

"I can't be here," I whispered to Tommy.

Then he walked me home.

Thirty-One

For days I'd been practicing with an eyebrow pencil after school, filling in the spaces on my eyebrows. I wanted to master it before they completely disappeared, but ugh—what a mess.

"This is impossible!" I slammed the pencil on the bathroom vanity.

"What's the matter?" Mom called from the hall.

I scrubbed off my third set of gross-looking caterpillar eyebrows. *Forget it. Next wig, long bangs.* When I'd finished drying my face, Mom was standing in the doorway and she'd noticed the eyebrow pencil.

"This is one of those times when less is more," she said and picked it up. She sharpened the pencil until it was pointy enough to skewer a steak. Then she rounded her fist and stippled tiny dashes of color on the back of her hand until it formed an arch. "Going the other direction is always trickier," she said, concentrating on the symmetry, "See?" Then she blended the color with her pinky, adding a few more strokes. "There, not bad."

"That looks great," I said.

"Well, uh—" she said, surprised by the impromptu art lesson, "—I have to get dinner started." She replaced the cap on the pencil.

"You were right," I said. "Sometimes less *is* more."

In the days that followed, it was clear from the announcements in homeroom that Darlington track was doing fine without me. Two of the boys had broken school records for the javelin and the eight hundred meter. And the girls' varsity was undefeated.

At night, Tommy and I talked a lot about him meeting his new half-sister, Lindsay. He was having a hard time agreeing to it; his brothers were willing to go, but they wouldn't go without Tommy.

One night we were at the mall with Eric and Dina, just there to walk around. Tommy challenged me to a penny skipping contest at the fountain, where I got one to skip four times, and Tommy's best was only three—so now he owed me a slushie.

Eric and Dina were strolling a few stores ahead when we started walking again.

"I don't know," Tommy said. "It'd be like stabbing my mother in the back to meet this kid." He was thinking about Lindsay again.

"But what if your mom remarried and had another baby—a girl," I said. "She'd be your sister, wouldn't she?"

"Yeah, I guess."

"Isn't it the same thing?"

He nodded thoughtfully, as if he was warming up to the idea.

"A-a-a-nd, here's the best part," I said with a sly grin.

"Having a little sister promotes you from the annoying little brother to one of the annoying *big* brothers."

Tommy shot me a fake scowl and started chasing me. I shrieked and laughed until we caught up with Eric and Dina. We stopped in front of Once Upon a Time, the bookstore where Silk City had played. Tommy turned to me and said, "Think she'd like a book?"

I told him, "I think Lindsay would love a book from her awesome big brother." Then we went inside.

❧

Most days after school, when Tommy was rehearsing with Silk City, I'd go running. Lately, I'd carved out two new routes for myself, ones around my neighborhood that took me nowhere near Falcons, or Cougars.

One day I walked up the driveway, just back from a four-miler. I didn't have on a wig—just a bandana that was soaked at the temples. Kyle was in front of the house flipping his skateboard and landing a new move while Mom knelt in the grass, cutting back her tulips.

Inside, I chugged a glass of water and carried the laundry basket upstairs. Then I filled the bathroom sink with warm water and shampoo, dropped one of my wigs in and swished it around so it could soak while I showered. I still used shampoo on my head, which smelled better than regular soap and it felt good to let it ooze over my scalp. When I got out of the shower, I rinsed the wig and hung it to dry. My dry wig waited for me on the stand as I dressed and I thought about how many times those foam heads holding the wigs startled me into thinking someone else was in my room.

I stood in front of the mirror and smoothed my hands over my scalp, the skin still warm from the shower. My ears didn't stick out, which was good, and my lips didn't seem gigantic anymore. I slipped on my wig and put away my laundry, took the basket to Kyle's room, then went back and turned on some tunes in my room. A few minutes later, Kyle's dresser drawers slammed open and shut several times.

"This was in with my stuff," he said. And tossed my uniform to me.

"I have to turn it in," I told him.

Kyle rummaged through his pockets and offered me a handful of Skittles, which I politely declined.

"You miss it?" he asked, eating the red Skittles first.

I nodded and flopped on my bed. "There's this one girl on the team," I said. "She totally psyches me out. I see her and I practically pee in my pants."

"How about the rest of the people?"

"They're okay. Nobody ever gave me a hard time. When my hair was falling out and it got really bad, I knew they could tell, but nobody said anything."

"You want to go back?" Kyle asked.

"Coach said I could." I shook my head. "I just don't know if it's worth it."

"Is staying home worth it?" he asked.

I folded my uniform to the size of a sandwich and didn't answer him.

"When's the next meet?" Kyle asked.

"Tomorrow, at home."

"You know what? Maybe you should hang on to that." Kyle pointed at the folded uniform in my lap. Then he left and I heard the laundry basket tumble down the stairs.

Maybe he had a point. What was I afraid of? Robin?

They'd all seen my naked head and nobody'd treated me different afterward. I was dealing with it. Best part was Tommy, who was amazing. No pressure or questions about what was under my wig. He was into me, like he'd said.

Still…why drop myself into that nightmare again?

I traced the edge of my wig around my face. It wasn't just Robin—there could always be some jerk pointing, making fun of my wig. But what was I going to do? Run away every time something like that happened?

The Cranford meet was the next day, and I packed my uniform into my gym bag.

The next morning, as I was leaving the house, something in the family room caught my eye: a small, new frame on the shelf, studded with pink Austrian crystals. It held one of the pictures I'd found from when I turned four—*hat off*.

Yup, Tara was right. I *was* a cute kid.

❧

At school, the Darlington marquee read, "GO FALCONS. TRACK MEET TODAY AGAINST THE CRANFORD MUSTANGS." My heart rate seemed to double as the bus pulled around to the back of the school that morning. I squeezed my gym bag and slung it over my shoulder. *Only eight periods between the track and me.*

The school day went by at warp speed; I focused on the finish, and all the rest was a blur. After art class, Tara and I hustled down to the gym locker room. I ran my fingers over the tiger's eye beads before I changed, and the silky polyester uniform felt like liquid against my skin. I slipped into a stall, removed my wig, and tied on a bandana.

"Did you tell the coach that you were coming back today?" Tara asked.

I opened the door and went straight to the mirror.

"You're the only one who knows. I needed to keep my chicken-out option open."

"All you have to do is get out there. I know you can do it," she said.

It was a gorgeous spring day with just a slight breeze. We jogged to the field, did one quick lap, then sat in the grass to stretch. The poster from the hallway was hung above the top bleacher seats on the announcer's box. The Falcon's wings sparkled with silver and blue glitter.

"All right, Cassie," Lauren said. "We're gonna burn it up out there."

"Hey, glad you're back," Suzanne said.

Ron Sperling came up to me. "Break a leg," he said. "Wait—that's for acting, isn't it?"

"Yeah," I said. "It doesn't sound right for runners, does it? Thanks, though."

Coach Minnelli heard the chatter. "Donovan, you're in?"

"I'm in."

"Coach, what's *she* doing here?" It was Robin's voice, snaking up from behind me.

My muscles tensed.

"She's not racing today, is she?" Robin struck a pose, her hands on her hips, as she shot me a snotty look. "She hasn't been to practice in weeks."

"Donovan's racing," he said.

"That's not fair," Robin whined.

"Enough, Lakewood," he told her.

"But Coach..."

He glared at Robin and turned to the team. "Let's go, folks. You know the drill. Stretch it out. You've worked hard to get here and you can make it happen. But you gotta fight if you want to win. The State Championship is right in front of you. Do you want it?"

"Yes!" we cheered.

"I can't hear you."

We roared and clapped and whistled, then Coach Minnelli ran down the roster. Robin was right about one thing: I hadn't been to practice in weeks. But I'd been running all along, only the coach didn't know that; he might think I was out of shape. I'd be lucky if he put me in at all.

Then he called my name for the hundred and the four hundred meter races—same as Robin.

The Cranford Mustangs warmed up before the rows of packed bleachers as still more spectators squeezed in. And high in the stands, under the Falcon poster, I couldn't believe what I saw: Mom, Dad, and Kyle. They waved their arms over their heads. Kyle must've taken a chance and told them I'd be racing today. That kid was smarter than I thought.

And Tommy stood leaning against the fence with his buddies, holding a bouquet of bright pink carnations.

"Varsity girls' hundred meter," a voice announced.

Our team lined up first and the Cranford coach gave some last-minute tips to his runners as I adjusted my blocks. Then I checked the bandana—secure.

The official motioned for Cranford to fall in.

"You're going down, loser," Robin told me.

Without flinching, I stared into her cold eyes. "Think so?" I said. "Just try and take me." And then I sensed it— fear. She broke eye contact first and for the first time, it felt like the balance of power might be shifting from Robin to me.

"Runners." The official raised his arm.

I locked in.

"Set."

Crack!

A Cranford runner blasted ahead instantly. I stayed on her, pulling with my arms, extending my legs to their max with long, steady strides. Her shoulder was just an inch from mine when I sloppily thrust myself over the line. She leaned in and had it; the Mustangs took first, I'd grabbed second for the Falcons, and Robin placed third.

"Donovan, I told you never to open up like that," Coach Minnelli said. "You hold it together out there. I wanna see a clean finish next time."

"Got it," I said. I'd screwed up. I should've had her. Running alone those weeks, I'd never worked on the finer points of finishing. If anything, I'd built up stamina for distances, but I had to remember to finish right.

"Great run," Tara said. "How'd it feel?"

"Good. That Cranford girl was tough, though."

"You almost had her. Don't worry, you'll get her next time."

A few feet away, Robin was bitching.

"That was *my* race," Robin said. "Cassie Donovan cheats. She jumped the gun."

"No, she didn't," Lauren said. "The official would've called a false start. You came in third, Robin. If Cassie didn't race, you'd have finished *second*. Ease up, already."

"Why do you stick up for that freaky little freshman?"

Lauren waved her off like a mosquito and turned away.

Robin glared at me and wouldn't back off. She was so obvious, trying to psyche me out, but Lauren wasn't buying into her crap, and neither was I. Not anymore. And I wasn't just competing against Cranford; I was also winning back my place on the team—something I'd handed to Robin all too easily by quitting.

Two boys' events followed and Darlington wiped up the field with Cranford. Hurdles were next. Tara took first in the freshman girls' hundred. After her win, we found a patch of shade and sucked on our water bottles, cheering on the boys' hurdles and pole-vaulters.

Then Robin pulled out the big guns, whispering to the guys, and pointing to me and laughing. But Adam tapped a couple of guys on the chest and led them away from her, disgusted. But she just wouldn't let up. I caught the words *bowling ball, baldy, bubble head.* Her spurts of venom were meant to send me running for the hills, and my pulse quickened as my hands curled into fists. I started walking.

"Where are you going?" Tara asked.

"To talk to Robin," I said.

"Just ignore her, Cassie," Tara called to me.

But a tank couldn't have stopped me. Tara caught up next to me; I knew she wouldn't interfere. She was there as a safety net, in case I did anything really stupid.

I went straight up to Robin and planted myself just inches from her nose, close enough to smell her mint gum.

"What do *you* want?" she said.

The potential catfight drew more attention than I wanted, but so be it.

I looked her square in the eye and said, "Know what the difference is between you and me?"

I'd backed her into a corner, and she came out scratching.

"Hair?"

I stood up straighter and pressed my shoulders back.

"No, that's not it, Robin. The difference is, when I look in the mirror—" I peeled off my bandana and let it drop. "*I'm* not ashamed of what I see."

Her face contorted; no one here was on her side. She kicked the bandana and took off behind a wall of Falcon uniforms. And suddenly, I was being pelted with pats on the shoulder and back, accompanied by shouts of "You go, girl!" and "You tell her!" and "Way to go!"

I absorbed all that good energy right through my skin

and every muscle in my body tingled with electricity. Even Adam winked at me in a big-brotherly way.

"Varsity girls' four hundred meter." I heard the announcement and floated to the starting line.

People stared, craning their necks from the bleachers for a closer look. I could feel my family and Tara pulling for me as the warmth of the sun caressed my head.

Tommy blew me a kiss and I set up my blocks, then shook out my arms and focused on the race I was about to run.

It was no big deal and I'd want to look, too. After all, a freshman running varsity track wasn't something that happened every day.

Acknowledgments

Thank you, Terry Wassel. Your random act of kindness, cutting and donating your long hair, set me on this incredible journey. I am forever grateful.

Bunny Gabel, you were there from word one and encouraged me to *Keep going!* Your guidance and patience through most every draft was indeed a gift from the editorial gods. Thank you.

Thanks to George Akshar, Janice Chandler and Jamie Perkovich for sharing your stories with me and for reading a very early draft of this novel.

Thanks also to Martin Kassir, M.D., F.A.A.D., and Mary DiTore, RPh, for answering medical questions.

Hugs all around to the talented, generous writers in my Wednesday Night critique group: Susan Anthony, Roberta Davidson-Bender, Stephan Boyar, Selene Castrovilla, Sheila DeCosse, Stephanie Ferreira, Alice Golin, Emily Goodman, Michele Granger, Laurent Linn, Arlene Mark, Mary Rattray, Kathy Roche, Vicky Shiefman, Marcia Shrier, Erika Tamar, Susan Teicher, Seta Toroyan, Pat Weissner, and Niki Yektai.

A special shout out to wonderful writers Karen Dowicz Haas, Richard Spector, and Seta Toroyan who provided countless, insightful comments and just as many laughs. Thank you!

Thanks to my parents, Richard and Viola Sperling, for always supporting my creativity, then and now (my mom still has all my creative writing assignments from middle school to prove it). Mom and Dad, I love you.

Patsy and Patricia DelleCava—best in-laws ever! Thanks for all the love and support.

And much love to my dear friends and family who have been cheering me on from the get-go.

Evelyn M. Fazio, my fabulous publisher, thank you for shining your light where I needed it most. Mega thanks for your confidence in my work and for making my dream come true!

Patrick and Nicholas, you brought so much to this novel, whether you realize it or not. I love you. And, yes, guys, you totally have to read this entire book now.

Pat, you're a constant source of love and support for all my creative endeavors. Okay, except when it comes to planting flowers in the yard. Thank you for reading various drafts of this novel and for always giving me your honest opinion. You are the best husband, best friend ever! My greatest joy comes from sharing this whole experience with you.